The Sons of Killian have hunted my ancestors for centuries. The same way they hunt me now.

Descended from an Irish demigoddess, Brianna has fled to Ireland to escape destruction at the hands of her sworn enemies, the Sons of Killian. Taking refuge at the estate of her former nemesis, Austin Montgomery, Brianna discovers a rift in time that opens to an era before the feud began.

Wrestling with her newfound feelings for the younger Austin—whom she meets a thousand years back in time—Brianna begins to wonder if altering the past could change her future. But when Brianna and the present-day Austin learn that the Sons are raising an army of mythical beasts, a tragic destiny may be their only fate.

Also by Talia Vance

Silver

GOLD

TALIA VANCE

GOLD

flux
Woodbury, Minnesota

First Edition
First Printing, 2013

Book design by Bob Gaul
Cover design by Ellen Lawson
Cover illustration by Brenda Meelker/Embrision Arts
Cover image: 96106883/Patryk Kosmider/Shutterstock.com
Title art © Llewellyn art department

Flux, an imprint of Llewellyn Worldwide Ltd.

This is a work of fiction. Names, characters, places, and incidents are either the product of the author's imagination or are used fictitiously, and any resemblance to actual persons living or dead, business establishments, events, or locales is entirely coincidental. Cover model used for illustrative purposes only and may not endorse or represent the book's subject.

Library of Congress Cataloging-in-Publication Data
Vance, Talia.
  Gold/Talia Vance.—First edition.
      pages cm.—(A Bandia novel; #2)
   Summary: "Brianna, a seventeen-year-old Daughter of Danu, flees to Ireland to escape her sworn enemies, the Sons of Killian, and finds herself in league with another former nemesis in her battle against the Sons"—Provided by publisher.
   ISBN 978-0-7387-3471-2
   [1. Supernatural—Fiction. 2. Mythology, Celtic—Fiction. 3. Goddesses—Fiction. 4. Ireland—Fiction.] I. Title.
   PZ7.V39853Gol 2013
   [Fic]—dc23
                                                            2013015754

Flux
Llewellyn Worldwide Ltd.
2143 Wooddale Drive
Woodbury, MN 55125-2989
www.fluxnow.com

Printed in the United States of America

Acknowledgments

First, a huge thank you to everyone who read *Silver* and came back for more of Brianna's story. You make everything possible.

Thank you to the wonderful team at Flux, especially to the editor who does it all and then some, Brian Farrey-Latz, and Sandy Sullivan who finds the devil in the details. Thank you to the design team, Bob Gaul, Ellen Lawson, and cover illustrator Brenda Meelker, for giving me another gorgeous book. Special thanks to Mallory and Katie, who have done a wonderful job of getting my books out into the world.

Thanks to my amazing law partners, associates, and support team, who supported my writing with genuine enthusiasm and excitement from the beginning. I'm proud to be part of the greatest place to work with a law degree. You're the reason I'll never quit my day (and night) job.

This book wouldn't exist without the brilliant and talented Sarah Davies, agent extraordinaire, who is always ready to lend a supportive ear or tweet a hedgehog photo when it's most needed. And this journey wouldn't be half as much fun if I didn't get to share it with the YA Muses, Bret Ballou, Donna Cooner, Katherine Longshore, and Veronica Rossi. Thank you for everything and then some. I am blessed to count you as friends.

Thanks to those who read early drafts and lent support along the way, Jenn McCoy, Jaime Arnold, Rachel Clarke, Kristen Held, and Beth Hull. And, lastly, thank you to my family, who continue to cheer me on.

To Jeff, who made me into the
hopeless romantic I am. Sorry about making
you the bad guy and then killing you off.

ONE

Ireland is magic. There's no other way to describe it. The air is alive, so cold it cuts right through skin and bone, even though it's supposed to be summer. Ever-present clouds move across the sky, dampening the ground with fat drops of rain that make everything glisten. The earth smells of loose dirt and something richer. The elements converge and meld, coming together so fiercely that even a human must feel their power.

I am drunk with it.

I ride in the back of a black BMW driven by a tall guy with ginger mutton-chops and a tight blue suit. Apparently the full facial sideburn is making a comeback here. His name is Mikel, which rhymes with pickle, but he had to tell me three times before I got it right, so I'm just going with Mick. He doesn't smile, but he keeps glancing at me in the rearview mirror. His eyes are rimmed with a sadness that makes him seem older than his eighteen years.

"Did Joe tell you why I'm here?" I ask.

Mick shakes his head. "Not my business."

"Don't you want to know what I'm running from?"

"Nope."

When Joe left me at LAX yesterday and told me his friend would be there when I landed in Dublin, I assumed that Mick already knew what he was getting into. That he understood the danger.

"Well, you should. You might change your mind about helping me."

"Doubt it." Mick concentrates on the narrow road in front of him.

The houses get farther apart as we drive. Sheep graze in pastures so green they make my eyes hurt. I blink back a tear. I refuse to let myself cry.

It wasn't my fault.

I take a deep breath and concentrate on pulling myself together. "Where are we going?" I ask, trying again to engage Mick. Trying to distract myself.

A hint of a smile teases at the corners of his eyes. "A place I think you'll like."

"Thank you, Mr. Vague."

"Lorcan Hall on the Dingle Peninsula."

The unfamiliar names mean nothing to me, but at least we have an actual destination. It's not enough to ground me, but it's something. I lean back against the seat and suck in another taste of the wild air. I need to tell him what's coming. "The Sons are looking for me."

He doesn't take his eyes off the road. "Figured as much."

"You get what that means, right? They want me dead. And I won't go down without a fight."

He sighs. "You never have."

What's that supposed to mean? He sounds so certain. "I'm sorry, have we met?"

"Yes." He must catch my look of confusion in the mirror because he adds, "Perhaps not yet."

"What do you mean, not yet? Either we've met or we haven't." And I'm pretty sure I would remember meeting a red-headed Elvis Costello with mutton chops.

"We have a mutual friend."

"Joe. I know. That's not the same as actually meeting. Did Joe tell you about what happened?"

"I wasn't thinking of Joe. I meant Lord Lorcan."

"Not ringing a bell." I don't know a Lord anything. I mean, Blake can be holier than thou at times, but he's only a demigod.

"You probably know him as Montgomery."

The cold air fills me until I'm nearly numb. I haven't heard his name in weeks. Austin Montgomery. A murderer. A god. The air in the car swirls around me before it occurs to me to summon it. I fight against the urge to blow out the windows, struggle to keep my power under control. It's what got me into this mess in the first place. Besides, Austin is safely locked up in the underworld.

I start counting in exponents of seven until the wind

settles around me. I don't speak until I'm certain I can say his name without losing it. "Austin Montgomery is not my friend."

Mick lifts his chin stiffly. "Sorry to hear that."

I wonder if this means he won't help me. "You can just drop me off at the next town."

"Can't."

Crap. I don't even know this guy. Maybe this was a set-up to begin with; Blake was furious when he sent me off with Joe.

"Okay, let me out here then." I look out the window. There's nothing but fields and sheep and rain.

"Easy, bandia."

It's what Blake said to me the first time he saw me. The tears are back all at once, streaming down my cheeks in long lines, little waterfalls of saline that I can't stop.

Mick doesn't say anything more. He keeps his eyes firmly on the road. I don't have much choice but to trust him. I'm halfway around the world with no friends and a bunch of demigods out to kill me.

I don't know how long I cry, but it's a good half hour later before Mick tries to talk to me again. "I don't know what happened with you and ... " He pauses, biting back Austin's name. "It doesn't matter. I am sworn to protect all that is his."

My anger is back tenfold. My body burns with fire, but it's a welcome relief from the hurt that squeezes my heart. "I am not his," I say. "Not even close. Austin killed my horse. He nearly drowned my best friend. He made me kill my boyfriend. I sent him back to the underworld where he belongs."

Mick covers his mouth with his hand. "Oh my."

"Are you laughing?" Blue flames start to spark on my fingertips, my power there before I can stop it, ready to strike. I take a deep breath and concentrate on another element: Water. Ice.

Better. I can control this. I have to.

Mick shakes his head, but he keeps his hand firmly over his mouth.

"It's not funny."

Mick removes his hand and looks as stoic as ever. "The path to your destiny never is." Then he does laugh. "I think I'm going to like you."

That makes one of us.

TWO

"We're almost there," Mick says from up front.

I open my eyes, trying to focus. I glance at my watch. Nearly four hours have passed since we left the airport in Dublin. The rain stopped somewhere along the way and the sun peeks out from behind fluffy white clouds, making everything even brighter.

We drive through a little town that looks like something straight out of a theme park, with cobblestone streets and rows of old buildings in bright colors. The pub on the corner has a suit of armor standing guard at the front door. Tiny little iced cakes dot the window of a bakery across the street. As we turn up a hill, I get a perfect view of the harbor, filled with fishing boats and a few pretty schooners.

"Cath is beautiful, isn't she?"

"Cath?"

"The town. The prettiest stop on the Dingle Peninsula. But then I'm biased."

"It is pretty."

"Wait until you see Lorcan Hall."

"Is it here?"

"About ten kilometers north. The ancestral home of the Montgomerys."

"So we're going to his house." As much as I don't like this idea, I have to admit it's the last place the Sons will look for me. Joe is kind of brilliant.

"It's more of an estate. But you needn't worry—a Montgomery hasn't set foot on the property for at least a thousand years." As he drives, Mick gives me a history of the estate and the improvements that have been made over the last few centuries. I'm sure it's not uncommon for people to know the history of the property they manage, but he talks as though he personally oversaw the work.

And then it occurs to me—he has. Joe isn't the only giolla around. While Joe has always served the Sons of Killian, it makes sense that the gods would enlist giolla to help them, too.

"You're like Joe?"

"Not at all. I'm far more outgoing."

I'm not letting him evade the question. "You're a giolla?"

Mick sits up straighter, the top of his head brushing the ceiling of the car. "In the service of Arawn."

Arawn . . . Austin's true name, the name that serves him as the god of the underworld. Before he showed up in my hometown, he'd been banished for a thousand years, confined to the underworld for taking a mortal life. After only three years of being able to once again traverse the gateway between his realm and ours, he was banished a second time. By me.

Not that I feel bad about it. The underworld can have him.

"How long have you been in his service?" I finally ask.

"A long while."

The road narrows as it winds higher, twisting and turning through a forest of trees until I can't see the town or the ocean anymore. "Can you remember the last time Austin came here?" The giolla are keepers of the history they live, so Mick should know this.

"Aye. The lord graced us in the year of our gods 1009. The house never got a wink." Mick's eyes crinkle in the corners, and I wonder how he manages to keep from getting crow's feet given the centuries he's been alive.

"What was he like then?" I can't imagine Austin as some kind of medieval lord.

"Fancied himself quite a lad."

"Figures."

Mick nods his head like he's made a decision. "I give him a new name and persona every sixty years or so, even though he never comes back to claim it."

"Did you know he was back? In California?" It's kind of sad that Mick has been maintaining Austin's life on earth for all these years for nothing.

Mick doesn't answer. He straightens a little more, though there's barely room in the car for him to do so. "Are you truly a bandia then?" he asks, changing the subject. "Is that what's stirred the Sons?"

The Sons of Killian have hunted my ancestors for centuries. The same way they hunt me now. "Who else knows?" I demand. "About the bandia?"

"Even the most stalwart of the people here know our town's history. The bandia are part of that." Mick smiles. "Best you don't go throwing your power around where anyone can see."

Maybe Joe did fill him in on why I'm running. "So you're saying my one-woman magic show is out?"

"Perhaps not. I imagine most folks would pay a small fortune to see it."

Just when I think I'm going to be carsick from all the turns, he pulls the car off the road, stopping in front of a huge pair of iron gates. Each gate has a giant metal sun at its center and is flanked by a high stone wall that goes on as far as the eye can see, on either side. Mick hits a button on the rearview mirror and the gates open with a creak. He picks up his phone and says something in a thick brogue that I can't understand at all.

After a mile or so, we crest the top of a hill. The ocean is visible again, stretching out beyond a flat expanse of land that ends in a steep drop to the thrashing waves. The house sits on the bluff. Grass and stone pathways dot the land around it, ending at a low stone wall that follows the edge of the cliff. The jagged hillside matches the fierceness of the white caps and rocks below.

The house itself is more of a castle than a home, a giant

stone building with two immense wings that fold behind it, walling in a courtyard on three sides. Matching round turrets flank the corners, like something out of a fairy tale. To the right is a large barn, encased in matching stone. A man lunges a shiny bay horse in an adjacent field. It's a home fit for a king.

For a god.

"You like it?" Mick stops the car so I can take it all in.

My chest expands as I breathe in the salty air. "It might be the most beautiful place I've ever seen."

"I know exactly what you mean." He eases the car down the hill, gliding to a stop at the front of the house.

Eight people are lined up along the stone drive. They look perfectly starched in their black uniforms, but on closer inspection they all seem to fidget, shifting in their places as they try to get a glimpse past the dark tint of the car windows.

Mick gets out of the car and walks around to open the rear door. The eyes of the assembled staff settle on me as I step out, in my slept-in jeans and sweatshirt. I push a strand of brown hair behind my ear in a useless attempt to tame it.

Mick goes down the line, introducing me to each person in turn. I follow, bowing my head and extending my hand. I try to commit their names to memory, but by the time we get to the frizzy-haired, freckled woman on the end, a cook named Rhiannon, their names are swirling around my head in a jumble.

Rhiannon takes my hand. I'm about to let go, but she tightens her fingers, trapping me in a painful squeeze. She stares at the silver charm bracelet around my wrist, taking in the small horse and horseshoe charms before settling on the silver wolfsbane blossom dangling from the chain.

Her eyes go wide, and she drops my hand just as suddenly as she trapped it. She backs up a step. "I'll not work in the house with her."

Mick puts a hand on Rhiannon's shoulder. "She is a guest, and you will treat her as one."

"I don't serve witches."

The word stings.

So much for running. I can't escape what I am. The eyes of the assemblage are all on me now, still curious, but wary too.

The stable manager, a short, rough-looking man who I think is named Malcolm, laughs. "Can't you see she's American?" This draws a laugh from the other four men in line.

"Enough." Mick's voice is barely above a whisper, but everyone stops laughing immediately, recognizing it for the command it is. Even Rhiannon looks chastened, her eyes focused firmly on the ground in front of her. Do they know what Mick is? Or is he using compulsion?

A light rain breaks free from the clouds, but no one moves. Mick takes my hand in his and I let him, grateful for the acceptance.

"Brianna is a guest of his lordship. If you cannot respect her, leave now."

I don't want to be Austin's guest, even if he's trapped safely in the underworld. I don't want to be Austin's anything. I pull my hand away from Mick.

Rhiannon glances up from the ground, her eyes narrowing

on the pendant hanging at my throat, a silver circle the size of a quarter with a wolfsbane blossom etched on it. "Accept my resignation then." She reaches for the arm of the girl next to her. "And Shannon's. No daughter of mine will work here."

The rain comes harder now, but everyone stands in place. I shiver as the water soaks into my hair, turning the straightened locks into wild curls. There will be no taming it here.

Shannon doesn't move. She makes eye contact with me from beneath her blond bangs. Her lips curve in a shy smile. She wants to stay, but her mother is right—she should run far away from this house while she can. I am exactly what her mother says.

A witch. A Seventh Daughter of Danu, who can control the elements and leave destruction in her wake. A danger to them all.

Just ask Blake.

Rhiannon crosses herself as she drags her daughter toward the road. She stops and points a long, crooked finger at my chest. "She will bring a plague on this house."

The chill that fills me now has nothing to do with the rain. It's bone deep. Austin used to call me Juliet to his Romeo, but it was Blake and I who were doomed from the start. Rhiannon's words echo in my head, and all I can think is that Shakespeare only had it partially right.

I am a plague on both their houses.

THREE

Sleep is sporadic. I can't close my eyes without seeing the fury in Blake's eyes when he sent me away. I thought he could forgive me for what I did to him on the beach. I killed him, but I found a way to bring him back. Maybe we could've trusted each other after that, but his family was a whole other story.

What did he expect me to do? Just let them keep hurting me? A bandia can fight back. But I wouldn't hurt innocent people. How could he think that I could?

I'm left alone in a giant house that's basically a castle, with a staff that's afraid to look at me after Rhiannon's outburst. I spend most of my time in the huge room that Mick designated as mine. The bed is so high, it has its own stairs. The floors match the stone walls, making the room seem more cold than cozy, an elaborate cave softened by feather comforters and pillows. I pass a good seventy-two hours fueled by nineteenth-century science texts from the library and lots of room service.

At first, I jump at every sound, as if the Sons are right around the corner, waiting to catch me off guard. It's not like my fragile truce with the Sons was going to last forever, but I expected it to last more than a few short months. I don't even know if anyone was hurt in that fire. Or if Blake means to kill me too.

By the third day, I'm more restless than wary, and I set out to explore. I stick to the halls, taking in the paintings and furniture which make the house feel more like a museum than a home. Even with all the elaborate furnishings, there's an emptiness here, one so vast that even the thickest tapestry can't wall out the drafts and echoes. It's a house without a family. Without a soul.

It's not until I get outside and make my way to the barn that the cold chill that's settled around me since I fled Rancho Domingo starts to dissipate. The familiar smells of oats and leather chase away the darkness. Malcolm, the stable manager, nods at me as I walk down the barn aisle. He looks even rougher in the half-light of the sun peeking through the clouds, his face pockmarked and scarred.

I stop at every stall, taking a minute to introduce myself to each horse. A thick bay flicks his ears at the sound of my voice and walks over to lift his nose over his stall door. I stroke his cheek.

"I see you've met Tally." Malcolm steps beside me. "Don't let him fool you. He's all charm on the ground, but he's a handful under tack. A tiger in a horse's body."

"I know the type."

"You ride, then?" For someone who looks like a back-alley thug, the man's voice is light and friendly.

"I had a horse back home." I smile and hold out my hand.

Malcolm takes it without hesitation. He was the one who stood up for me when Rhiannon called me a witch. I don't know whether he doubted her or was just trying to score points with Mick, but I like him either way.

"Can I ride?" I feel almost shy, asking.

"Aye, the horses will be glad for the company. But not Tally; start with Molly. She knows her way around the property and she won't give you any trouble."

Molly turns out to be a thick black mare with three white socks and a small star in the middle of her forehead. I groom her myself, but Malcolm insists on saddling her. He gives me a leg up and then points me in the direction of a path that disappears over a hill.

I ease Molly into a trot and then a canter. On a long stretch, I let her have her head and gallop. Everything goes by in a blur of green and gray, and my mind goes blank as it registers only the beat of Molly's hooves on the soft earth and the cold wind on my face.

By the time I bring her back down to a walk, I can no longer see the house or barn behind me. A small trail branches off to the right of the main path, narrowing toward the ocean. I taste the salt on my lips, and I'm seized with longing to be closer.

I turn Molly the opposite way. I can't afford to indulge my instincts. Not anymore.

I find a trail that disappears into rows of neatly planted trees before twisting up a steep hillside. I ride up, looking back every now and then to admire the view of the estate below.

A small clearing sits at the top of the hill. The remnants of two stone walls meet at a right angle in the middle of the field. The strange ruin is six feet at its highest point, three feet at its lowest. The longer wall stretches for about fifteen feet before turning the corner and going five feet farther. The stones are odd shapes, but they fit together like a jigsaw puzzle, forming neat rows.

I set Molly loose on a patch of fresh grass and approach the crumbled structure on foot.

The gray sky turns darker. Wisps of white mist crawl along the ground, breaking off in opposite directions where they meet the base of the wall. The stacked stones sealed with mud remind me of the wall I saw in the field with Danu . . . in the vision I had when I tried a love spell with my friends at home. Only this wall is smaller and in disrepair.

The wind is cold, cutting through my light sweater. As I step closer to the ruin, I feel dizzy. I place my hand against the wall to regain my balance. The smooth stone is marred by deep lines cut into it, carved into primitive shapes. The first shape is a circle with lines pointing out, like a child's drawing of the sun. Next to it is a crude lightning bolt. The last shape is more detailed—the silhouette of a horse, its mane and tale flowing behind it as it runs.

I know that horse.

I finger the little horse charm hanging from my bracelet. I lift my wrist, holding the charm next to the stone carving, marveling at the similarities. The charm brushes the stone, and there's a flash of bright silver light before everything disappears.

Everything.

I'm surrounded by fog, so thick I can't make out anything but the cloud of choked air around me. The ground beneath my feet gives way to air, as if I'm floating. I close my eyes to try to orient myself, but that only makes me dizzier.

When I blink my eyes open, I'm back at the ruin, the solid ground under my feet. I catch my breath. Okay—I'm right here. Only everything looks different. The south wall is taller, reaching over my head nearly twelve feet or so. The mist and gray sky are gone and bright sunshine lights the little clearing, which is filled with spring flowers. Molly is nowhere in sight.

A girl laughs in the distance. When I turn to look, there's nothing, just the wind whistling through the trees, which are thinner and sparser than I remember.

I hear the laughter again. Now I see the girl. She's about my age, maybe a little younger, with dark hair that flows to the middle of her back. Her dress is long, made of thick brown wool that brushes the ground. It's belted at the waist with a long strip of matching fabric. Her neck is adorned with a thick silver chain, accented by three distinct charms I recognize well: a horse, a horseshoe, and an odd-shaped flower.

I glance at my bracelet. The charms are identical, except for scratches and tarnish from years of wear.

"Gwyn," a boy with a thick Irish accent calls from behind her. "Come back." He doesn't speak in English, not exactly, but I understand him perfectly.

The girl's name is Gwyn? Danu had a daughter named Gwyn. Supposedly my charms belonged to her. Is this Danu's daughter? My ancestor?

The girl laughs again and runs toward the ruin. Toward me. She stops and turns toward the boy's voice before she sees me. "Come on, Aaron. The grass looks soft enough to lie on."

That gets the boy's attention. He peeks around the trunk of a tree, a mop of brown hair covering his eyes. "Is that so?"

A squeak catches in my throat. The boy's hair is long, brushing his collarbone, but it still falls across his forehead in a familiar, unruly way. His smile is crooked, the little imperfection that made Austin's otherworldly beauty feel almost human.

Impossible.

Gwyn laughs again and runs toward the field of grass and flowers.

The boy starts to run after her, but stops when he sees me. Gwyn is already across the field, darting into the trees, but he doesn't follow. He takes a tentative step in my direction.

I lean back against the wall, reaching for fire, wind, any weapon. For the first time in weeks, the elements are not there in an instant. There's nothing but cold fear.

"Austin?" My voice shakes. It can't be him. She called him Aaron, not Austin. Austin is banished to the underworld. He can't hurt me anymore.

"Would that I were." His eyes rake down my legs. "Do I know you?"

I'm wearing jeans, but suddenly feel like I need more clothing. "It's me. Brianna?"

He cocks his head to the side. "Are you not from around here then?"

"Of course not." The sunlight does little to warm the air. I shiver.

He steps closer. "Are you an angel?"

A laugh escapes before I can stop it. Does he really not know me? "Hardly."

Gwyn calls from across the meadow. "Aaron!"

"Aaron?" I take in his clothes. The belted wool shirt that hangs almost to his knees, the coarse leggings that look almost like tights. He's dressed like one of Robin Hood's merry men.

He bows slightly. "Lord Lorcan."

If that girl really is Danu's daughter, then is this boy Austin before he was banished? One of the personas created by Mick as the current Lord Lorcan?

He doesn't look away from me. "And you are?"

"I think I'm from the future."

"My future?"

"Don't you know?" This is where Austin should make one of his cracks about how we will end badly.

He smiles, the familiar crooked one. "Your ambition is admirable, but I'm not exactly on the market."

He thinks I'm hitting on him? Please. "Get over yourself."

"Pardon?" There's an air of innocence to him that's unexpected. It's hard to imagine this boy as the boy who put my friend's life in danger and tricked me into killing Blake. But I know it's him. It has to be.

Gwyn comes out of the trees. She moves across the meadow, dragging her skirts behind her. Austin's eyes flit toward her.

The dizziness I felt earlier is back tenfold. I double over with nausea, falling into the wet grass. When I open my eyes, the sky is gray again. My clothes cling to me, soaked through from the ground. My teeth chatter as I push myself to my feet.

Molly grazes in the patch of grass where I left her. The wall is smaller, six feet at its highest point.

What did I just see? It was Austin, I'm sure of it. He was here with Danu's daughter.

I make my way across the little field. "You okay, girl?"

Molly continues chewing, unfazed. So it's just me then.

I swing into the saddle and glance back at the ruin, half-expecting to see a ghost, but there's nothing.

I've traveled to places I couldn't understand before. I've met Danu and even Killian in visions. But this felt different somehow. I wasn't trying to hold back my power or attempting to cast a magic spell. And Gwyn and Austin didn't seem to know who I was. They weren't part of my present.

I'm pretty sure I intruded into their past.

FOUR

I should leave this place. The last thing I need is the ghost of Austin Montgomery's past haunting me from across the centuries. It's bad enough that the ghost of Blake Williams' present keeps invading my dreams.

I could go back home to California and fight the Sons. It's not like I'm afraid. I'm not alone, either. There's another bandia—Sherri Milliken is out there somewhere. God knows she's up for a fight. But I've never wanted a war with the Sons. I never wanted any of this. I just want a normal life. A normal boyfriend, one who trusts me. Is that too much to ask?

Apparently it is, if Blake is any indication.

I didn't want to go to his little sister's fifteenth birthday party, but Blake was so adamant. I get that he wanted me to be part of his whole life, not just some girl he kept hidden away, and I wanted that too. Still, it was one thing to want it, and another thing to try to make conversation with the backs of his parents' shoulders. I'd only met Mallory once, and I was pretty sure she hated me as much as the rest of the family. It had only been three months since the Sons initiated me into their Circle, and I was ready to fold. Yet Blake kept insisting we go all in.

It wasn't just Blake's family, either. The Sons had only allowed me into their ranks because they thought I could lead them to Sherri; they thought I was under Blake's thumb. And maybe on some level, I was. I thought I loved him, anyway. I thought he loved me.

I'd only been at the party for a few minutes. Blake hadn't even seen me yet. He was talking to a group of breeders, next to a built-in barbecue made of stacked stone that matched the exterior of his parents' McMansion. Without the soul bond that we once shared, I could no longer feel his emotions, so it was impossible to tell if his dimpled smile was real or a mask.

Sierra Woodbridge, the self-proclaimed leader of the Brianna Paxton Not-a-Fan Club, flipped her cherry-striped hair away from her face and curled her lip as I walked toward her and her boyfriend, Jonah Timken. I would've kept my distance, but they were blocking the narrow path that cut across the yard. Jonah tightened his arm around Sierra's waist, pulling her closer. She melted into him, completely oblivious to the fact that the squeeze was not a sign of affection.

Jonah succeeded in distracting Sierra while his gaze followed the line of my floral skirt to where it draped along the curve of my hip. He winked at me, over Sierra's shoulder.

Gross.

"Keep walking, witch," Sierra said. "No one wants you here."

The comments used to be murmurs, malicious whispers I wasn't meant to actually hear, but in the weeks leading up to Mallory's party, the breeders had become more confrontational. Still, I tried to ignore her. Sierra and I would never be friends, even if we weren't on different sides of the war on magic. It was better to keep walking.

"That's right," Sierra said. "Run to your boyfriend. He's the only reason you're still alive. Might as well enjoy it while you can."

Jonah's grin got bigger.

My fingers tingled with a fiery itch—desperate to unleash a torrent of flame, to wipe that smile off of Jonah's face. To wipe Jonah off the face of the planet. I should've been used to these flashes of power, given the months of hanging out with my mortal enemy, but they seemed to grow stronger with each passing day, impulses that were becoming harder to control. I ducked behind a large palm tree and started counting.

6. 36. 216. 1296. Better. By the time I got to the seventh exponent of six, I was sure the itch was snuffed out.

I should've known better.

———

Mick walks into the kitchen, where I'm fumbling with a complicated piece of machinery that's supposed to be a coffeemaker. If a degree in mechanical engineering is a prerequisite to making a cup of coffee, it's no wonder everyone here drinks tea.

Mick wears a dark gray suit today, with pinstripes and pants that taper in at the ankle. He looks like a nineteenth-century hipster. All that's missing are a pair of nerdy glasses. "You settling in?" he asks. At least he doesn't comment on the pajama pants, oversized sweater, and three pairs of knee socks that I'm trying to pass off as an outfit.

"Define settling in." Holing up in a castle on the far coast of Ireland would've sounded like a dream vacation a week ago. Now it just feels lonely. And cold.

Mick takes the coffee grounds from me and presses them into a small metal cup. "I've been wondering if Joe was wise to send you here."

"Why?" As far as I can tell, no one knows where I am. I checked in with my parents online, but even they knew better than to ask where I went.

Mick adds more grounds to the cup and slides it into the contraption, in no hurry to answer my question. He places a small glass underneath the spout before he presses a button and looks up. "You saw how Rhiannon reacted when you arrived. The people here know well enough the destruction that a single bandia can bring. They're at least as a much of a danger to you as the Sons are."

"You mean the locals? But they're humans."

"You shouldn't underestimate them. Humans were responsible for defeating the gods the first time."

"But I'm on their side."

Mick arches a brow. "Are you sure you're a bandia?"

"I wish I wasn't."

Mick focuses on the dark liquid as it finishes pouring into the little cup, but he has a curious look in his eyes. "You are an enigma."

"An enigma?"

"An enigma inside a mystery, wrapped in magic that you're afraid to use."

"I'm not afraid to use it." That's the problem. I can't seem to stop myself.

Mick hands me the tiny cup of black sludge. "It's probably best if you don't go into town. There will be rumors. We can't stop them, but there's no need to fuel them either."

"So I'm trapped here? Like some girl in an ivory tower?"

"It's just a suggestion."

"Of course it is." I add two cubes of sugar to the tiny cup of coffee. It won't be enough to mask the bitter taste, but Mick doesn't keep vanilla syrup on hand, and the odds of my getting some steamed milk are less than zero. "Can I take the car?"

"I think there might be a bit of the bandia in you after all. I suppose you won't listen when I say you should stay in one place for a while."

I can't stay cooped up here forever. I stride toward the door, but stop halfway. "Who was Aaron?"

"Ah." Mick leans against the stone countertop.

"He was Austin, wasn't he?"

"The last incarnation of Lord Lorcan, before the thousand years he was locked away in the underworld."

How did I manage to see Austin from over a thousand years ago? And why?

All I know is that I shouldn't be here. "If you won't give me the keys, will you at least take me into town?"

"It's not a good idea," Mick says.

"I won't stay here."

He almost smiles. "I didn't say I wouldn't take you."

FIVE

The town is even more magical up close. It looks the same as I imagine it did centuries ago, with stone streets and stone buildings and wood facades painted in bright colors. We stop at the bakery with the little cakes, and I eat three of them while Mick sips a cup of raspberry tea.

No one pays any attention to us. "I don't know what you were worried about," I say as I bite into yet another little cake. It's sweet without being sugary.

"No sense taking risks if you don't have to."

"The Sons don't know where I am, do they?"

Mick shakes his head. "I told you, the Sons aren't your only concern. The Milesians are every bit as dangerous."

"The Milesians? But the Sons are the Milesians." The Sons were the descendants of the warriors who'd been tasked with ridding Ireland of the last vestiges of magic.

"*Were* the Milesians. After Killian bonded with Danu,

he became something more. More than a human—a demi-god, like Danu herself. Cursed with the dark powers of a god, he and his descendants became the very thing the Milesians sought to destroy."

"I get that, but Killian went on killing demigods," I say. Killian's new, godly power made him very successful; he eradicated all the remaining demigod lines except for Danu's. Ironically, while the bandia descended from Danu believed that Killian had killed Danu, and therefore swore eternal vengeance on the Sons, I knew the truth: *Austin* was the one who'd killed Danu, to spark a war between the bandia and Killian's heirs. Austin wanted the bandia on his side, fighting against those who'd conquered the gods of Ireland. If the bandia defeated the Sons, according to Austin's logic, the gods could one day return to earth.

Mick stirs a cube of sugar into his tea. "Killian wasn't the only warrior. The Milesians—the merely human Milesians—still exist, Brianna. As I said, they are at least as dangerous as the Sons."

"Does anyone actually like the bandia?"

"I like you fine."

Shannon walks into the little bakery. She sees me and smiles warmly before coming up to our little table. "How are you?" She strings the words together so fast they sound like one word.

"Good." It's hard not to smile back.

Shannon's hair is plaited in a long braid that falls between her shoulder blades, but her bangs nearly cover her eyes. "I wanted to apologize for my mum. She's not as off her nut as she sounded. She's only marginally insane."

"It's fine," I say. *Your mom was exactly right about me.*

"I work at the dress shop around the corner now. We have some beautiful party dresses. You should come."

"Thanks, but I don't think I'll be going to any parties while I'm here." I don't think I'll be going to any parties for a while. Not when the last one ended up in a blaze of blue fire.

"You should come anyway." Her smile is so genuine that I'm tempted to take her up on it.

Mick waits until Shannon leaves before he tries to talk me out of it. "She's harmless, but her mother is a different story."

"I like her."

"You need to lay low."

"I'm not going to spend the rest of my life under house arrest. It's not like I can't defend myself."

"That's what I'm afraid of."

"Oh." I stare down at the tray of tea cakes, my appetite gone. Is that why Mick doesn't want me around the villagers without a babysitter? Does he think I'll lose control of my power?

I'd really thought I had my power under control. There was no question that it seemed to come at me quicker, stronger, the more I was around the Sons, but I was always able to keep it to a low simmer. Maybe if Mallory hadn't chosen that exact moment, when fire still lingered at the edge of my self-control, to confront me at her party, I could've stopped it.

Blake's little sister marched up to me as I stood behind the palm tree, counting. Her arms were crossed tight across her chest, wrinkling the smooth lines of her designer dress. "I don't want you here," she said. Mallory had the same silver-blond hair as Blake, but that was where the similarities ended. Blake's easy confidence and friendly smile drew people in. Mallory was pretty, but her features were sharp, her body stiff. Untouchable.

She probably thought her statement was some shocking revelation. I almost wanted to laugh, but since she was only fifteen, I tried to appease her instead. "I think Blake wants us to get to know each other."

"Why? I know everything I need to know about you. You're a witch."

I took a breath, checking to be sure the fire inside me wasn't going to fight me for control. I was pretty sure that taking down the birthday girl in a ball of flame was a party faux pas. "And you feel the need to tell me this because...?"

"I know what you are. Everyone knows. You might be able to lead my brother around by his dick, but you're nothing to me. Less than nothing."

Her words shouldn't have hurt—they weren't anything worse than what I'd heard a hundred times from Sierra or Portia or any of the breeders. But I couldn't help the bitter laugh that escaped my lips. Everyone thought Blake was with me for the sex. The truth was, we hadn't been alone together since we'd broken the bond. The one time we were,

Blake wouldn't let it get that far. He denied it, but we both knew the truth: he was afraid that we'd bind our souls again.

I couldn't expect her to understand Blake and me. Not when I didn't understand it myself.

"There's no such thing as 'less than nothing,'" I said, trying to ignore my blood's rising temperature and focus on something more rational. "Under the theory of infinite small-ness, things can always be halved, shaved into smaller and smaller parts."

Mallory blinked. "Whatever. Why don't you go find my brother so you can screw him and leave?"

I glanced toward the barbecue. Portia Bruton stood next to Blake, her eyes flitting from her sandals to Blake's charming smile. He looked relaxed, almost happy. More comfortable with the daughter of the Sons' leader than he could ever be with me.

I used to know exactly what Blake was feeling. Hell, I felt every emotion he did, when we were bonded. But that was before. All I had at Mallory's party was my own loneli-ness as I navigated a house full of people who'd prefer me dead; my own jealousy, as I noticed how genuine Blake's smile appeared as he talked to Portia.

Mallory followed my gaze and let out an unkind laugh. "Maybe my brother's finally coming to his senses."

I didn't need this brat rubbing it in. "You better hope not." I turned to face her, letting the fire come. I raised my hand so she could see the blue flames arc between my fingers. "Right now, he's the only thing keeping you alive."

She backed up a step, eyes wide. "Witch."

For the first time since I'd gotten to the party, I felt empowered. Strong. Mallory might be a descendant of Killian, but only the Sons—the seventh-generation Sons—manifested Killian's demigod power. She was just a breeder.

Human.

I moved my hand to the right, letting the fire fly from my fingers. The blue flame sailed past Mallory, but she screamed anyway. The fireball hit the center of the large swimming pool with a blue flash that fizzled and vanished almost as soon as it sparked. The loss of the fire made me instantly cold.

A group of breeders standing by the pool looked around with mild panic, trying to find the source of the blue flash. I stepped out from behind the palm tree and smiled.

Let them look.

Let them see that their months of persecution had not rendered me weak. It only made me stronger. They shouldn't hurl stones as if I were a defenseless girl.

I shivered, but not from the cold. Was I seriously considering hurting these people? What was I becoming?

I hadn't been lying to Rush when I'd told him I was no threat to his people. I'd been lying to myself.

Blake saw me now. His blond hair glowed against the setting sun, shading his face in darkness.

I reached for his emotions, finding, of course, only my own anger and frustration and fear. Blake's body language gave away nothing. Ever the poker player, he kept his expression a mask of polite interest. If I was closer, I might have seen the vein along the line of his neck stand out, the one tell he couldn't master.

It was only a matter of seconds before Rush and Jonah appeared in their demigod forms. I knew they wouldn't let my display of power go unchallenged.

Everything happened so quickly after that.

A flash of blue light flew over the people gathered outside and exploded in flame on the roof of Blake's house. People screamed and ran as another explosion rocked the west side of the home. Blue fire was everywhere.

I couldn't feel it.

I couldn't stop it, either.

SIX

When Mick and I get back to Lorcan Hall, I'm still restless. I pull on a jacket and walk out a back door of the house, toward the edge of the bluff. The waves below crash and churn against the rocks, sending sprays of water straight up. It's nothing like the rhythmic sounds of the waves rolling in to the beach in California. There's no order to the swirls of riptides, to the waves colliding and attacking before being swallowed by another rush of water from behind.

Water stirs inside me, there before I even call it, a power as strong as the ocean. As wild. I conjure a wall of water and push it over the bluff with as much force as I can summon. It rushes out across the rocks before collapsing and merging with the sea.

This small display of power does nothing to curb the ache in my chest. I want to be closer, somehow. Part of the sea. I walk along the bluff until I find a worn switchback trail that leads down to a rocky beach. I pick my way down the trail slowly. By the time I get to the bottom, the sun has dipped behind dark clouds, making the early afternoon look more like night. The days last forever here, the sun clinging to the earth until nearly midnight as if to make up for the constant cloud cover.

Something calls to me, singing to my blood. It's a pounding in my chest, a drumbeat that pushes me forward. The water looks even wilder from down here on the shore; waves crash against tall rocks that soar above me. The wind carries the sea in its grasp, creating its own icy current that pelts my cheeks. This beach has no sand, just rocks of all shapes and sizes arranged haphazardly. A small passageway veers between two boulders, large enough for a person to pass through.

I make my way across the rocks, slipping through the boulders to another, smaller beach. The air swirls in circles, trapped against the bluff and boulders, creating a natural wind tunnel. It should be freezing, but steam is billowing from a crack in the rock wall that rises up at least a hundred feet from where I stand. There's a glint of gold behind the cloud of steam, and I move toward it instinctively.

Wind, water, fire, and earth converge at once—all my powers harnessed into one chaotic surge. It's overwhelming and incredible. I lift my hands up to the sky, wanting to take it all in, alive with the elements pulsing through my veins, pulsing through this place.

The power that fills me is stronger than any I've felt before, yet I feel peaceful, calm. This wildness is who I am. I let fire, wind, and water out to the ocean in one burst as the ground shakes beneath my feet. A flash of blue lights up the darkening sky, creating lightning-like arcs that flare out in several directions at once before my power settles back inside me.

The wall beside me rumbles and shakes.

I freeze.

I reach for the earth, finding it quiet and undisturbed beneath my feet. I can't feel the wall as it shakes.

No.

It can't be happening again.

I instinctively move away from the wall. The rumbling continues. Not in the wall but *behind* it. The sound gets louder. Something is coming.

I take a few more steps backward, not taking my eyes off the shaking cliff. A rock falls to the ground a few feet away from me. I run to the shelter of the two boulders. The opening in the wall groans and shakes, widening with a loud crack that sends another shower of rocks to the ground.

A dark shape sails through, landing with a hard thud on the ground, barely missing the boulder that I'm crouching behind.

The wall cracks and groans again before sealing itself tight with a final shudder.

I stare at the dark figure on the ground, waiting for it to rise up and attack. It doesn't move. I take a tentative step forward. A shirtless guy lies on his stomach, still and unmoving. A body?

I kneel down and place my hand on his neck. There's a pulse. I pull on his arm, rolling him on to his back.

Austin's lips curl up into a familiar, crooked smile.

He's draped in ancient plaid, a thick piece of fabric around his waist, but he's not glowing gold like he normally does when in his true form. His jeweled broadsword is nowhere to be seen. He's filthy, still covered in clumps of rock and debris from the cliff wall. Yet the dirt can't mask the sculpted lines of his face and the perfect proportions of his body. He is a god, after all.

I drop his arm, letting him fall back against the rocky ground.

"That hurts." He blinks, propping himself up on an elbow. "That shouldn't hurt."

"And you shouldn't be here," I say. *Should. Not.* I banished him to the underworld for a thousand years. By my count, he still has over nine-hundred ninety-nine years to go.

Austin groans and closes his eyes. Beneath the smudges on his face, his skin looks sallow and pale. Sweat beads along his brow. I touch my palm to his forehead. He's burning up.

The ocean fills me, cooling my hand before I can think to call it. It's becoming so instinctual—the elements come to me almost unconsciously now. Like I'm part of them. Except when they take on a life of their own.

Austin opens his eyes. "And Juliet is the sun."

I jerk my hand away from his forehead. "You need some new lines."

He rubs his temples. "Best I can do with this vise on my skull. Does pain always feel so bad?"

"It's called pain for a reason."

Austin lifts his head, his crooked smile in place despite the obvious effort it takes him. "Says the girl with a death wish."

"Are you threatening me?" He doesn't look like he's in any condition to threaten anyone.

"'Course not. I would never threaten you," he grunts as he pushes himself up into a sitting position.

"Oh, that's right, you prefer to threaten the people I love."

"For your own good."

"I'm the only one who gets to decide what's good for me." I take a step forward, flames simmering under my skin. "You shouldn't be here."

He watches the blue flames arc between my fingers. "Right. I've made quite a mess of things, haven't I?"

"How did you get here?" The spell I used to trap him in the underworld had worked. I know it. "You shouldn't be able to cross over."

"Perhaps fate has other plans for me."

A ball of flame appears in my hand. "A fireball to the head?"

He laughs and then stops himself, rubbing his forehead. "I hope not."

The sky darkens as more clouds roll in. Everything is wrong. I'm half a world away from my parents, my friends, Blake. For what? To postpone a war that will come for me anyway? To spend my last days alone, or worse, in the company of the very god who made me kill Blake?

The fire burns hot, my blood searing my skin from the inside. Austin watches the flames dance in my hand, and I swear there's something that looks a lot like fear in his eyes. Good. He should be afraid of me. But since when is Austin afraid of anything? He may be weak, but he's immortal.

"Go on," he says. "It's about time you acted like a bandia."

No. I am not a killer. I may have killed Blake, but only because I tried to save him. And I brought him back, too. That has to count for something.

I turn and throw the fireball as hard as I can at the water. It sails for fifty feet before it hits a wave with a bright blue blast and dies out.

Austin sighs and falls back against the rocks. "Perhaps there's hope for us yet."

I reach for the wind, gathering it with such strength that I have to wrap my arms around the boulder to keep from getting swept up in the strong gust, and send it flying at Austin. He soars into the air, his back slamming against the wall of rock behind him. I keep the wind on him, pinning him there, five feet above the ground.

I have to shout to be heard. "There is no us. There will never be any us. And if you come anywhere near me or anyone I care about, I will find a way to kill you."

I stop the wind as quickly as I called it, and Austin drops like a stone, landing hard on his side.

"There's my girl," he says as he rolls to his back and closes his eyes.

SEVEN

Mick watches me maneuver my roller bag down the winding staircase. He doesn't offer to help me. "You're leaving?"

"I've already booked a room over the pub in Cath," I say. Tomorrow I'll head back to Dublin. And from there, anywhere but here.

"I'll get the car."

Mick doesn't lecture me about safety or keeping my power in check as he drives me back into town. I don't know if he knows that Austin is back, but it hardly matters to me now. I just need to get out of here.

"I'm the first number on speed dial." He hands me a cell phone as I step out of the car in front of the Ornery Knight.

"Thanks, Mick."

"Mikel," he corrects. "I know there's no point arguing, but you should stay at Lorcan Hall. The Sons will be here soon."

"The Sons are coming here?" Why does he think the Sons are coming? Did Joe contact him?

"The call of the gateway is strong. They won't be able to ignore it."

The "call of the gateway" was undoubtedly why the Sons and the bandia were all living in San Diego County. The gateway was sealed when Austin was banished, but Austin isn't banished anymore. He's here. Along with the gateway. I've managed to come to the one place where the Sons are certain to be.

"Do the Sons know I'm here?" I ask.

"Doubt it. The power will draw them. Just as it draws you."

"I'm not staying."

"We'll see." He does that thing with the corner of his mouth where he almost smiles.

My room over the pub is tiny, with barely room for a twin bed and small nightstand. Apparently, it's the height of luxury in Cath because it has its own bathroom, although the shower consists of nothing more than a handheld sprayer next to the sink and a drain in the floor.

I wrap a threadbare blanket around my shoulders and curl up in the corner of the bed, flipping through the train schedule on the phone Mick gave me. In the morning, I'll take a taxi to the station in Tralee and catch a train to Dublin. By this time tomorrow, I'll be in London. Or Paris. Tuscany. Maybe Berlin.

Anywhere but here.

Still, some sick part of me wants to stay. My twisted

heart clings to a small tendril of hope, an undeniable spark of longing at the thought of the Sons coming here.

Blake.

I stomp on the thought and crush it into a billion microscopic shards. I will rip this little wish to shreds until there is absolutely nothing left. Screw infinite smallness. My heart is a vacuum, as dark and empty as a black hole. As lethal. I can't afford to indulge a stupid crush on a boy who doesn't even want me.

Not after what happened.

The explosions of blue flame at Mallory's party seemed to come from everywhere and nowhere, bright flashes of heat and fire. The back windows, near the Williams' living room, shattered. Acrid smoke choked me as people ran in every direction at once. I tried to stop it, but it was like the fire had a mind of its own, arcing and shooting back at me in rebellion.

Water.

I could feel water. I sent water at the flames in large waves, but it was too little, too late. The fire simply danced away, evading my efforts to tame it.

Blake appeared next to me in a flash of silver. He grabbed my hand and spun me toward him. "What did you do?"

"It's not me." Panic laced my words, but I believed what I said. The fire burning the house wasn't mine. I couldn't control it.

"Like hell." Silver sparks lit up Blake's green eyes. I'd seen him in his demigod form before—his perfect body clad in a swath of plaid fabric and illuminated in silver light that seemed to come from within—but his face was harder now. There was nothing beautiful about the pure hatred in his expression. "I saw you with my sister."

I opened my mouth to respond, but before I could say anything, another flash of silver flared on my right.

I needed to move.

I ran past Blake just as Jonah appeared where I'd been standing, his jeweled knife drawn. There would be no pretense of peace now. Jonah or Rush or Levi or one of the other Sons would kill me.

Blake ran after me and grabbed my elbow. "This way." He turned the opposite direction from the crowd making its way out the back gate, guiding me instead toward the burning house. "Can you clear a path through the flames?"

I could if they were mine, but this fire was beyond me. "I can't control it."

"We'll have to take our chances." Blake ran straight into the burning house.

I followed without hesitation.

The heat of the blaze was stronger inside. Flames were devouring an exterior wall and a couch in the corner. The hallway filled with dark smoke. I pulled my cardigan over my head, covering my mouth and nose with it.

Blake held tight to my wrist as he dragged me toward a large window that would take us out to the street. He stopped as a burst of flame came through the wall a few feet in front of us, spinning me around and pulling me back the way we came. We didn't get far. Blue flames had already filled in behind us. We were surrounded by fire.

I tried not to breathe, but my lungs fought me, the

instinct stronger than my will. I sucked in smoke until I could do nothing but choke and cough into my sweater.

I had to focus. I closed my eyes and concentrated on water running through my veins, becoming one with it. The wall of water I conjured was the largest I'd ever made, and I sent it at the flames in front of us.

It wasn't enough. Although the flames directly in front of us sputtered and died, they were soon replaced by another wave of fire rolling in to take their place.

I tried wind, whipping the air around us in an attempt to keep the fire and smoke at bay. It kept the fire from getting closer, but it also fed the flames, making them higher, stronger, hotter.

Blake's arms came around me as the heat and smoke became unbearable.

"Go," I rasped, pointing to the window. Blake had the power to disappear and reappear anywhere within his line of sight. He could transport himself to safety.

He kissed me instead.

I sputtered and choked against him, pushing at his chest. He needed to get out of here. A flash of silver lit behind my lids, and then the air around us turned cold and damp. I opened my eyes to find us floating in gray mist. I shivered against the cold, and Blake's arms held me tighter. He was still in his demigod form, but he was no longer lit up with starlight.

I knew where we were—that place that hovered between life and magic, where the Sons went when they disappeared while changing form or transporting themselves. I had been to the spirit realm before. Blake and I had come here together once, when we bonded.

I inhaled the damp air in large gulps. Blake held me against him until I stopped coughing. I curled my arms around his neck, clinging to him. Afraid to let go.

"I'll bring us back to the front porch just outside the window," Blake said into my neck. "That's the best I can do. You won't have much time. They'll be looking for you. Joe's car is parked near the intersection about four houses down. Hide in the back seat until Joe can meet you."

I listened to his instructions, not missing the iciness in his tone. We'd barely gotten out of the fire alive, and we were nowhere near safe. Blake had just kissed me, but when I looked into his eyes, all I saw was anger.

"It wasn't me."

His hands tightened on my arms. "Don't."

"But—"

"Don't lie to me now." His laugh was harsh. "Or was it all a lie?"

"What? Of course not. You can't believe that." I could see in his face that he did. He believed I could burn down his house and attack his family. He believed I could pretend to care about him as a way to get close to the Sons. "Your sister and I had a fight. The fire was there before I could stop it."

"She's human."

"Your sister can be pretty annoying." My attempt at a joke fell flat. Blake dropped his hands to his side. My arms still hung around his neck, but they felt awkward, heavy.

I didn't need Blake to tell me that my calling fire against

a girl who was no threat to me was a bad, bad sign. However close I'd come to starting a fight with one of the Sons, I'd never lost it like that with a human before. I'd never lost control of my elements.

But I'd sent my fire into the pool. I didn't attack the house.

Blake stiffened beneath my arms and I finally let my hands fall to my sides, too. I didn't need the bond between us to know that he didn't trust me.

"So you decided to burn down the whole damn place and everyone in it?" And there it was. Right out in the open. He didn't even pretend to trust me.

"No."

"What's wrong with you, Brianna? Did you want to kill them all?"

"I wouldn't do that," I whispered, though part of me wondered. The truth was, I didn't know what had happened.

"You just did."

My anger drove me forward, pushing him hard in the chest. "You've spent the last three months letting me be ridiculed and ostracized by your so-called friends while deliberately keeping me at a distance." It wasn't until I said the words that I realized how true they were. I was willing to risk bonding again—Blake wasn't. "And *I'm* the one that can't be trusted?"

Blake lifted his broadsword between us, the cold steel pressed against the skin covering my heart. "Looks that way."

He didn't make a cut. He didn't need to. The distrust in his eyes did the cutting for him. He leaned closer, glaring at me. "Assuming you can make it to Joe's car, he'll get you out. Then you better hope you never see my face again. You might've fooled me once, but I know exactly what kind of monster you are. If anyone back there is dead, I'll find you, and you'll wish like hell I'd let you burn in that fire."

I was already burning. Each word choked the air from my lungs and seared my heart, branding it with a black mark that would leave a permanent scar. I'd thought that loving him was enough. That we would find a way to be together. But I'd been so, so wrong. Blake didn't even want to try anymore. If he ever did.

"I love you."

"Don't." His voice was soft, but his eyes were hard.

"You felt it." There'd been a moment, before I killed him and broke the bond, that we'd both felt love. I didn't imagine it.

"I've felt a lot of things. That doesn't make them real." Blake stepped closer, wrapping his arms around me. There was no tenderness in the way he held me. His arms tightened.

"How did you get me out of that fire?"

"Like this." He lowered his head to mine and kissed me. Hard.

Even though we weren't bonded anymore, I could feel his anger just the same. It was there in the way his lips crushed mine with a force that rocked me backward. When my mouth opened against the assault, his tongue thrust inside and I swore I felt his anger mix with sharp desire, the one constant he couldn't deny.

It wasn't enough, but I reached for it anyway, kissing him

back with the same ferocity until the only fire I felt was the one that burned for Blake. My hands were in his hair, pulling him closer. He groaned into my mouth. I closed my eyes against the bright silver light that was growing around us.

The kiss ended as suddenly as it began, leaving my mouth cold and bruised. Before I could adjust my eyes against the light, there was another blinding flash. I could feel the emptiness where Blake had stood. He was gone.

Black smoke billowed out of the broken window, creating a screen that kept me hidden. It burned my nostrils and throat.

I turned toward the street and ran.

EIGHT

The sun breaks through the clouds, sending rays of light through the cracks in the blinds of the pub's main dining hall. The light casts the morning in a golden glow that's much too bright for my dark mood. A half cup of milk does nothing to temper the too-strong coffee, but I sip it anyway. I'm beginning to understand this country's fascination with tea. At least the coffee's better than the runny eggs and the chunk of igneous rock they try to pass off as a biscuit.

I slept little, spending half the night trying to work out how Austin could be back and what it might mean, and the other half planning my escape to nowhere in particular. All that matters is that I won't be anywhere near here when Blake arrives.

A shadow falls across my coffee. Austin stands over me, looking far better than he did when I left him on the beach. His hair is combed into some semblance of style, despite the unruly strands that fall into his eyes, and he's wearing a pair of dark jeans and a form-fitting cream sweater that appears calculated to show off the perfect proportions of lean muscle that define his chest and shoulders. He grabs a chair from an adjacent table and pulls it next to me, straddling it backward and placing his elbows on the backrest.

He glances at my suitcase. "You don't have to leave on my account." His accent is softer than I remember, still more English than Irish.

"I'm pretty sure I do."

His brown eyes meet mine, specks of gold reflecting the morning sunlight. "Why did you come here then? To my home?"

I stare down at my coffee. I don't owe Austin an explanation.

"You're not going to talk to me?" He leans forward and lowers his voice. "I don't know what I expected, but it wasn't this."

The bandia in me is there in an instant, all fire and vengeance. "I'll find a way to hurt you," I snap. I want to do more than hurt him. I want to destroy him. It's a fight to keep the fire from leaping to the surface and flambéing my breakfast.

He sighs. "You think you haven't?"

"Not nearly enough, or you would still be locked in up in the underworld."

He doesn't respond except to gesture at the mess on my plate. "You going to eat that?"

"I've lost my appetite." I push the plate toward him.

He pulls a fork from the setting next to me and digs in,

shoveling the slop of eggs into his mouth in a way that is anything but godly.

"That's attractive."

"Is it?" He winks at me but doesn't lift his head from the plate. He doesn't try to talk to me again until he's cleaned the last bit of egg with a large hunk of biscuit. "You can't get a breakfast like that in the underworld. No chickens."

Curiosity gets the best of me. "What do you eat?"

His lip quirks. "Forbidden fruit."

I don't know why I bother. I reach for my suitcase. "It's been fun, but I have a train to catch." A life to live that doesn't include a war between the gods and the Sons of Killian. And certainly doesn't include the god who forced me to kill Blake.

Austin stops me with his gaze, his brown eyes nearly black as they bore into mine. "Your destiny is here."

"It's not."

The hint of gold in Austin's eyes glows with an other-worldly light, and I realize that the cloudiness I feel is a sign that he's trying to get inside my head. I close my eyes and turn my back on him. "Stay the hell out of my head."

"I'm not your enemy, Brianna."

"Sorry, but it's not your call. I'll pick my own sides, thanks."

He reaches for my wrist as I step away. "Don't go."

I jerk my arm from his grasp and spin to face him. A crease forms between his eyebrows, breaking up the sculpted lines of his face. The tiny flaw is magnified on him. He looks almost broken.

I want to hurt him. I want him dead. I should not want

to reach out and touch that little imperfection, to smooth it away. I grab my roller bag and walk out of the dingy pub, past the dusty suit of armor that gives the place its name.

Cath is about as far from a thriving metropolis as you can get, so it's not like there are little yellow cabs cruising up and down the streets searching for wayward bandia in need of a lift. At least a sign across the street proclaims *Taxi* in big black letters. I dutifully stand by it, staring at my watch. Austin steps out of the pub a few minutes later. He stays on his side of the street, but I feel his eyes on me.

I turn to face the other direction.

After ten minutes, there's still no sign of anything resembling a taxi. The only traffic consists of a tiny beige car, slightly bigger than the Barbie Jeep I had when I was five. I glance at the clock on my phone.

"Do you need a lift?" Austin walks across the street even though I'm shaking my head. "I could drop you at the station."

"I don't accept rides from strangers."

"Then you're in luck. I'm hardly a stranger."

"Just strange. And evil. I'll pass."

"You think I'm evil?"

I meet his gaze, raising my eyebrows. After everything he's done, what am I supposed to think?

He opens his mouth and closes it again, before it falls open on its own. "For God's sake, Brianna. I'm not evil."

"Tell it to someone who is too blinded by your inhuman good looks to recognize the snake who thinks it's okay to kill to get what he wants."

"To protect what I care about."

All Austin cares about is his stupid war against the Sons. "Murder by any other name…"

He places his hand on the *Taxi* sign and moves closer to me, invading my personal space. "Are you so different? If I recall correctly, you were perfectly willing to kill me to save your bloody boyfriend."

"That was different."

"Was it? Because you killed him instead?"

His words sting. It's true that I would've killed him to save Blake. It's what Austin had counted on and used against me, so that when I lobbed a fireball and Austin disappeared at the last second, it was I—not Austin—who was the one to kill Blake.

But Blake's alive now. I saved him. "I brought him back," I say.

"What are you talking about?" Austin's eyes narrow. The crease is back, deeper than before.

"Blake. I brought him back. With the reversal spell you used to save my horse."

Austin's hand curls into a tight fist before he catches himself and straightens his fingers. He looks past me, out at the harbor beyond the buildings dotting the street. "Then you have to run."

Since when does Austin not want me to fight the Sons? It's the only thing he's ever wanted from me.

"What happened to 'stay and face my destiny'?"

"You've already let them win."

"Maybe the earth is better off without bunch of gods turning humanity into indentured servants. Has it ever occurred to you that maybe the Sons *should* win?"

Austin flashes me a rueful smile. "Actually, it has."

Not the reaction I expect. At all.

A small silver hatchback pulls up to the taxi stand. Austin makes sure the driver knows the way to the train station in Tralee as I pull my bag into the seat beside me and shut the door.

He leans in through the window. "Get as far from here as you can. No matter what you feel, just keep going. The pull to come back will get weaker over time."

"I'm not coming back." I need to get away from here. Away from Austin. Away from Blake. Away from all of this.

"The best laid plans of mice and men." He chews on his lower lip in a way that makes him look almost human. Then he smiles and the effect is ruined. "I could go with you."

Gods.

"How do I put this in terms you can understand? Wait. Got it. *No.*"

His smile fades by a fraction. "Worth a shot. Do you know how to reach Mikel?"

I hold up the phone. "Covered."

He lifts his chin and backs away from the car. As he walks back across the street, his shoulders slump forward.

Once the taxi is a good mile out of Cath, I lean my head against the window and let my cheek settle against the cool glass. Everything about Austin seems wrong. It's not like him to let me go so easily. One minute he's telling me I have to stay, and the next he's giving the driver directions to the train station. I should be glad, but all I can do is wonder what it is he thinks he knows that I don't. And since when does Austin *slump*? I push the thought away. None of it matters. What matters is that I'm getting far, far away.

I get a whole twenty miles out of town before I'm hit with the first pang of longing to go back.

NINE

I do my best to ignore the driving beat of my heart, an insistent pounding that gets stronger with every mile that stretches between me and Cath. I won't stay in Ireland and wait for the Sons to come find me. I definitely won't sit around and wait for Blake. Whatever the magic was that brought us together, it wasn't love. Love means giving someone the benefit of the doubt. Blake doesn't trust me. He never did.

And there's no way I'm going anywhere near Austin Montgomery. No. I will get on the train to Dublin and then take a plane to somewhere far, far away. I still have the money from selling my horse, Dart. I can survive for a long time on that money if I need to. I can go to college, have a normal life.

I flip the phone Mick gave me around in my hands a few times before I dial my parents. Mom picks up on the first ring. She sounds so normal. So much like home.

"It's me." I have to work to keep the emotion out of my voice. No sense worrying her.

"How are you doing?" she asks.

"Good." I don't know if it's true. I'm alive, and I'll be long gone before the Sons get anywhere near me, so the chances of me staying alive for the next few weeks at least are promising. "I'm on the move again, but I don't want you to worry. I'll call again in a few days."

Mom and Dad didn't argue with me when Joe brought me home from Mallory's party and I started throwing things in a suitcase with no idea where I was going or what I was doing beyond running. They know what I am, and they don't want me to fight the Sons any more than I do.

Still, it's hard to be away from the people who care about me. The people I love.

I imagine Mom's pasted-on realtor smile as she talks. "Jenna and Dart took reserve champion in their division this weekend," she says. At least her ability to change the subject to more comfortable topics hasn't left her.

"That's great." I wish I could've been there to see it, but I don't say anything. I can't go back to Rancho Domingo any more than I can go back to Cath. I can only go forward.

To what? My future is shrouded in gray fog. Nothing feels certain. I have nothing to go toward. Nothing that matters.

Everyone I love is behind me.

The taxi pulls into the train station and parks next to the curb. I grip the phone tighter. "I've got to go." I hang up and shove a handful of bills to the driver.

Every step toward the ticket counter feels heavier than the

last. The pounding in my chest becomes more pronounced, an ancient beat that calls to my soul. I need to get on that train. And then on a plane. To where? A prickle at the back of my neck makes me look over my shoulder. A man with dark, greasy hair and a weathered face winks at me. I look away quickly.

All at once, I see my future unfolding with perfect clarity. Another train station, another airport. Constantly looking over my shoulder while I race off to another strange city in another strange country, away from anyone I've gotten to know or care about. Always starting over, never safe. Never anywhere that feels like home. There is no such thing as normal for me.

I board the train. Given the number of stops there are along the way, the ride to Dublin will take longer than the drive from Dublin to Cath did.

About an hour outside of Dublin, a petite woman takes the seat across from me. Her hair is short, cut into a stylish blond pixie cut with spikes on top. She's wearing a severe black pantsuit and never looks up from her phone as she maneuvers her bags into the seat next to her.

The woman's eyes flit from the phone screen to my silver bracelet. "That's lovely," she says in a thick Irish accent.

"Thanks." I cover the charms with my palm, instinctively.

"Are you traveling alone?" She crosses her legs and smiles without opening her mouth.

I flash back to a lecture from fifth grade about not giving too much personal information to strangers. I hadn't thought much of it at the time, beyond relief that we weren't getting the sex talk, but now it all comes back at once: *Lie*. "I'm meeting some friends."

"Very good," she says. "It's not safe for a girl like you to be traveling alone."

Goose bumps rise on my arms. I just nod. She's probably just trying to be nice. She has no way of knowing that I could wipe out this entire train with a flick of a wrist. She stares at the silver pendant at my throat. I stifle the urge to hide it, too, and stare out the window, concentrating on counting the sheep on the hillside.

"It must be hard being so far from home."

My blood burns with the itch to ignite, my body reacting automatically to the fake sweetness in the woman's voice.

Focus. Reaching for air to cool my blood, I temper the heat that threatens. It's not like I can go torching every person who makes me uncomfortable. I may be deadly, but I can control this power. I have to.

But I couldn't control the fire at Mallory's party.

I couldn't even feel it.

I would've been able to feel it. I know it.

Sherri Milliken is the only other bandia I know. While I wouldn't put it past her to try to take out a party full of Sons and their minions, Sherri would make damn sure that everyone knew it was her. Besides, the Sons were already looking for Sherri. She's the reason they let me into their fold in the first place, to find her. Someone would've seen her at the party.

According to Occam's razor, when you're faced with

multiple hypotheses you should always start with the simplest one and try to rule it out first.

There was only one bandia everyone saw at the party. One angry bandia who let a fifteen-year-old human girl get under her skin enough to send a ball of blue fire right through the middle of the backyard into the pool. A second later, another fireball lit up the house. The math is easy. If *I* can't rule out the most obvious cause of the fire, how can I expect Blake to?

Because I would never do something like that.

Would I?

"You're American, right?" The woman says, completely oblivious to how close she came to meeting the business end of a ball of fire.

I nod. That much is obvious, so there's no point denying it.

"Our ways must feel very strange to you." She reaches across the space between us and places her hand on my wrist. "Can I look at your bracelet?"

There's no preventing the heat that fills me now. "I'm sorry." I stand up and pull my roller bag from the overhead bin. "My stop is coming up."

I walk away from her as quickly as I can, moving toward the door to the next car. When I look back, the woman is texting away on her phone again. I'm overreacting. I take a breath and count in exponents of seven until my power cools down. I hustle off the train when it stops five minutes later, wanting to put as much distance as I can between myself and creepy corporate Tinker Bell.

The "station" here consists of a few stone benches on a raised cement platform and an automatic ticketing machine. A schedule on the side of the machine indicates there won't be another train for an hour, so I settle in on one of the cold slabs. The air isn't as damp this far from the ocean, but the wind blows just as hard and I shiver against it. I steal a glance over my shoulder, but there's no one there.

This is what alone feels like—cold and gray, with a dash of paranoia to remind me that there are worse things than being alone. But there are better things too.

I flip on the phone Mick gave me. It's after midnight back home. Haley is probably trying to sneak into her house without waking her mom, while Christy interrupts her with a dozen text messages about a crisis with her boyfriend Matt. Haley will talk her down, and Matt will send some ridiculous poem that will melt Christy's heart, and all will be good again. I never thought I'd miss Matt's pretentious spoken-word poetry, but I kind of do.

I fight the urge to text them. The less communication I have with my old life, the safer we'll all be. But it's hard to embrace this new life with my butt growing numb against the stone. A week ago, my life was messy but it was mine. It wasn't *all* Sons and breeders and trying to maintain a fragile truce. I had friends, and parents, and a boy I loved. Now all I have is heartbreak and strangers and the looming threat of my own murder.

I may not be able to do anything about the heartbreak, but I can get my family and friends back. I can take out the threat. I can stay and fight.

Once made, the decision seems so clear, so right, that I can't believe it took me so long to figure it out. Austin was right about one thing: we are not so different. I would kill to protect those I love. For my right to love them.

I don't get on the next train to Dublin. I wait an additional forty minutes for the train headed back the way I came. As the train heads west, the pounding in my chest eases a little, the rhythmic beats slowing to a softer thrum. By the time I'm back inside a taxi in Tralee and on the road toward Cath, I feel almost normal. It's not until the taxi stops at the gates of Lorcan Hall that I start to question what I'm doing.

But I'm not stupid enough to think I can take out the Sons alone. I need allies.

It's time to make peace with the enemy of my enemy.

TEN

Mick meets me in the drive and takes my bag. He doesn't say anything, but I can almost make out a hint of a smile at the corner of his mouth as he rolls my bag back into the house.

I don't follow him. If Austin is inside, I'm not ready to face him. What would I even say?

You win.

Maybe if I play it cool, make him think I'm less certain than I am, I could make him promise not to hurt Blake. Austin may be a manipulative god, but as far as I can tell, he's never outright lied to me.

The wind blows across the bluff, carrying drops of moisture that spatter against my cheek. My blood pulses erratically, mimicking the cacophony of waves in the distance, power moving through me in bursts and shocks. I walk away from the house and pick my way down the switchback trail to the rocky beach below.

The water mirrors the black clouds overhead, creating a colorless landscape where water and sky blend together, separated sporadically by white caps as the waves crash against the rocks. I feel like I've stepped into a black-and-white movie, everything distinguishable only by their varying shades of gray.

Foam coats the rocks at the water's edge in a blanket of bubbles before dropping back and surging forward again to cover more ground. The dark water is so much more than two parts hydrogen and one part oxygen, and for once I'm glad for it. For a girl who spent the last three years trying to explain the world by breaking it down to its barest elements, there's an unexpected freedom that comes with embracing its magic.

Some choices are made. Some are made for you. I didn't choose to be a bandia. I didn't choose to be a part of the war with the gods, but I won't run from it, either. If the Sons want a fight, they will damn well get one.

I walk between the boulders to the small beach beyond. The tide is high enough that only a narrow path of rock along the edge of the cliff wall remains dry enough to walk on. I follow it to the place where the earth opened yesterday, letting my fingers trace the crack.

My hand goes right through a space that's too small for this to be remotely possible, and I jerk it back.

The gateway.

If I slipped through the crack, I would be in Avernus, a barren wasteland full of waterfalls that converge in a powerful river—a river that bears souls to their final resting place. Before I learned what Avernus was, I thought it beautiful, unspoiled, with its stark rock landscape and rushing water. Now I shrink back from it, remembering the three huge wolf-hounds with razor-sharp teeth that patrol the perimeter.

A flash of white light burns through the dark sky. I've never connected with lightning, but the electricity tickles the edges of my own power, igniting it. I close my eyes against the light. The hum of power that flows through me is achingly familiar, a hint of what it feels like when Blake touches me. I open my eyes abruptly. Spots dance in front of them.

"Ah, a welcoming committee." The voice comes from nowhere and everywhere.

I spin around, but see no one. As I drop my hands, the air goes suddenly still. Even the ocean seems tame as it slides into the rocks. My blood is quiet, my power muted.

"Here, love."

As the spots in my vision fade, I make out the shape of a man leaning against one of the large boulders that mark the path back to the main beach. Not a man, exactly. He looks about my age, maybe eighteen, but he's definitely not human.

Freezing water swirls around my ankles as the tide rushes in to meet me. My blood runs just as cold.

He's bathed in his own cold light, which casts shadows that only serve to accentuate every beautiful cut of muscle and bone in his chest and arms. His long dark hair flows past his shoulders, tied back in a ribbon of green plaid that matches the cloth draped around his waist. His blue eyes flash with white. I've only seen one god before, but even if I hadn't, I would recognize him for what he is.

"Where are the others?" His voice is melodic, royal.

"Others?" I look around me. We're alone on this rapidly disappearing scrap of beach. Is he expecting more gods? Impossible. The gods are trapped in the underworld, at least as long as the Sons are still alive. Trapped there by their own long-ago promise to split the world with the Milesians. Tricked by the Milesians' insistence on taking the top half.

"You can't be the only one who felt my call to arms." His accent is not as refined as Austin's. He rolls his R's in a way that sounds vaguely pirate.

"Call to what?" The water swirls at my calves now, the current pulling at my legs. I need to get off this beach before it disappears completely. I step toward him, though every instinct tells me to keep far away. This isn't right. Even if Austin found a way back into the human realm, only the god of the underworld can cross over.

Unless the Sons are dead.

Blake.

My pulse jumps in time with my panic. I shouldn't have left Blake. Over the past few days I've had plenty of time to think about him, and I have, but I haven't once worried for his safety. It never occurred to me that Blake might not survive. Shouldn't I feel something if he's dead?

But my soul can't feel Blake anymore. I would never know if something happened to him.

"Call to arms. That's still an expression, is it not?" The god wrinkles his nose, destroying the perfect lines of his face.

Sharp, icy stabs prick at my skin as the water covers my knees, soaking through my jeans. The ocean curls around me, grasping and not letting go. I lean on a boulder to keep from losing my footing. I have to stay calm. This god wants to talk, and I need answers. "And you would be ...?"

He throws his shoulders back even though he's already standing perfectly straight. He looks pissed that I have to ask. "I am Pwil. You can call me Liam."

The water comes in faster. I wedge my numb foot against the boulder for support. "Well, Liam, I suggest you move out of the way before we both get sucked out to sea."

"Perhaps if we were mere mortals, I would agree with you." He tilts his head at me. "But then, you are mortal, aren't you? Pity. No matter how powerful you are, your human side will rob you of your youth and then your life."

He knows what I am. Of course he knows. He thinks I answered his call to war.

The water reaches my thighs, tugging with such force that I grab onto Liam's arm without thinking.

He pulls me against him roughly. "You don't need my help, bandia." His fingers tighten on my arms. "If you are going to fight for me, you will have to be stronger than this."

Fire fills me, heating my skin so quickly he lets go with a start.

I fall back into the water and the flames in my palm disappear in an instant. The current snatches me in one swift pull, dragging me under. I gasp at the cold. Water rushes in before I can close my mouth. I fight the urge to swallow, slamming my jaw closed and trying to push the water out before it can make its way down my throat. The cold stings so much it burns, crackling against my skin. My legs start to go numb, relieving the pain but slowing my fight against the current. As

I roll and twist with the ocean, it's difficult to tell which way is up. My shoulder smacks against a wall of rock, sending a welcome burst of pain that distracts me from the freezing water. It takes all my strength to swim away from the rock. I push off, but I'm thrust back into it a second later.

The pain and the cold quickly become secondary to my need to breathe.

I fight down the burst of adrenaline that urges me, once again, to swim away, and concentrate on the water instead. The force of it begins to feel different as it rushes through my veins; it becomes part of me. Bends to me. The current changes directions. With one last effort, I push off the rock and kick toward what I hope is the surface.

A shadow moves in front of me. Something huge and white is swimming through the rocks. Are there sharks in Ireland?

God, I need air.

I try to kick, but my numb limbs don't cooperate. The white creature comes closer. It's not like anything I've seen on Shark Week. Does it have legs? The lack of oxygen must be going to my head because, in the dark, the animal swimming toward me looks just like a horse. As he reaches me, the horse bares his teeth and grabs at my charm bracelet, jerking hard enough to draw blood where the chain hits my skin. I hit the creature in the nose and he loosens his grip, enough for me to yank my wrist away.

Maybe the horse isn't even a boy. The incoherent thought is the last thing that crosses my mind before I open my mouth and breathe in the sea.

The dark water turns almost gold. A shockingly warm arm wraps around my waist. There's a bright flash, and then I'm coughing, spitting and retching, sucking in huge gulps of air. I shiver, even though the cold air around me is warm in comparison to how icy the water was. I'm surrounded by the misty weightlessness of the spirit realm.

The arm around my waist loosens. "Are you insane?" Austin says from over my shoulder. "Entire ships have gone down in that cove."

The nerves in my legs start to wake in shocks of pain. My clothes are weighed down, chafing against my skin. All I can do is cling to Austin's warmth and breathe.

He doesn't wait for an answer. "I saw the flash from the house. Who was here? Blake? Jonah?"

I shake my head. "Not a Son." My throat is raw. "A god."

Austin holds me closer. I tremble as his warmth begins to reach other nerves, breathing life and pain into parts that I would rather stay numb. "You're sure?"

"Yes."

"Bloody hell. I thought we'd have more time."

Another burst of gold light surrounds us. When I open my eyes, we're standing on the rocks at the base of the trail that goes back up the bluff. The entire beach is submerged in water. There's no sign of Liam.

My breath comes faster. "He was just here."

Austin nods. "Go back to the house and warm up."

I reach for fire, using its heat to start thawing myself from the inside, even as the wind batters my soaked hair and clothes.

It's not until I'm safely in my room, wrapped in layers of blankets with a steaming mug of hot chocolate between my palms, that I look out at the ocean churning below my window. The water looks ominous, less a part of me than a force to be respected. I may be able to access the power of the ocean, but I'm a fool if I think I can control it. Control anything.

If it weren't for Austin, I probably wouldn't have made it out alive.

Not good. I don't want to owe Austin any favors. I don't want to owe Austin anything.

ELEVEN

Austin lounges on an antique chair in the sitting room down-stairs, his legs draped casually over one ornately carved arm. A fire roars in a fireplace that is taller than I am.

"Thank God," is all he says when I sit down on the couch across from him.

"You talk to God?"

"Not literally. He doesn't visit the underworld, and he certainly isn't here."

"I didn't mean literally." It's almost a relief to see Austin. The familiar is welcome, even the bad.

He gestures to a tray of hot tea and some kind of pastries that look like little berry pies. "Mikel can't seem to stop feeding me."

I reach for a dainty china cup and pour the hot liquid into it. "I feel like I've stepped into another century."

His smile catches me off guard. He looks disarmingly like he did a thousand years ago. "Trust me, you haven't."

But I did step into another century, another millennium, up at the ruin. Does Austin remember meeting me back then? I watch him as I sip my tea. He pushes his wild bangs out of his eyes. I catch myself before I smile back. Austin is not my friend. He's a means to an end.

"Who was it?" The crease is back between his brows. "The god you saw at the beach? Did he say anything to you?"

"He said his name was Pwil, but he's going by Liam."

"Liam," Austin repeats. "What an arse." He swings his legs around so his feet are on the floor.

"You know him?"

"I probably don't need to tell you this, since you met the bastard, but this is bad."

"Who is he?"

"My best friend." Austin grabs one of the tiny pies from the tray and bites into the flaky crust.

"You don't have friends." Blake had been Austin's so-called friend. And then Austin made sure I killed him.

"There's the rub." Austin arches an eyebrow.

It still doesn't make sense. Austin is the only god who can cross over from the underworld. "Why is Liam here?"

"Why are you here, Brianna?" Austin ignores my question. "You were supposed to be on a plane out of Dublin by now. You promised you wouldn't come back."

"I couldn't just run."

"You could. You still can."

"I want my life back." I don't expect him to understand. Austin can't know what it means to want to be close to the people you care about. All he cares about is taking back the earth for the gods. "My human life."

"Careful what you wish for." His smile is sad. He eats the last of the pastry, licking the crumbs off his thumb. "I'm afraid I'm much too selfish to make you go, so we'll have to come up with a new plan. Liam's a bastard, but right now he's the least pressing of your worries. The Sons will gather here, Brianna. The call of the gateway is strong."

Mick already told me as much. But Austin is the god of the underworld—he can stop all this. "What the hell are you doing, then?" I demand. "You knew that if you opened the gateway, you would bring the Sons straight here. Or is that what you want?"

Of course it is.

I should've known that Austin would try to force a fight. The only thing I accomplished by banishing him was to make him more determined. He still wants me to be his pawn in a war against the Sons. To kill for him.

The sick part is that I *want* to fight the Sons now. And not for him. For me.

He leans forward, resting his elbows on his knees. "I didn't open the gateway. Liam did."

"How is that even possible? You're the god of the underworld."

Austin laces his fingers together. There's no trace of his usual confidence as he stares down at his hands, worrying his thumbs against each other. "*Was.*"

"What do you mean?"

His crooked smile is meant to reassure me. It doesn't. "I had a good run, didn't I?"

"What happened?"

"I suppose I've lost my immortality."

"You realize that whole sentence is an oxymoron. Immortality is supposed to be a permanent condition."

"Are you not a believer, then?"

There's little left to believe in. I thought I believed in logic, but not everything can be compartmentalized in numbers and scientific theory. I believed in Blake. But once our bond was severed, he kept me at a distance. Then he immediately assumed the worst about me the first time the opportunity arose.

"What exactly am I supposed to believe in?" I ask.

"Magic."

Our eyes meet, and for a second I'm back in the field by the ruined little wall, remembering his smile in another time. I push the memory away. I can't afford to think of Austin as anything more than the danger he is.

"You're sure it's Pwil?" he adds.

"And just who is Pwil, again?"

"A minor deity with a major dose of ambition." Austin puts his hand in his hair, pushing it off his forehead. "He was my second, covering for me while I was topside. I trusted him once."

"But you don't anymore." It's not a question.

"He won't be as patient as I've been."

"You've been patient?" This from a guy who's killed or

orchestrated the death of more than one demigod to advance his cause.

Austin watches me with an intensity that makes me shiver. "More than you know."

There's something raw about his stare, like a layer of veneer has been pulled away to reveal the imperfections underneath.

"So if you've lost your immortality, does that mean you can die?"

Austin's crooked smile is back in place. "Don't go getting ideas."

TWELVE

I resist the urge to spend another three days holed up in my room, now that I know the Sons are coming here and a new god is on the loose. Austin and Mick work together in an office at the end of a long hall, and I spend most of my time at the barn with the horses. I ride in the fields close to the house, giving the trail to the ocean a wide berth. After two days with no new Liam sightings, I venture farther, turning Molly up the trail to the trees.

I dismount as soon as the crumbling walls come into view. Once Molly is set loose to graze in the meadow, I circle the stones. Maybe I only imagined seeing Austin in the past. None of it seems possible. But it wasn't as if finding out I was descended from a goddess seemed possible six months ago. Bringing Blake back from the dead shouldn't have been possible either. Blake sending me away without listening to my side of the story—completely impossible. But all of it happened anyway.

The little carvings in the stone mock me. The horse carving seems lighter than the others now, as if it's fading somehow. I finger the matching charm on my bracelet. I stand unmoving, pretending that I'm not going to press the silver horse against the stone. Then I do.

At first nothing happens, and I let myself breathe. My lungs have barely filled when the wall disappears into fog and mist and I go with it, floating in the cold, gray nothingness until the sky brightens and I feel damp grass beneath my feet.

"I was beginning to think I'd imagined you."

I turn toward the soft Irish voice. Toward Austin. Not Austin, exactly—Aaron, with his soft eyes and innocent smile. He's wearing the same style of belted wool shirt that brushes his knees, only this one is green. His long, wild hair falls past his shoulders.

I came here to see him, but I don't have a plan exactly. What if this is the last chance I'll have to talk to this Austin from a thousand years ago? I could warn him about the war with the Sons. How the Sons kill most of the bandia. Maybe if he knows how things will turn out, he'll think twice about killing Danu to spark the war in the first place.

Maybe I can change everything.

"Don't do it," I finally say.

"Do what?" He tilts his head to the side.

"Don't kill Danu. It won't work. The Seventh Daughters will fight the Sons, but they won't win."

Austin laughs. He leans on a low portion of the wall,

his eyes filled with a mix of curiosity and fascination. "Why would I kill Danu? She is the last of her kind."

"Not the last. That's supposed to be me."

"Then the future is not so dire."

"You believe me? That I'm from the future?"

"I know better than to run from fate." His easy smile is contagious.

"What if you could change it? The future, I mean."

He laughs again, and when he looks at me his eyes are unguarded. Unspoiled. This Austin hasn't killed Danu. Hasn't killed Dart. Hasn't hurt me. "Why would I want to change my future if it includes you?" he asks.

It doesn't. I bite back the words. This boy doesn't seem to want anything from me. He just seems to like talking to me. There's something simple and easy about that, but I can't afford to think this way. "I don't think you're supposed to know your future," I mutter.

"Are you here to stop me then?"

Can I? Can I stop him from killing Danu, and find a way to bring the Sons of Killian and the Seventh Daughters together before centuries of death and destruction make peace impossible? I'm supposed to end the war—I'm the seventh generation of the Seventh Daughters. Maybe this is how I do it. I can stop it before it starts. I'm giddy with the possibility. Why else am I here?

"One decision could stop future generations from killing each other off," I say. "Maybe I'm here to change everything." His future. Mine.

"So I've made a royal mess of things, have I?"

I stare down at my boots. "Not just you." Austin may have orchestrated things, but I am still the one who killed Blake. Tears come before I can stop them.

Austin reaches for my hand, gently holding my fingertips like he's afraid I'll break. The gesture somehow makes me cry more. I don't know why I'm crying, exactly. For Blake. For me. For all the bandia and Sons who will die in the centuries between Aaron's time and mine.

He waits until my cries fade to sniffles. "I wish I could make it right," he says. "But I'm afraid you already know how it ends."

Do I? I know he'll kill Danu to spark a bloody war that will continue down the years, a war I'm supposed to end but unlikely to win. The bit of hope I felt only a moment before is already out of reach. "If I can't stop it, why am I here?"

Austin's laugh is warm and comforting. "I know better than to question a gift from the heavens."

I look up, and for a dizzying second I'm lost in his eyes.

Everything fades to gray and he's gone.

I'm back at the ruin. The small ruin. Alone, except for Molly. I fight for breath.

I have to find a way back again.

I could change everything. Austin might not think so, but it's a chance I have to take. No one has to die. I press my fingers to my lips, remembering the feel of his hands on them before I slam my arms back down to my sides.

Austin is a necessary evil, an ally against the Sons. I

can't let myself forget who I'm dealing with. After everything that happened with Blake, I should know better than to let the devil draw me in.

THIRTEEN

After another week without any sign of Liam or the Sons, I need to get away from Lorcan Hall. I've stayed far from the beach and even farther away from the ruin. After days of riding in circles in the field, I ask to borrow the car. Mick insists on coming with me and I don't argue, mainly because I don't know if I can drive on both the wrong side of the car and the wrong side of the road.

Mick follows at a discreet distance as I walk down Main Street, gazing into the shop windows. I stop in front of a dress shop, admiring a long red sheath that's too fancy even for prom. Not that I'm going to prom anytime soon. Or ever.

Shannon waves from inside the store, where she's talking to a customer, and I wave back.

Mick pauses in front of the leather shop two doors down and pretends to look interested in something inside, but I catch him watching me out of the corner of his eye. I move along to the bakery. As much as I want to talk to Shannon, it will be better to wait for an opportunity when Mick isn't looking over my shoulder.

I purchase a small white cake with a blue flower on top. The flower looks like a misshapen bell, a near-perfect match for the silver wolfsbane blossom on the pendant at my throat. In real life, wolfsbane is deadly if ingested, but I bite into the icing anyway. It's barely sweet, yet delicious.

I smile at the boy behind the counter. His face turns rosy, magnifying the freckles that dot his nose. Embarrassed, I look out the window, just as a familiar flash of blond hair moves out of view.

He goes by so fast I can almost believe I imagined him, until I hear his laugh.

Blake.

Blake is here.

I shake with an odd combination of dread and anticipation. I throw the rest of the cake away and rush outside.

Blake is already two stores down. His back is to me, but I would recognize him anywhere. The way he moves, with the smooth gait of a predator. The way his hair falls in long layers that brush past his ears, looking slightly messy but somehow perfect. He wears a weathered leather jacket that looks soft to the touch. I want to touch it.

I want to touch him.

I shouldn't. After everything he said to me during the fire, the last thing I should want is anything to do with Blake Williams. But seeing him here, thousands of miles from Rancho Domingo, tugs at my soul. We're so far away, but the inescapable truth is that Blake still feels like home.

I stop myself from running to him. For all I know he still blames me for the fire at Mallory's party. It's not like he's here for me. I knew he would come. All of the Sons will. But I can't prevent the surge of hope as it rises from the ashes with the strength of a Phoenix. Maybe he's looking for me. Maybe he came to warn me that the Sons are coming. To apologize. To tell me he believes me. To tell me he loves me.

It's not too late. We can fix this. I walk after him quickly, desperate to close the distance until there's nothing between us but our breaths.

I'm stopped by a hand on my shoulder.

Mick looms over me, following my gaze to Blake's retreating back. "We need to get you back to Lorcan. Now."

"It's just Blake." He keeps walking, getting farther away now.

"It's not *just* anything. He's a Seventh Son of Killian."

"He's my friend." It might not be true, but I have to find out. I break free from Mick's grasp and keep walking.

He follows, using his longer strides to keep pace. "The fewer people who know you're here, the better."

"He might have news." I can't stop myself from adding, "He might be looking for me."

"That's what I'm afraid of. We can't risk it. With the gateway open and the Sons—" Mick stops mid-sentence.

"What?" But I'm only half listening, my breath catching as Blake stops next to a gift shop and turns his head to look in the window. I can see the side of his face, the corner of his lips. I've missed those lips. I want to run to him, but Mick's hand is on my wrist, cuffing it.

"Wait," Mick says.

A dimple appears on Blake's cheek. My heart melts a little. I know that smile, the one that's charmed a thousand girls, the one that charmed me. But he hasn't seen me. His smile is for someone else.

Portia Bruton walks out of the store and launches herself at him, drawing him into a hug. Blake's arms come around her easily.

Fire floods my veins in an instant. Mick lets go of my wrist with a start. I take a few steps closer, ducking into a stone archway that forms a small alcove in front of a bookstore. I lean against the cold wall and try to breathe. Blake and Portia are friends. So they hugged. It doesn't mean anything. I push back the fire, giving in to the urge to look around the corner.

Portia looks prettier than usual. Her chestnut hair is cut in flattering layers that accentuate her big amber eyes. I don't think I've ever seen her smile. Now that she does, it lights up her whole face, and she's gorgeous.

I want to kill her.

18. 324. I concentrate on calculating the third exponent, but I can't think with the fire raging inside me, burning to get out.

Blake, *Blake*, lowers his head and kisses Portia right there in the street. Not a peck, but a deep, soulful kiss that's too intimate for the sidewalk.

The fire in me is gone in an instant, replaced by ice. I'm trembling. The tears on my cheeks freeze into little icicles, so cold they burn the skin.

Mick ducks into the alcove beside me. He takes off his heavy black coat and pulls it over my shoulders. The little archway crackles as more ice forms a thin layer over the stone wall. "Not here," he says.

I barely hear him. Portia whispers something in Blake's ear as they move down the sidewalk toward me, their arms wrapped around each other in a public display of affection. It's the kind of territorial show that Blake never once put on with me. Not even when our souls were bonded.

I wish we were bonded now. I want Blake to feel the cold that crackles and twists its way through my chest. I want the despair that strangles my neck to choke the air out of his lungs the same way it does mine. I want his heart to break into a thousand brittle shards.

But he doesn't feel me. He doesn't even see me. As he passes by my little ice cave, he doesn't even bristle. He's too busy smiling down at Portia Bruton like she's the most perfect girl he's ever seen.

Two weeks. That's how long it took for Blake Williams to forget I ever existed.

Five seconds is all it takes for him to rip my heart from my chest as easily as if he'd stabbed me with his broadsword.

I slide down the icy wall to the frozen ground below.

Mick sits down, shivering beside me. "We need to get you back to Lorcan."

I don't argue with him. I just breathe in the cold, praying for it to numb me on the inside. Praying for peace that can never come.

FOURTEEN

It's hard to imagine that some part of me still believed Blake and I would work everything out. That Blake would realize he was too quick to blame me for the fire, that we would figure out what happened together. Yes, I was hurt by his lack of trust, but some part of me always thought he would come around. I was the worst kind of stupid, hanging on to the fantasy that Blake would learn to trust me. That what we had was real.

Now I question everything—not just the night of the fire, but every night we were together. Did Blake ever really care about me, or was everything just a by-product of the supernatural bond we'd forged, an artificial connection based on the fact that we shared a soul? After the bond was broken, he stayed with me for a couple of months, but he never let me get close. He didn't want to share his emotions with me again, so he hadn't. I heard him call me a witch to the other

Sons, and then convince Rush Bruton that they should keep me around long enough to lead them to the other bandia. And now that the Sons no longer had a use for me, neither did Blake.

As soon as I get back to Lorcan Hall, I change into breeches and boots and go down to the stable. Malcolm grabs Molly's bridle, but I hold up my hand to stop him. "Not Molly. Tally."

He starts to shake his head, but when he meets my gaze, he thinks better of it. He sets the bridle down and reaches for a larger bridle with a Pelham bit. "You're sure?"

I nod.

Malcolm saddles Tally wordlessly and hands me the reins.

Tally shies to the left when I mount, but I find my stirrups and stroke his neck until he stands still. When I squeeze my legs against his sides, he moves off into a strong trot. I can feel the tension he holds in the muscles of his back, like a spring ready to uncoil. He kicks out a hind leg as we approach the open field, nearly jarring me off balance. It takes all my concentration to keep Tally from breaking into a run. I stroke his neck again. "Easy, boy."

Alone on the trail, I try to make sense of my feelings. They are purely mine now, so there's no confusion over what's really mine versus Blake's. Anger and betrayal mix together with grief and disappointment, forming a black hollow that starts in the center of my chest and spreads until I am nothing but an empty shell.

Once Tally steps onto the wide dirt road that crisscrosses the field, I lighten my grip on the reins. Tally explodes into a gallop without any urging. I stand in my stirrups and grab a handful of mane. He answers with a joyful buck, increasing his pace until he's moving at a dead run, head and back stretched out as he barrels down the road at full speed.

I couldn't stop him if I wanted to. The physical sensation of being out of control drowns out the swirl of dark feelings that roar inside of me. We run at this pace for nearly a mile before Tally's stride starts to shorten. I tighten my fingers on the reins and pull back gently on the bit until Tally comes down to a walk. His nostrils flare in time to his labored breaths.

I settle into the saddle, waiting for my heart to slow to a normal rate. I focus on every pulse as my blood pumps through me, each beat a reminder that I'm not completely broken.

As Tally approaches the edge of the bluff, the air gets thick with sea water. I breathe it in and imagine unleashing the power of the ocean on the Sons, letting it rain and rain and rain until the sea rises to meet the earth and swallows them whole. A smile plays at my lips before I realize that black clouds are moving in from the west.

No.

Seven generations ago, my grandmother's great-grandmother's grandmother destroyed an entire village with fire after her heart was broken by one of the villagers. Forty-nine generations ago, Danu was said to have created a famine when Killian rejected her. But I won't kill innocent people. I concentrate until the sky returns to a normal light gray.

There is only one person I want to hurt. And I know

exactly how to hurt him. My revenge will be much more personal.

Fire with fire.

"Back already?" Liam stands at the top of the trail down to the beach, his long hair loose and blowing in the wind.

Tally stops and lifts his head without any prompting, his muscles tense.

I straighten my spine instinctively. "Enjoying your promotion?"

Liam's blink is the only indication I've caught him off guard. "Indeed. I thought I'd head into town. It's been some time since I've enjoyed the pleasures of human flesh."

I cringe at his words despite my best efforts. "Maybe you should change into something a bit more modern," I say. He's still dressed in a plaid cloth, draped across his waist and chest.

"What do you suggest?" The bored look in Liam's face is mixed with something darker.

"You might want to start with pants."

Liam smiles, his beauty on full display. He disappears in a flash of bright white and then reappears, dressed in a pair of dark slacks and a tailored button-down.

"So is there a Nordstom in the spirit realm now?"

Liam ignores my comment. "Do you want to come meet your sisters?"

"I don't have any sisters."

"Oh, but you do." He crosses in front of Tally, heading toward the main drive. "Together you will defeat the Sons."

Tally shakes his head, sidestepping away.

The dread I felt on first meeting Liam is tempered. Liam

is here to orchestrate an end to the Sons of Killian. We're more aligned than I first thought.

I am a bandia. Blake will pay for breaking my heart.

FIFTEEN

I find Austin in an office in the west wing of the house. He sits at a giant wood desk that looks as old as the house itself, his attention absorbed in something on the monitor in front of him. He wears a pair of dark-rimmed glasses I've never seen before.

I hesitate in the doorway. He hasn't seen me; there's still time to turn back. I finger the skirt of my blue silk dress. The material is too thin in the cold air, transparent.

This was a stupid idea. I should go.

Austin looks up from the laptop. "This is a surprise." He takes in my dress and his eyes widen.

"I was just coming to see if you were going to join Mick and me for dinner." The slight quiver in my voice gives the lie away. This shouldn't be so hard. If Blake can kiss Portia in the middle of the street, I can kiss Austin. At least Austin will want me.

He takes the glasses off and sets them on the desk, flashing me his crooked smile. "I don't think you've given me a choice."

"We always have choices." Choices are all I have.

Austin stands and takes a few steps toward me. "I don't know. I think I would follow you anywhere in that dress."

"A choice." Blood rushes to my cheeks in spite of the cold. Not good. I don't want to feel anything. I just want to get this over with. I force myself to smile, stepping all the way into the office. The heavy door seals shut with a click that echoes in the large room. I stand up straighter. "Or we could make another choice. We could just stay here."

Austin's eyes turn serious. "What are you doing, Brianna?"

He's not supposed to ask questions. He needs to let me do this. I close the distance, standing just in front of him, close enough that I could fall into him if I leaned forward.

"Does it matter?" I brush my fingertips along his cheek and slide them down his neck until my hand rests on his shoulder.

"Doesn't it?" His smile is wicked. He covers my hand with his own.

I move a step closer, although there's barely room to do so, until our chests are nearly flush. His body heat contrasts sharply with the cold air, and I shudder.

He bends his head toward me. I lift my chin and close my eyes, waiting. But he doesn't kiss me.

When I open my eyes, his lips are right there, less than an inch from mine. I lean closer, but he puts his other hand on my shoulder and holds me in place. He doesn't move away. If anything, he moves closer. His chest touches mine, so lightly I might imagine it. I want him against me, but he holds me in place.

I bring my free hand to his waist and let my fingers trail down his hip, savoring his swift intake of breath. His reaction is exactly what I'm after.

"Kiss me," I say.

His hand at my shoulder still keeps me from stretching up to him, but his head dips lower. I feel the heat of his breath against my mouth. I can almost taste him. "No," he whispers.

I push back against his shoulders with both hands, backing away from him. "What's your problem?" None of this is going the way it's supposed to. Austin wants me, and God knows I need to feel wanted right now. "This is what you wanted," I snap.

Austin rubs his temple and closes his eyes. "Not like this."

"What do you mean?"

"Forgive my skepticism, but the last time you said you wanted to kiss me, you banished me to the underworld for a thousand years."

Oh yeah. But it's not like it worked. "You think I'm going to hurt you?"

"You think you won't?"

I told him I'd find a way to hurt him, but the idea of hurting someone like Austin is absurd. He's not human. Or at least, he wasn't. "I'm giving you want you want," I say.

"You're not."

We'll see about that. I reach for him, placing my hand

over his heart. His muscles tense against my palms, but he doesn't push me away. I drag my hand along his chest and lower, past the lean muscles of his stomach, until I feel the hard ridge behind his zipper. The proof of his desire.

I lift my chin. "Liar."

He grabs my wrist, pulling my hand away. At the same time, he wraps his other arm around my waist and thrusts forward, pressing me against him. Every cell in my body stirs at once, tingling with anticipation.

He pushes me backward until we crash against his desk, sending his laptop smashing to the floor. He lifts me onto the desk, ignoring the clattering as his glasses fall off. In one quick move he's over me, trapping me with his body. His eyes are dark. Wild.

"Is this what you want? Like this?" His words are hot against my neck.

An electric thrill jolts me awake. For the first time since this afternoon, I'm warm. Alive. "Kiss me," I say again.

He brings his lips to the spot just below my ear, lightly brushing the sensitive skin on my neck. "No." His teeth graze the skin along my throat as his hips drive against the thin cloth of my skirt between my thighs.

I gasp.

"You like that?" His words are rough. Raw.

"Yes." My voice is a scratch, my body a riot of sensation. Every nerve burning. Every cell aching to be touched. I lift a leg around his hip, arching my back so I can feel more of him.

His breath comes harder as his hand works its way up

my calf to the bare skin of my thigh. "Do you want me to make you forget him?"

"Yes," I say, though I barely remember who I'm supposed to be forgetting.

Austin lets out a strangled growl. His fingers tighten on my leg. Then he pushes himself off me and backs away.

I prop myself up on my elbows. "What?"

His dark eyes follow the line of the strap of sleeve that hangs off my left shoulder. "You're using me."

"Does it matter?" I sit up, letting my legs hang from the front of the desk. I struggle to slow down my breath.

He looks away. "As it happens, it does."

It doesn't make any sense. Austin has never cared about me. He wanted me for his army. He was willing to hurt me to make it happen. He may have wanted me a little, but that's all.

My legs wobble as I slide to my feet. I slip past Austin to the door, embarrassed now that the moment has passed. Did I misread him? I don't know anything anymore.

The thick wood door opens with a creak.

I feel Austin's gaze on my back. When I turn around, I catch him watching me. I don't imagine the desire in his eyes as he licks his lower lip.

I tighten my hand on the doorknob. "What do you want from me?"

He sighs, and for a second I think he's not going to say anything. Then his lips curve into a sad, crooked smile.

"Everything, Brianna. I want everything."

SIXTEEN

When I wander into the kitchen for breakfast, Austin is already seated at the giant wood table, sipping a cup of tea. He watches me warily, like he's not sure if I'm going to slap him or throw myself at him again.

There's nothing to worry about. I'm too exhausted to slap him, and there's no way in hell I'm going to try to kiss him again, even if my stomach tightens when I look at his lips.

Austin thinks he wants everything from me, but he doesn't mean it. Not really. He wants an ideal, a fantasy who doesn't exist. This sad, angry girl is everything I am right now. I am heartbreak and vengeance. It's all I have room for.

Austin sets down his cup. "Have you been to Rome? It's lovely in the summer."

"No." So we're not going to talk about what happened. Good. I don't need a second dose of humiliation.

"If the Sons are here, we don't have much time."

"Then we fight. Isn't that the point?"

"The point is to keep you alive."

"Since when?"

"Since always." His gaze is warm.

I focus on the basket of muffins in the center of the table, battling the fire that starts in the pit of my stomach and flows outward. "You can fight now that you're no longer immortal, right? You can interfere without being banished to the underworld. I'll find Sherri Milliken. We can beat them."

"It's too risky."

"It's what you wanted. For me to fight the Sons." For me to fight Blake. "What's the matter? Now that you can die, a war doesn't seem like such a great idea?"

"It's not just my immortality that I'm losing." The shakiness in his voice is what makes me look at him. His face is pale, drawn. What's happening to Austin?

Mick hurries into the kitchen. "My lord, I tried to stop him, but he insisted on seeing you now." He looks back over his shoulder.

"Who?" Austin asks.

Before Mick can answer, Liam storms in behind him. He's dressed in modern clothes: a pair of skinny jeans and a fitted blue sweater. Seems like the spirit realm also has an Urban Outfitters. While Liam looks hipper now, he still looks out of place. He can't quite mask the otherworldly air that lingers in the way he holds his perfectly sculpted chin.

"Well, isn't this domestic?" Liam practically throws himself on the seat beside me and reaches for a muffin. He takes a bite so large that half the muffin is gone.

I scoot away, putting as much distance between us as I can.

Austin sits up straighter, his face now a mask of haughty pretense. "Has it been so long you've forgotten your manners?"

Liam brushes the crumbs from his shirt. "It has been much too long." He glances at me. "I see you've met my warrior."

"I'm not your anything," I say.

"She's not your anything," Austin says at the same time.

Liam looks from me to Austin and laughs. "Isn't this interesting? You're even weaker than I thought, Arawn."

"Austin," he corrects.

"Such a human name. It does seem more fitting." Liam shoves the rest of the muffin into his mouth and chews. He talks with his mouth full. "I'll be staying here for the foreseeable future. Have your man make up your best room."

Mick still stands awkwardly in the doorway. "Sir?"

Austin takes a sip from his tea, looking outwardly calm. "I don't recall issuing you an invitation. This is still my house."

"Best to hold on to your earthly possessions while you have them." Liam grins. "You can't take them with you."

Austin disappears in a flash of gold light so bright I have to cover my eyes. The light barely dims when he reappears, shrouding the entire room in its brilliance. "You presume too much. I am not some withering human."

Liam brings his arm up to cover his eyes. His face looks pale even in the golden light.

I can't stop staring at Austin. It's impossible to look at him and not understand why the gods were worshipped. He wears only a plaid cloth that drapes across his hips, revealing smooth lines of golden skin that look like they were carved by a master craftsman. His hair is still wild, and the juxtaposition with his perfect features makes him seem almost touchable. One look at his eyes, lit with gold light that seems to come from within, makes it plain that Austin is not a forgiving god. His gaze is both regal and deadly as he glares at Liam.

Then he lifts his jeweled sword until the edge of the blade meets the skin above Liam's collar. "You are not welcome here," Austin says, as if the sword to the neck isn't sufficient to convey the message on its own.

Liam bows his head, but his mouth is contorted into a sneer. "My lord."

Austin returns to human form and casually sits down, picking up his cup of tea. "Mikel? Can you show Liam out?"

Liam doesn't look at either of us as he stands and walks to the doorway. "You always were more reckless than bright. Today's petulance is tomorrow's sorrow."

Austin rolls his eyes. "You're not my god, Liam."

Liam laughs at that. "Then it is as I thought. You are becoming human."

Austin meets Liam's gaze. "Not yet."

"Soon." Liam blows Austin a kiss before he follows Mick down the hall.

Austin waits until the last of their footsteps fade into silence before he speaks again. "We're running out of time."

I'm not following any of this, but I don't miss the way Austin's brow furrows. He's worried. "What was that about?"

Austin pours himself another cup of tea. "Liam's been coveting my throne for centuries. It's just like him to want to lord it over me now."

"How did he overthrow you, exactly?"

"I'm losing my power, Brianna. All of it."

"But I've seen you. You might be mortal, but you're still a demigod. Like the Sons. You saved me from drowning, and just now…"

"It's more of an effort every time." Austin stirs a cube of sugar into his tea.

Liam meant it literally when he said that Austin was becoming human? Not only mortal, but powerless? I try to process this. "How?"

"Magic is easily conjured, not so easily undone."

"Undone?"

"The reversal spell I used to save your horse was deceptively easy to perform, was it not?"

I nod. I used the same spell to bring Blake back from the dead. All I had to do was say a few ancient words.

"Such powerful magic does not come free."

"What are you saying? You're losing your power because of what you did to save Dart?"

Austin won't look at me. He rubs his temples and stares at the brown liquid in front of him. He finally sighs and lifts his eyes. "And what you did to save Blake."

"Blake? How does what I did with Blake affect you?"

"Not me."

It hits me all at once. The spell I used had consequences.

"I'm going to lose my power because of what I did to save Blake?"

"I'm afraid so."

I've barely had time to come to terms with what I am. It's not fair—I'm finally ready to fight. And now I might not be able to.

"How long do I have?"

"At first, there's just a delay. Barely noticeable. Soon it will be an effort to bring forth even the simplest spell. It only gets harder to break through. Within weeks, we'll both be powerless."

"It hasn't happened to me yet. Maybe it won't."

"It will."

I pull my shoulders back. "Then we have to move fast."

"Brianna, it's not that simple."

"It is. I still have power. So do you. We don't have to wait for the Sons to find us. We'll find them first and take them out one by one. While we still can."

Austin sighs. "We can't."

"Why not?"

The furrow in his brow is back. "Because we're on their side now."

SEVENTEEN

I don't want to be on the Sons' side of anything. But the more I think about it, the more I realize that Austin is right. If we take out the Sons, the gods will return—but we won't be counted among them. I can't stand the thought of Liam lording over us anymore than Austin can. If the other gods are anything like him, we're in serious trouble.

"So what now?" I ask. "We can't run, and we can't fight."

"We do what every army in need of an ally does. We make nice."

He wants me to be nice? To Blake and Portia? To Jonah and Rush? To Mallory and Sierra and the rest of the breeders who spent the last few months making sure I knew exactly how much they hated me? "Impossible."

He laughs. "It's for the greater good. To protect humanity."

"I'd rather live under Liam's thumb."

"You wouldn't. He's a sadistic bastard."

"And Jonah Timken's better, how?" Austin saw Jonah's assault on me last spring.

"Liam kills for the fun of it."

"Like Rush Bruton?" Rush's restaurant in Rancho Domingo is a taxidermist's wet dream. He kills animals for sport and has them stuffed like sick trophies.

"Liam won't stop at animals. People might as well be game when it comes to him. The only thing stopping him from attacking right now is the threat of personal banishment. He won't kill a human and jeopardize his ability to move between the realms, but if he gets free rein up here, no one is safe."

"So what do we do?"

Austin closes his fist into a tight ball. He stares at it for a moment and then moves his hand below the table. He looks up at me, his expression steady. "You could talk to Blake."

"No." No way in hell.

"He's the only one of them who will listen to you. He'll give you the benefit of the doubt."

"He won't." Blake will give me exactly nothing. If he ever gave me the benefit of the doubt. If he ever gave me anything. "He hates me."

Austin's eyes glisten. Not with gold. He takes a long sip of his tea. The cup clinks against the table when he sets it back down. "I'm not wrong about this. He's your best chance to survive—he was ready to risk anything to keep you. That's not something a person can just turn off. He'll help, if you ask."

That may have been true once, but everything was different when Blake was bound to me. He's already moved on. In fact, he'll probably be the first in line to stab me in the heart. I open my mouth to protest, but stop myself when Austin wipes his eyes.

"You have to try. We need his help."

"Are you okay?" I ask.

Austin laughs. "I'm still not sure what to do with these damned human emotions."

"You knew."

"What?"

"Last night." When I threw myself at Austin like an idiot. "You knew I was going to have to go back and ask Blake for help." No wonder he wouldn't let me have my revenge. He wanted me to go back to Blake.

He doesn't answer. He closes his eyes against me.

"What about Joe? We could talk to him. He can arrange a meeting with Rush."

When Austin opens his eyes, he looks stronger. Resigned. "Joe doesn't have the influence Blake does. The Sons will listen to Blake. He's a natural leader."

I'm suddenly furious. "So that's it? You expect me to go crawling back to Blake and beg for his mercy? Didn't Mick tell you we saw him with Portia yesterday? He's moved on. Even if he wanted me once, he doesn't now."

"I seriously doubt that."

"Here's what you missed while you were hanging out in the underworld with Liam and company. When I made the truce with the Sons, Blake told Rush that he was using me to find the other bandia. After we nearly bonded again, he made sure we were never alone because he didn't want to be tied to me anymore. He never wanted us to be together like that in the first place, and he didn't want it to happen again. If he helps me now, it won't be because he loves me. It will be because I can help the Sons."

Saying the words out loud brings everything into razor-sharp focus. Blake never loved me. Not really.

"Of course you can help the Sons. Even an idiot can see that." Austin takes another sip of tea, but the cup in his hand trembles.

"I won't."

"I'd kill him myself if I thought it would help. But I've been over this a million times. The best way to the Sons is through Blake. Even if he doesn't want you back, he will never let them hurt you. You have to trust that."

"Fuck trust." It's not like Blake ever trusted me.

Austin stands up and walks around the table. He raises his hand as if he's about to place it on my shoulder, but drops it before touching me. "We have to try. If I'm going to die, it won't be for nothing."

"You're going to die?" The thought of Austin's death should make me happy. I've wanted him dead. Now I'm filled with a panic that doesn't make sense.

"I'm mortal now. My death is as inevitable as anyone's. If I only have this life to live, I want to make it count."

"Oh." Of course. He's talking in generalities. Mortality is new to him.

"I had Mikel do some checking. Blake is staying at the inn above the Ornery Knight on Main."

"You want me to go to his hotel room?"

"Well, it's private. We don't know if the other Sons are here and you don't want to risk a public confrontation." Austin stares at the ground. We both know that it's more than that. He wants me to get Blake back the old-fashioned way.

"You expect me to get back together with him?" Like that's even possible. Blake doesn't want me back. He never really wanted me to begin with.

"If that's what it takes." Austin turns his back to me.

"What about me? What if I don't want him?" I say the words, hoping that if I got the choice, I would make the strong one. The one that ends with me walking away.

Austin turns around, his eyes dark. "Don't play with me, Brianna."

Play with him? This has nothing to do with him. "Forgive me for not being excited about throwing myself at the guy I just saw kissing Portia Bruton."

Austin grasps the back of the chair next to mine, leaning forward. "It's the logical choice. Surely you can understand logic. Blake is your best chance of staying alive. I've already made arrangements for Portia to enjoy a complimentary spa day today. She won't be in the way."

Austin has already *planned* this little reunion? How thoughtful. "What exactly am I supposed to tell Blake?" How exactly am I supposed to win back the boy who hates me? The boy who's already moved on? Who never loved me to begin with?

"The truth."

"The truth doesn't work with Blake." I stand up, but Austin doesn't back away. There's barely an inch of space between us as I face him. Heat radiates off his chest, and my cheeks burn with the memory of his body pressing against mine. "You really want me to do this?"

"No," he says, "I don't."

"But you're sending me anyway?"

He swallows. "And if I didn't?"

I don't have an answer for that. I take a step back.

"It doesn't matter. I'll try." I stalk past Austin. "But whatever happens, I'm blaming you."

"Fine."

I pause in the doorway. "You should've kissed me last night when you had the chance."

He meets my gaze. "I know."

I'm barely out of the room when I hear the cup smash against the wall behind me.

EIGHTEEN

The entrance to the inn is through the pub. Only a few people sit at the bar, and none of them are Sons. A stout woman with short curly hair pours ale from behind the counter. She winks at me when I ask for Blake's room. At least she holds her tongue as she leads me to a narrow wood staircase in the back.

"Second on the right," she says.

I try to ignore the creaks in the stairs as I climb, but every sound is magnified, grating on my ears like shrill screams. I wipe my palms on my jeans when I get to the door. There's no sound from inside, and I let myself imagine he's out. The ruse is the only thing that allows me to raise my hand and knock on the door.

There's a rustling inside. "Did you forget your key again?" Blake says from the other side of the door.

I can hear the smile in his voice. My stomach flips over before I can remind myself that his smile is not for me. It's for Portia. Despite what I saw yesterday, some part of me still hoped there would be some perfectly rational explanation for him and Portia, like that's even possible. But it's pretty clear I saw exactly what I thought I saw. Portia has a key to his room, and Blake is happy she came back.

He flings open the door carelessly, a smile still on his lips. He's wearing a pair of faded 501s and nothing else, his blond hair pointing out in odd angles like he just woke up. My chest tightens into a ball, robbing me of breath. I want to launch myself at him, to hold him and never let go.

Pathetic.

I keep my feet anchored to the floor in the hallway.

His smile fades. "What are you doing here?"

"Nice to see you too. Can I come in?" I step past him into a room without waiting for an answer. I resist the urge to touch him, pressing my hands into the pockets of my jeans.

The room is dominated by an unmade full-sized bed and a small night table. Blake's bag sits on a wooden stool, its contents spilled around it. There's barely room for the two of us to stand.

Blake glances down the hall and shuts the door behind him quickly. He runs his hand through his hair, which only makes it stick out worse. "How'd you find me?"

"You found me. I've been here for the last two weeks."

He stares at the floor. "You need to leave."

I don't know what I expected from him, but it wasn't this indifference. There's no emotion in his voice. Not even anger. Doesn't he feel anything? I reach for his emotions without meaning to, trying to feel something, anything that will give me a clue what he's feeling. Of course there's nothing but cold, empty air. The hole in my heart where his soul used to be. "I was here first."

"I'm serious. The Sons will all be here on Friday. They have a lead on Sherri Milliken." His eyes meet mine for a second, but he looks away just as quickly.

Oh yeah, this will be easy. He can't even look at me.

Good. I don't want to be with someone who doesn't trust me. Portia can have him and his fake fucking feelings. "This was a bad idea," I mutter.

"Brianna?" For the first time since I got here, he looks at me. The vein in his neck throbs, but it's his eyes that give him away. His green eyes are sad, broken. "Why are you here?"

I meet his gaze, and I'm lost in it. I step toward him without meaning to. I close my eyes, fighting the urge to take the step that will bring me into his arms.

Remember. Remember what he did. "I saw you with her."

When I open my eyes. Blake's face is as impossible to read as ever.

"Was any of it true?" I add, blurting out the one question I really don't want answered. But now that it's out, I can't stop myself. "Was *everything* a lie?"

Blake sits on the edge of the bed and rubs his palm on his cheek. "How can you even ask that?"

I inch back until I'm pressed against the wall, keeping as much distance as I can between myself and the bed. "I don't know. Maybe it has something to do with the fact that you automatically assumed the worst as soon as things got crazy at your sister's party. Or the fact that you started dating

Portia Bruton the second you got rid of me." A new panic sends my heart racing. "Maybe you never *stopped* seeing her."

"Stop it." Blake's voice is finally angry. "The fire was bad, Brianna. Don't blame me for thinking what everyone in that room was thinking. I saw you with my sister. We all did."

"So? I get why everyone else thought it was me, but I told you I didn't do it. That should've been enough. Forget it. It's fine. The truth came out—I know you don't trust me. You never did." A tear drops onto my cheek. I turn to face the door, rushing to wipe the tear away before he sees.

Blake gets up and walks behind me. My traitorous body warms at his proximity. "How can you say that? I risked everything, including my life, to be with you. I loved you."

I don't miss that he's talking in the past tense. I grip the doorknob so tightly that my fingers hurt. "When did you stop? When the bond was broken? At your sister's party? When?" I'm talking through tears, but it doesn't matter now. Let him see. If I can't make Blake feel how broken he's left me, at least I can make him see it.

He turns and kicks the bed. "I don't know."

He stopped? He really stopped loving me? I want to scream. I choke it back as I turn on him. "I gave up everything for you." My heart. My power.

He pins me further against the door with his hard stare. Then he takes another step toward me, stalking me like prey. "No, you didn't. You killed me, remember? Then you sulked around my family like they were poison. You didn't even try to get along with them. All you wanted was for us to bond again. You wanted my soul, but I was never good enough."

"And Portia? She gives you what you want? Can you screw her brains out without having to worry about losing your soul in the process?"

"You don't even know what you're talking about."

"I know what I saw." Wind whips around my hair. My wind.

"Stop it." Blake backs up a step, but his legs hit the bed frame. "I don't want to fight you."

"Why? Afraid I'll kill you again?"

"Brianna." Blake's eyes plead as the wind picks up the clothes on his suitcase and flings them to the bed. The lamp on the nightstand smashes against the wall. "Stop."

I lift my palm, stopping the wind as quickly as it started. Blue arcs of electricity spark between my fingers. It would be so easy to turn everything into a flaming ball of fire. To watch it burn. To end this once and for all.

Blake grabs my wrist. "Don't."

We both freeze, his hand searing my skin with the strange, sick chemistry that draws us together. His touch fills me with a different kind of fire, a flame that licks at my core and makes me want to melt into him.

"I hate you," I say, but the sparks in my hands recede. My blood is still hot, charged with the heat of Blake's touch. He closes the distance, and then his lips are on mine and his chest is against mine and his hands are on my shoulders and my waist and my hips. I kiss him back instinctively, my body responding to the call of his soul even as my brain screams for me to stop. His hands tangle in my hair as he brings me down on the bed underneath him, pushing and pressing until his legs twine through mine and our bodies connect at every possible point. I claw at his bare back, lost in the electric heat of his touch as his hands move underneath my shirt, turning me to molten lava.

We are fire and fire.

The kiss is full of his anger and my anger, grasping for each other through the physical connection, feeding off each other. We shared our souls once, and my body aches to feel him again. I barely notice the silver thread of light that spins around us, getting faster and faster as Blake's hips press into mine, as his kisses get wilder.

Yes.

Wind whips around us, urging us closer.

He wants me. I can take him for myself. I can bind Blake to me and never let him go.

The goddess in me urges me to do it. To take everything he once promised. To wield my power over him in a way he can never escape. While I still can.

The girl in me fights to the surface. Blake accused me of forcing the bond on him last time. I don't want to feel his anger and resentment and bitterness, all of which will inevitably follow.

I don't want to be bound to someone I can't trust.

All at once, I understand exactly why Austin pushed me away last night. I thought I wanted Blake, but I don't want it to be like this. It's not enough for Blake to want me—I need more. I need something Blake may never be able to give, bond or no bond.

It takes every bit of strength I possess to push against his shoulders and break the kiss. The silver thread of light dances around us still.

"We have to stop," I say.

Blake starts to protest, his lips moving back against mine. Then he notices the way the light folds around us and stops abruptly. He pushes off of me, sitting up on the bed, his breath coming in quick gasps.

The wind dies first. After a few seconds, the silver light fades to nothing.

"You stopped it." Blake lifts his hand, and for a second I think he's going to reach for me, but he jerks it back and runs his fingers through his hair instead. "Why?"

I scramble off the bed, retreating to the relative safety of the wall by the door. "For someone who used to share my emotions, you don't know me at all." I need more than this physical connection. I need more than to feel his emotions as if they were my own. I need something Blake has never been able to give me.

I unclasp the silver necklace that he gave me for my birthday.

He doesn't resist when I walk to the bed and take his hand. We both feel the heat that flows between our fingers, but this time we don't act on it. His eyes are dark as I place the wolfsbane pendant in his palm, closing his fingers around it.

"I never lied to you," he says.

"It doesn't matter." Whatever we had, it wasn't enough to make him trust me. I run my fingers through the layers of his hair, doing my best to smooth it back into place. "I'm sorry."

I don't know why I'm the one apologizing, but it feels

like the right thing to say. I am sorry. I wish to God things could've been different for us.

He stands up, and we're so close that for a second I think he's going to kiss me again. I drop my hand to my side and walk to the door before he gets the chance.

He doesn't say anything when I leave his room. He doesn't need to.

We both know this is goodbye.

NINETEEN

I couldn't ask Blake to help. I couldn't ask him for anything. There has to be another way to make the Sons understand that we're on their side.

I'm halfway through the pub when I see Portia coming from the other direction. I can't help wishing I'd stayed in Blake's room just a few more minutes, that I'd let that kiss stretch a little longer. As it is, I feel a sick little twinge of pleasure when she sees me and her pretty amber eyes darken. I'm a horrible person.

"You!"

"Me." I smile. Let her wonder.

"Does Blake know you're here?" She can't hide the panic in her voice.

"Yes." I finger-comb the snarl in my hair where Blake's hands had been. "Sorry if I ruined the surprise."

"You ruin everything you touch."

"Even Blake?" I let my meaning hang in the air.

Portia's beautiful face turns ugly when she's angry, and she's angry a lot. "He's over it."

Her words hurt more than I want to admit, stinging the open wound like saltwater. "Is he?" I force a smile onto my lips. I don't know why I want to hurt her—it's not her fault Blake wants her. Still, the little seed of doubt I plant is nothing compared to what I could do.

But there's no fire flowing under my skin. No ice threatening to break free. No dark magic bursting to get out.

Maybe I'm getting better at controlling it.

A fireplace near the far wall flares to life with blue flame.

Maybe not.

I watch the fire grow, but I don't feel it. At all.

No. I should be able to feel it. I concentrate, but I can't reach it. All I can do is pray it doesn't spread and grow like the fire at Mallory's party.

Portia walks past me and disappears up the little staircase. The fire shrinks and dies behind her, and I still don't feel anything.

I reach for the embers. The fire doesn't respond.

I try for water, since it's usually the easiest element for me to access. I concentrate on filling my veins with ice, a trick I've learned to do quickly as a defense against the Sons.

It should be right there.

But there's nothing.

Austin said it would get harder to access my magic, but I wasn't expecting this. I can't reach it at all.

Rhiannon walks past me, wearing the Ornery Knight

shirt that the servers wear. At least both she and Shannon found jobs after my arrival at Lorcan Hall drove them away. As she clears glasses from an empty table, she watches me with dark eyes. "We don't serve witches here."

"Lucky for me I'm not a witch." It might even be true now. I laugh. I can't help it.

Rhiannon crosses herself as I walk past her out the door.

The sun has made an appearance for the first time in days, casting everything in a warm glow. Austin is pacing in the narrow street. He nearly jumps when he sees me step outside.

"What are you doing here?" I ask.

He smiles, but it looks forced. "Trying to keep myself from running upstairs and dragging you out of his room."

"It was your idea."

"It was a stupid idea."

"The lamest. So what's plan B?"

Austin steps closer, studying my face. "He said no?"

"More or less." It's not like I asked, and it's clear to me now that I can't. Blake and I are not getting back together. I'm not asking him for any favors.

"We'll find another way to reach the Sons," he says.

"We have a bigger problem at the moment."

"Bigger than the fact that Liam is roaming the countryside in search of a supernatural army?"

I nod. "You were right about me losing my power. It's done."

"Done?"

"One minute the elements were at my fingertips, as strong as ever. And now, there's nothing."

"That's not how it's supposed to work."

"I don't know how it's supposed to work. I just know how it is."

Austin leads me to a black sports car I haven't seen before. He holds the door open for me and walks around to the other side. He drives too fast for the narrow streets, not slowing until we turn into the gates for Lorcan Hall.

He drives past the house and stable, veering onto a dirt road that heads toward the ocean.

"Where are we going?" I ask.

"The gateway is the center of all power. It might be easier for you there."

We park at the head of the trail that leads down to the beach. Austin grabs my elbow when I stumble on a loose rock. He doesn't let go until we reach the rocky shore below, and then it's only to take my hand as we navigate through the boulders to the small beach beyond. The tide is out, but the water still spits and swirls against the rocks nearby. I haven't been here since I nearly drowned. Even with the tide out, the beach feels too small. I keep my back pressed firmly against the wall of the hillside, clinging to Austin's hand.

Austin stops in front of the crack in the rock wall. "Here."

"What now?"

"Concentrate."

Austin disappears in a burst of gold. I feel a surge of magic as he starts to reappear, but it's Austin's, not mine. A black shadow forms inside the gold, shifting and turning until Austin takes shape in all his godly glory. I have to remember to breathe. There's nothing vulnerable or flawed about Austin now. His crooked smile does nothing to mask the perfection of his high cheekbones and chiseled jaw, and the golden flecks in his eyes glow. He's so achingly beautiful that I want to look away, but I can't. The plaid covering his waist and hips only serves to emphasize the smooth skin stretched tight along the muscles of his chest and stomach. He carries the ancient broadsword in his right hand, but his left hand is extended out to me.

I lift my hand to his, marveling at how human his skin feels in spite of its brilliance. "Reach for the sea," Austin says, in a voice that covers me like crushed velvet.

I close my eyes against his light and listen to the waves as they crash against the rocks. My breathing gets shallow, but my blood remains still. "Nothing. It's gone."

Austin's index finger brushes my lips for an instant. "Never. Your power will diminish by halves until you can't feel it or call it, but a part will always remain. Make no mistake about it, Brianna. You are magic."

I open my eyes. "The theory of infinite smallness."

"What?"

"It's a theory. So long as something has mass, it can be halved, and halved again, into perpetuity. It never really disappears."

"Smaller and smaller pieces?"

"Exactly."

"So find a way to reach that piece inside you. Try again."

I close my eyes, concentrating on the sound of the waves. I can almost feel the water flowing in my veins, but whether it's really there or just a memory, I can't say. Austin squeezes my hand lightly.

I inhale deeply. It's not the sea that fills me, but something richer. Apples and spice and fire mix together in a scent that's at once strange and familiar. I open my eyes and all I see is Austin. He's closer, but I don't remember moving toward him. His golden light is warm as it licks against my skin and sends my nerves into overdrive.

"Feel anything?" he asks.

Just you. I swallow. "I'm not sure."

He leans closer, his breath dancing along my neck. "When was the last time you felt your power?"

"In Blake's room."

"You used your magic against him?"

"Against his suitcase. And a lamp." I shift my weight, stretching toward Austin. He doesn't try to stop me. If anything, he pulls me closer.

Austin grins. His lips are so close. "Poor lamp. So that was the last time you felt it?"

I shake my head. I shouldn't be embarrassed that I kissed Blake, but I am. It wasn't my finest moment. Aggrieved ex-girlfriend gets revenge by making out.

Austin's lips are in my hair, as soft as his voice, a whisper. "When was the last time?"

He's going to make me say it. I step away from Austin, biting my lip. "When Blake and I kissed. We nearly bonded again."

Austin drops my hands and steps away. The crease between his brows is a deep line, marring his golden face. He no longer looks like a god. He looks like something altogether more dangerous.

"I stopped it."

I don't know if he hears me. There's a brilliant flash of gold light, and then nothing but spots in my eyes.

"Austin?" By the time the spots clear up enough for me to look around the beach, there's no sign of him.

Just me and the rocks and the waves and the air. So potent, but just out of reach.

TWENTY

I eat dinner in the kitchen by myself. According to Mick, Austin hasn't come back to the house. Fine. I don't want to argue with him right now anyway. He was the one who had the brilliant idea to send me to Blake's room, to prey on Blake's supposed feelings for me. What did he expect?

Screw them both.

On to Plan B. I take out the cell Mick gave me. It takes a few tries before I remember the number, but I finally do.

Joe answers on the second ring. "Hello."

"Are you in Cath?" I ask.

"Might be. You?"

"I might be outside the bakery on Main Street at ten o'clock."

"Tonight?"

"Will you come?"

"You should lay low."

"I will."

"Nah, you won't. Don't suppose I can do anything to change your mind, though."

"Thanks."

Mick gives me the keys to the sedan with only a little prodding after I tell him I'm meeting Joe. The whole driving on the right side of the car is only weird for first few miles or so. By the time I get into Cath, I feel like I could get used to it.

The bakery is in the center of the block. It's easy to disappear into the shadowy alcove by the door, the street barely illuminated by the old-fashioned gas lamps that dot each corner as the sun finally drops behind the buildings. It's quiet except for peals of laughter that occasionally drift out of the Naughty Baron, a pub a block over.

The air is damp even though we're a few blocks from the ocean. If this is summer, I hate to think how cold winter must be. I hear footsteps approach before I can make out anyone in the darkness.

I peek out of the alcove, instinctively reaching for the wind but finding only the cold, impervious sky. The shadowy figure that approaches is tall and thin, with hair teased even higher. It's the right shape for Joe, but I duck back into the alcove until I can be sure.

He stops in front of the bakery and looks into the window.

"Joe?" I whisper.

He walks the rest of the way to me, his hands buried deep in the pockets of a long black coat that covers him to just below his knees. He nods toward the pub. "Drink? It'll be warmer." His voice is tinged with an Irish accent I haven't heard before.

"I didn't realize you had an accent."

"It's like a bad penny."

I follow him across the street and into the pub. The walls inside are lined with dark paneling. Darkness clings to the corners in the dim lighting, allowing us to make our way to an empty table in the back without drawing any attention.

Joe surveys the restaurant twice. "You shouldn't be out like this. Too risky."

"Are they all coming here?"

Joe nods. "Friday."

At least Blake didn't lie about that. I have two days before the Sons descend on Cath. "Looking for me?"

"Nothing's changed. They're always looking for your kind."

"Why did Blake come early?"

Joe takes out a cigarette from the red packet in his pocket. "Not much gets by you." He stares at the thin cylinder but doesn't put it in his mouth.

"You don't have to lie for him. I know about Portia."

Joe's irises get smaller, and I can't escape the feeling that he's looking through me. "You're taking it better than I expected."

"What did you expect me to do? Burn down the village?"

His cheeks redden.

"Oh my God, you did." He really thought I would fly into some violent rage. "Give me some credit."

He sticks the unlit cigarette between his lips. "I do. More than you likely deserve."

"I couldn't, anyway. Burn it down, I mean."

"You damn well could."

"No." I turn my palms up. "I really couldn't. My power is gone."

Joe orders a cup of coffee from a passing waitress. The quiet expression on his face never changes. He waits for me to continue. "And?"

"Did Blake ever tell you what happened, that night last spring when he fought Austin on the beach?"

"Just that you broke the bond."

"It was more than that. Blake was dead." It doesn't get easier to say the words. "I killed him."

I doubt much surprises Joe after centuries of living with the Sons, but the cigarette falls from his lips and lands on the table before he can close his mouth.

"I found a way to bring him back. Obviously. I mean, he's not dead now." God, I'm rambling. "But doing that drained my magic. I'm not a bandia anymore. Not like I was."

Joe smiles. "You never were the conventional type."

"Well, now I'm not the conventional anything. Do you think this will make a difference to the Sons? I'm no threat to them anymore."

"Brianna?" a guy's voice calls across the pub. "Brianna Paxton?"

I panic at the sound of my name. Both Blake and Joe said the Sons weren't going to be here until Friday, but plans change. I search the room for a familiar face, and stop when

I get to a boy two tables over. He's cute, and I know I've seen him somewhere before, but I can't place him. He waves and stands up, leaving two other boys at the table to their pints as he walks over to me.

I recognize him now: Braden Finley, baseball player and senior class stud. His dark hair is shorter than I remember, now a close-cropped buzz cut, but his easy-going smile and perfect white teeth are hard to forget. He went to my school, Rancho Domingo High, before he graduated this past spring. His locker was next to Haley's, and he used to ask her out to lunch every day whether he had a girlfriend or not.

I wait for him to get all the way to our table before I say anything. "Braden? What are you doing here?"

"Bumming around Europe before I start college in September. This is wild. What about you?"

"Staying with a friend." Austin's hardly a friend, but it sounds better than the truth: hiding out with a dethroned god and trying to figure out how to realign myself with a bunch of demigods before they make good on their threat to kill me. Or before the new god kills me.

Braden eyes Joe. "Him?"

"Oh, no. Austin Montgomery?"

Austin went to a different school than we did, but Braden nods like he knows exactly who I'm talking about. "I knew I should've made my move when I had the chance."

"I'm pretty sure you did." The day I went to school without my charm bracelet, which had kept me basically invisible to guys, Braden asked me out to lunch instead of Haley.

"Yeah, that's right. Shot down." Braden laughs easily. He nods toward his table. "You want to join us for a beer?"

"Maybe later?"

"Ouch. Shot down again!" His smile doesn't fade. He pulls a phone out of his pocket. "Give me your cell so we can sync up while we're both in town." When I don't do anything, he holds his hands up. "Just to hang out. It's nice to see someone from home. Someone who speaks English I can actually understand."

I can't argue with him. It is nice to see someone familiar. Someone who doesn't want to kill me or use me or hurt me or ask me for more than I can ever give. We exchange numbers before he walks back to his friends.

Joe watches him the whole way. "How do you know that guy?"

"From school. You haven't met? I should've introduced you."

Joe lifts his chin toward the table. "I know the bloke he's with."

I follow Joe's gaze to a tall boy with dark, spiky hair sitting at the far end of Braden's table. Either his eyes are rimmed with black eyeliner or he has the darkest lashes I've ever seen. It's hard to tell from here. When he lifts his beer, I recognize half of a Greenpeace tattoo on the part of his forearm bared by the pushed-up sleeve of his sweater. It's in the same place as Joe's tattoo. "Did you two serve together?" I ask.

Joe laughs. "You might say that."

Wait. Joe looks eighteen, but he's been alive for centuries, which explains how he managed to spend time with

Greenpeace in the 1970s. But the guy with Braden doesn't look any older than me. "He's a giolla?"

"Not surprising, really. What with the Gathering and all."

"The Gathering?"

"Austin moved the gateway to Cath. The reopening always sparks a Gathering of the descendants of the gods. That kind of thing will draw others as well."

"Austin didn't open the gateway. Liam did."

Joe's face looks blank.

"Pwil?"

Joe's face still doesn't change, but his fingers shake ever so slightly as he picks the cigarette off the table. "Bad time to be powerless."

"Why? What does the Gathering mean?"

"It means you won't be able to avoid the Sons, or even the other bandia. Pwil will call you all to the gateway and attempt to force a battle." He puts the unlit cigarette back between his lips.

"When?"

Joe shrugs. "Pwil and I aren't exactly on speaking terms. He's been below for a very long time. I imagine he'll do it as soon as he thinks you're ready."

"Me?"

"You and the other bandia. He won't set up a fight he doesn't think he can win."

Braden is grinning at me from across the pub. He lifts a glass of dark beer toward me in a silent toast.

I turn back to Joe. "Can you get me a meeting with Rush?"

He's silent for a long minute before he answers. "He's not your biggest fan at the moment."

"I know. But the Sons need to know about Pwil and the Gathering. I can help them if they'll let me."

"I'll see. How about you? You okay?"

"I'm really not."

Joe stubs the unlit cigarette in a small planter next to us. "Then God help us all."

TWENTY-ONE

Everything is quiet back at Lorcan Hall. It's strange to pass by the giant rooms without seeing anyone. I hear a footstep and spin around, but there's nothing there. Nothing behind me, and no magic to grasp. Every little sound sets me on edge. It's one thing to be hunted by a bunch of demigods when you're capable of taking them out in your own right. It's another to be powerless prey.

Mick took me to a library on my first day here, when I got the grand tour, but I can't for the life of me remember where it is. I search through both wings on the main level, but I don't find it. I head upstairs, and find only another drawing room and two empty bedrooms. I'm nearing my own room when I notice a light on under a large door across the hall. I knock, but no one answers.

I try the doorknob, and it turns. I push the door open just wide enough to stick my head through. The bedroom is huge, at least twice the size of mine. A king-size canopy rests against one wall, covered in brown drapes that match a plush duvet. An L-shaped leather couch and giant flat-screen television sit off to the right. The limestone floor is covered with a large, brown, faux-fur rug. At least I assume it's faux; it's too big to be real. An alcove in the opposite wall opens onto a stone hallway.

"Mikel?" I hear Austin say from somewhere down the hallway. "Is that you?"

"No, it's me."

Austin appears in the archway in jeans and a thick cabled sweater, the wool dyed a deep, rich blue. "Looking for me?"

"The library, actually."

"In my bedroom?" He raises his eyebrows, and I'm all too aware of how this must look.

"Right." I back out of the door and into the hall.

"Brianna."

I poke my head back in. "Yes?"

"I shouldn't have left you at the gateway. Liam could have . . . I'm sorry." His brows furrow, but he doesn't look angry. At least not with me.

"It's no big deal." I can't stop staring at the lines on his face. I'm not used to seeing any imperfections beyond his crooked smile. I'm sure that's all it is. It's a strange thing to see a god look this way. So vulnerable. The little pang in my chest is just a natural reaction to seeing someone weakened.

Austin leans against the wall of the alcove but doesn't move closer. "I'm not as patient as I used to be."

"You were never patient." That's one thing that hasn't changed.

"Was I always so jealous?"

"I don't know. Are you jealous now?" Of what? I have nothing for him to be jealous of. No family. No friends. No Blake.

"Eternally," he says.

"Ha."

"Ironic, I know. But some things survive even death. Especially emotions. They're tied to the soul. You humans can't ever seem to let them go."

"Well, you did keep trying to get me to kill Blake until you finally succeeded." I say the words matter-of-factly, without my usual venom.

"Then my jealousy has definitely gotten worse. Now I want to do it myself." He takes a breath and I realize that the lines in his face aren't the only thing that's changed. There's emotion behind his eyes; not jealousy, but something sadder.

"Austin?"

He closes his eyes. "I love the sound of my name on your lips."

I let myself smile while he's not looking. Last night, when I tried to get him to kiss me, it had been nothing more than a twisted attempt at revenge against Blake, a way to forget the pain and inflict some of my own. But now I can't stop thinking of the way he felt over me, his teeth grazing my neck. I shudder and close my eyes, trying to block the image from my mind.

"What are you looking for?" Austin asks.

I focus on my reason for searching out the library: research. "What's the Gathering?"

"Did you see Liam?"

"Joe. And also a giolla I've never seen before. He was with a guy I know from back home."

"One of the Sons? I never should have left you—"

"Chill. Just a guy from school who's spending his summer hiking through Europe."

"Who just happens to be passing through the Irish backcountry so soon after the gateway opened? With a giolla?"

It does sound odd, but why not? "Braden" is an Irish name—it makes sense that he'd want to see the land of his ancestors.

Crap. Braden is connected to Ireland. To all of this. "What is he?" I ask.

"More trouble."

"But he's not even a breeder from Killian's line," I point out. "And Killian killed off all the other demigod lines once he got his own power."

"The Seventh Daughters and the Sons of Killian are all that remain of the demigods," Austin says slowly. "But the gods weren't the only magical creatures to grace our homeland. Nor were they the only ones to suffer when the Milesians drove magic underground."

"The giolla?"

Austin nods. "The giolla have always aligned themselves with power. They blend easily with humans, since they can compel human emotions and create memories, but they prefer to surround themselves with magic. So that they don't have to pretend."

"But you can use compulsion, too."

"Not like they can. The giolla can create thoughts and feelings from nothing at all, although they don't like to. I can only bring forward feelings that are already present. More of a magnification."

So that explains why Austin couldn't make me want him after I'd bonded with Blake. "But Haley?" I asked. My friend nearly drowned herself under Austin's power.

"She's more troubled than you realize."

I sit down on the edge of the leather couch. "Poor Haley. I knew things were bad for her at home, but I never imagined."

Austin finally steps out of the alcove, into the room. "The Sons needed the giolla to pass down their history. A lot can get lost in seven generations. It's been a mutually beneficial relationship for them."

"But the giolla don't all serve the Sons," I say. "Mick has been here serving you, and the boy I saw today was with Braden."

"A thousand years is a long time. Even for the giolla. Especially for the giolla." Austin looks past me to a painting on the wall by the bed, a dark picture of a male angel being stabbed in the back by a handsome, smiling man. "Friends die. Loyalties shift."

"Braden is not a giolla." Joe, Mick, and the guy at the pub all had similar builds, tall and lean. And there was something else. Everything about Mick and Joe is slow and deliberate. Braden is too flirtatious. Too alive.

"I imagine not." Austin sits on the couch next to me. As he does, his thigh brushes my knee. His touch doesn't fill me with a rush of heat the way Blake's does, but it's nice.

I try to clear my head and focus on the stories my grandmother told me about ancient Ireland. "Are there faeries?"

"An old wives' tale."

"What, then?"

"Kelpie, maybe. More likely fuath, if he's here for the Gathering."

"Help me out."

"Kelpies are water horses. Dark creatures that lure people to their deaths by posing as horses and then taking the person on a ride to the bottom of the sea."

"Lovely."

"They haven't been active since shortly after the Milesians began their crusade against magic. They choose to stay below rather than risk detection and persecution topside. The fuath are more dangerous. They regularly mingle with humans. And they'll take more chances if they think they can advance their station with the gods."

"What *is* a fuath?" I ask.

"A more advanced form of water beast. They can appear as humans, but in their true form, they have the body of a horse and the tail of a whale. They're among the most beautiful creatures, and the most sinister. They can feed off human emotions, but they prefer to feed off magic. If they're here, it will be at Liam's invitation."

"The Gathering?"

Austin sets his hand down between us, but he doesn't touch me. "If Liam called the fuath, he means to align with them. He probably offered them a position in the new world."

"He's building an army." I stretch my fingers until I feel Austin's pinky on the couch next to me. I trail my finger from his nail to his knuckle.

"The Seventh Daughters have turned out to be a bit of disappointment." Austin looks down at our hands where I'm touching him. He takes my hand in his, flashing that crooked smile. His eyes flit to the giant bed. "I've never had a girl here before."

I pull my hand away. "You still don't."

"Don't I?" His eyes burn into mine.

I try to ignore the heat that rushes to my cheeks. I still need answers, and Austin has them. At least that's what I tell myself when I don't immediately leave his room. "So the Gathering…it's meant to bring us all together in one place?"

"Liam intends to speed things along. He will force our hand. Soon."

"Can the fuath take out the Sons?" I set my hand in my lap, clasping it with the other one. Anything to keep it from wandering back over to Austin's side of the couch.

Austin picks up a curl of my hair and twirls it around his finger. As he moves the hair away from my neck, his knuckles graze the skin. "Not alone, they can't. But they're clever. They've stayed hidden for centuries, biding their time while the Sons and Daughters killed each other. They won't fully align with any one side until there's a clear winner."

"So their loyalty is still up for grabs?" It's all I can do to keep from leaning into his hand.

"The fuath are loyal only to themselves." Austin drops the curl, like he's only just realized he was touching me. "You should stay away from them."

Stay away from Liam. Stay away from the Sons. Stay away from the fuath. Stay away from town. I may not have power, but it's not like I can be effective locked away and doing nothing.

"I'll find the other bandia," I offer. "The Sons think Sherri might be here. And I'll see what I can find out about Braden. Joe's going to set up a meeting for me with Rush."

Austin laughs. "I don't suppose there's any point to locking you in a tower."

"I'd find a way out."

"I don't doubt it." Austin's eyes dance with golden light.

I can't help but smile.

Austin brings his fingers to my chin, deliberately this time, letting them slide down my throat. "Ask me to kiss you again."

My lips part involuntarily, but he was right to stop things last night. We're not friends. We're not anything. Besides, I'm terrified of kissing him. I might want to do it again.

"No." I hope his ability to use compulsion doesn't allow him to see the little seed of longing that flutters in my chest.

From the way he smiles, I'm guessing it does.

I stand up quickly. "Where is the library, anyway?"

"Three doors down on the right." He waits until I'm at the doorway to speak again. "One question?"

I hesitate.

Austin leans forward, his elbows on his knees. His hair falls into his eyes. "Why didn't Blake agree to help you?"

"I didn't ask." I didn't bind Blake to me, and I didn't ask him for help. But maybe I got something else I didn't realize I needed: closure.

"And I won't," I add. My hand is fixed on the doorknob, but I don't turn it.

"You should go." Austin grins. "Or I might not wait for you to ask me to kiss you again."

I scramble out the door and into the hall.

Last night, I'd wanted Austin to make me forget. Today, I don't know what I want. But I do know that with Blake, I'd let myself think he was more to me than he was. I'd confused physical attraction for something more. I won't make that mistake again.

Besides, Austin has never cared for anyone but himself. He's a killer. He made me one. And no matter how much he seems to want to help me now, I can't let myself forget what he's done.

TWENTY-TWO

In the morning, I find the library right where Austin said it would be. It has floor-to-ceiling bookcases built into the walls, each shelf filled with both leather-bound volumes and more modern books.

My eye is drawn to a thick book on a table: *A Brief History of Cath*. I flip through the pages, scanning through stories of the town's heritage. I stop when I get to a story of a fire that destroyed half of Main Street a hundred and fifty years ago. The book describes a historic lightning storm and a strange blue fire, now believed to be caused by the natural gas that fueled the new street lamps.

My stomach twists into a tight coil. I knew that in coming to Ireland, I was coming home, but this is closer to home than I'd realized. This is the very town that my seventh-generation grandmother burned to avenge a heartbreak.

No wonder the townspeople don't want me here.

It's a relief to be powerless. To know I can't hurt anyone like that. But how am I going to stop Liam from assembling an army of fuath to kill off the Sons? If one demigoddess with a broken heart could inflict so much death and destruction, what will happen if the gods regained control of the earth?

Joe was right. Now is a really bad time for my power to be on the fritz.

I scan the shelves, pulling down an eighteenth-century physics book. I thumb through the parchment paper, simultaneously amazed at how much science was already known and how much was yet to be discovered. It's a wonder that so much information survived for so long, passed down and built upon by one generation after another.

The Sons have been building their knowledge, too. Not only using the giolla to keep their history, but conducting genetic research and intergenerational breeding to improve their numbers and strength.

The Seventh Daughters weren't so organized. Why not? Why didn't any giolla align with us? Why didn't the bandia keep a written history?

The only piece of history, the only legacy, that I was ever given is my charm bracelet. The wolfsbane-blossom charm used to serve as a talisman that shielded me from the Sons; men looked right past me until I turned seventeen and was able to control my power.

I twirl the bracelet around on my wrist. The flower doesn't shield me anymore, but I can't deny that it did its job well. And the horse. What did the horse do, exactly, out at that ruined wall? It showed me Austin a thousand years ago. Not just Austin, but Danu's daughter Gwyn. Before Austin was banished. Before Danu was killed.

All that has to mean something. And I have to find out what. But first I need to find Sherri Milliken. My *sister*.

"Breakfast?" Mick comes into the room, pushing a plate of scones at me.

"I'm going out. Want to come?"

He blinks.

"Come on," I say. "I'm taking the Porsche and I'll never figure out how to drive a stick left-handed."

I see the moment he gives in. His lip curves just slightly as he steps away from the scones. "I'll bring the car around."

I wait out front for Mick to pull up in Austin's black sports car. "How long have you known Austin?" I ask as we drive through the gates.

"A long time."

"You knew him when he was Aaron?" I want him to tell me more.

"He's had many names."

"But Aaron was the last one, right? Before he came back."

Mick's cheek twitches. "Aye." He concentrates on the road. "Are you planning to tell me the real reason we're going into town?"

"We're going on a witch hunt." If Sherri is in town, I want to find her before Liam or the Sons do. I want to try to convince her to fight on our side.

We start at the Ornery Knight. Sherri is a strong proponent of keeping your enemies close, so it's a good place to begin. We find a table in the back where I'm less likely to be noticed by other patrons. I avoid the eggs and just order some coffee from the same woman who directed me to Blake's room. Mick orders something that I think is made from pig intestines.

Rhiannon comes out with Mick's food, but without my coffee. She glares at Mick before turning on me. "I told you, you're not welcome here."

I smile in response to her never-ending hostility. "There are rumors of another witch in town."

Rhiannon blanches. "We all know what you are."

I can't blame her for distrusting me, not after my foremother burned down half the town. I'll never convince her that I'm on her side.

I try again anyway. "I'm here to stop the witch. The Sons are coming too." When she looks at me blankly, I add, "The Milesians? I want to help them."

Rhiannon's grin is smug. "The Milesians will be looking for you, then. They will drive you from here. If they let you live."

"Or the Milesians will finally lose."

"They won't."

"Even if the fuath join the fight?"

Rhiannon backs up a step. "You're lying. The Milesians drove the fuath underground centuries ago."

"Which is why the fuath might have an interest in the Milesians' defeat."

"Get out."

"I'm here to help."

"Now."

I stand up to face her. "How did you know? About me?"

She glances at the empty spot below the hollow of my throat. I reach instinctively for the pendant, but of course it's not there. Her eyes slide to the charm bracelet around my wrist, and she backs up another step and crosses herself.

"What's this about fuath?" Mick stands up.

"It's nothing concrete."

Portia comes out of the narrow hallway at the base of the stairs. She sees me and stops.

Rhiannon turns to look. She spots the pendant around Portia's neck the same time I do. I don't know who recoils faster.

My necklace. Blake gave her my necklace?

I reach for my own bare neck without thinking. None of this makes any sense. Not Blake and Portia, not Blake and me. Yesterday, he wanted me. I know it.

"Are you stalking us?" Portia raises her voice so it carries across the room, even though she's only a few feet away from us.

I catch a glimpse of Blake's blond hair on the stairway behind her. "It's a small town," I say, bracing myself for his entrance.

He steps up and places a hand on Portia's shoulder. He doesn't look at me. "Let's sit down."

I straighten my spine, reaching for Mick's coat. "We should go." It's one thing to know that Blake is with Portia in

145

theory. It's something entirely different to see them standing here together, looking so pretty it's like they're not even real.

Blake glances at me. A hint of fear crosses his face before he can remember to paste on a charming smile. I suppose having your girlfriend and your ex-girlfriend in the same room would strike fear into even the most heartless guy.

Portia leans into him, pouting. "I've lost my appetite."

I don't know what I expected to feel at seeing Blake and Portia together, but it's not this hollow emptiness. My eyes keep gravitating toward the chain around Portia's neck. Blake may never have been mine. Not really. But Joe gave him that necklace to give to me.

And I gave it back.

He can do whatever he wants with it now.

"I was just leaving." I push past them. My shoulder brushes Blake's arm in the small space, but there's no heat where our skin connects. My eyes fly to Blake's. This isn't right.

There's a flash of blinding silver light.

The room goes dark—pitch black and silent. I can no longer hear the sounds of the pub or see anything but an endless empty void. Gradually the pub comes back into focus, brighter than it was before.

Everyone is frozen. Completely still. I've been here before, in this frozen moment—and that time, Blake claimed the right to kill me. I look at Portia. She's watching Blake with a scowl on her face, her mouth open to say words that never come. Rhiannon stands back against the wall, her dark eyes narrowed on the necklace Portia wears. Her fingers pinch a ribbon of sea grass I hadn't noticed before.

Blake is frozen next to me, his eyes trapped in a look I can't decipher. His hand is halfway to my arm, as if he wants to stop me from walking away.

I'm trapped here too. My shoulder barely an inch from Blake.

Is Blake going to claim the right to kill me again? Why now? The bond has been broken for months, and while it's clear that we are more than capable of bonding again, the claiming thing hasn't happened. I wait for Blake to move.

He doesn't.

Portia does.

In the stillness, the slight lift of her chin looks more pronounced. She turns her head away from Blake to look right at me. Her lips curve into a closed-mouth smile. "Witch," she says. The word echoes in the silence.

In a burst of silver light, the room comes back to life. Blake drops his hand and backs into Portia. She stares at me, her eyes huge.

I take a tentative step forward. Blake told me that he'd been aware of that frozen moment when he claimed me. Only he swore that *I* was the one who'd moved and talked—that I had claimed him.

Did Portia see something like that too? I shake it off.

Rhiannon steps back to let me pass. She laughs again, and I stop.

"What's so funny?"

Rhiannon purses her lips and worries the sea grass in her hand.

"Tell me."

She spins around and nearly runs into the kitchen, clearly spooked.

Portia clutches Blake's arm, but her lip is trembling. She looks terrified. I grab Mick's hand and drag him out of the pub.

Portia saw me in the stillness. I know it. And if Blake's story is to be believed, I spoke to her. I called *her* a witch.

She has every reason to be scared. Whether the frozen moment in time was new to her or not, her cover's been blown.

Portia is a bandia.

TWENTY-THREE

Impossible. Portia is Rush's daughter, and Rush is a Seventh Son of Killian. Portia is just a breeder, a first-generation carrier of the Killian gene. Only the seventh-generation males manifest the Sons' power. Her descendants won't manifest power for another six generations; she's the weakest among the Sons' hierarchy.

It's not possible for Portia to be a Seventh Daughter.

Unless.

The Sons tested me for the Killian gene last spring. I was labeled a first-generation breeder too, before they knew what I really was. They'd somehow never accounted for the fact that my genetic link to Killian came through his son, Brom, who married Danu and had many children with her. So it's possible that I'm not the only descendant of Brom and Danu who they've misclassified as merely a carrier of the Killian gene. Dr.

McKay, their lead researcher, probably hasn't even isolated the genetic link to Danu, let alone looked for it.

Holy crap. Portia is a Seventh Daughter.

Who else knows? Does Blake?

I'm shaking when I climb into Mick's car. I text Blake before Mick even starts the engine: *We need to talk. Now.*

He responds a few minutes later: *Not a good idea.*

It's about Portia.

Do we have to do this?

Yes. Meet me at Lorcan Hall in an hour.

Make it two.

Done.

It occurs to me that telling Blake where I'm staying may not be the best move I've made, but it's not like it's a secret among the townspeople. Besides, I'm done running. Look where it got me—right smack in the eye of a hurricane. So I can't run from my fate.

I settle into a rarely used living room off the main hall, where hopefully we'll have some privacy. An hour and a half later, Mick raps lightly on the door. He raises his eyebrows as he announces Blake, a question in his eyes.

I ignore it. "Thanks Mick."

"Mikel," he corrects. He hesitates in the doorway, looking unsure as to whether he should leave me.

"It's fine."

Blake crosses the room and sits in an overstuffed chair in the far corner. It's the farthest place from where I'm sitting on the couch. He waits until Mick closes the door before he says anything. "Portia doesn't know I'm here, so we have to make this quick."

"You two seem close."

Blake stands. "I'm not going to have this conversation with you."

"Why not? We're not together now. You can see who you want."

His eyes get hard. "Is it that easy?"

"You don't get to care how I feel, Blake. Anyway, I have bigger problems than who you're hooking up with at the moment." My chest flutters with panic. If Portia is a Seventh Daughter and Blake is sleeping with her, have they bonded? The jealousy I thought I'd set aside is there at once, a parasite sucking my life's blood. But no—we almost bonded yesterday. I'm sure of it. He wouldn't be able to bond with both of us. I take a breath.

"The Sons landed in Dublin this morning," Blake says. "You have to leave."

"I'm aligned with the Sons."

"Not anymore."

"Now more than ever. It's Portia I'm not so sure about."

Blake's dimpled smile is there in an instant. It's meant to distract me, to mask the lie that follows. "Why? She's the daughter of our leader."

"Because she set fire to your house." I enjoy saying this way more than I should. *It wasn't me.*

His smile falters. I stare at him, daring him to deny it. He looks at the ground, running a hand through his hair. "What?"

"Portia is a bandia."

When Blake looks up at me, his poker face is back in place. "How did you figure it out?"

He already knows about Portia? That means he knows it wasn't me—he knows I didn't start the fire at Mallory's party. He *knows*, and he wasn't planning on telling me.

I'm totally lost now. "You knew? You knew it was Portia who burned down your house?"

"Not at first. After you left, I couldn't stop thinking about what you said. You were so adamant that it wasn't you. Then I remembered what you told the Sons during your induction—that you were a carrier of the Killian gene through Brom. They'd never figured it out on their own. There could be others, right?"

So Blake was one step ahead of me. But it doesn't excuse the fact that he's known this for a while; was he just going to keep letting me think he still thought it was me? Does he even care how I felt? Did he tell the Sons? Are they still hunting me?

Blake keeps talking. "Everyone at Mal's party was a breeder, and it made sense to start with the people who were there when the fire broke out. I got Dr. McKay to show me the tests for each of the breeders. There are only a few first-generations, and of those, Portia is the only girl."

"So Portia was the only possible Seventh Daughter among the breeders."

"Right. Plus, both her parents were seventh generation under Killian, which meant that she could've received the Killian gene from her mother's side, too."

"And if Portia's mother got her Killian gene through Brom, as opposed to one of Killian's other children, then her mother was a sixth-generation daughter of Danu."

Mystery solved. Portia started the fire. Why didn't Blake *tell* me?

"Exactly. But my speculation wasn't enough. I had to get closer."

My mouth is dry. Is he trying to tell me that he's only dating Portia to find out the truth? "You've been spying on her?"

"I'm trying to help. I still need proof."

"So you were just going to hook up with Portia until when? She confessed to being a bandia?" I feel sick. "And you weren't planning on telling me?"

"Because I knew you would freak out like this. Besides, the less people who know the better. I need for Portia to trust me. If she knew I was here talking to you—"

I stand to face him. "You're worried about her feelings? You let me think I set your house on fire!" I wish I had my power right now—I've never wanted to strike him down more than I do at this very moment. "You let me think you didn't trust me."

"I didn't."

Wow. It's nothing more than what I already knew, but still, it's like being hit with a flaming arrow straight through the heart. And then having Blake rip it back out while I lie bleeding out in front of him.

The door opens with a bang. Austin bursts through, his chest rising and falling with quick breaths. Two deep lines form at the bridge of his nose before he can mask it with a practiced look of haughty indifference. He turns to me. "Are you all right?"

Blake looks from Austin to me and back again. "What's he doing here?"

"He lives here."

The vein on Blake's neck throbs so hard it looks like it's about to burst. "You brought him back? I leave you alone for two fucking weeks and you brought this bastard back from the underworld so you could move in with him?"

"I didn't bring him back. The only person I brought back was you. And look how well that's turned out."

"Then how is he here?"

Austin raises an eyebrow at Blake. "Magic."

"Spare me." Blake's lip curls into a sneer. "Looks like your hero is here to whisk you away. Or to make sure you kill me. I can't be sure which."

"Stop it. Austin is helping me. You weren't here to do it. You're the one who sent me away, remember."

"I was looking for the other bandia," Blake growls.

"So you could sleep with her."

Austin leans back against the wall, a smile playing on the corner of his lips.

Blake collapses on the couch. "You have no idea what you're even talking about. You don't know Portia. She doesn't trust anyone. It's no wonder, given the secret she's been carrying. I had to get close to her in a hurry, okay?"

I can't believe he's trying to justify this. "I know exactly what you're doing. It's the same thing you did to me."

Blake's face goes white. "It's not."

I actually feel sorry for Portia. Blake is using her in the same way he used me, to gain information for the Sons. Maybe without the artificial closeness of the bond, Portia will see through him. I hope for her sake that she does.

Austin steps toward Blake. "What secret is Portia carrying?"

Blake looks at me, fear in his eyes. "You can't tell him."

"I trust Austin." I realize it's true. I don't know how it happened, but I trust him with this.

"Him?" Blake's green eyes flash with silver. "Have you lost your mind? You know what he's capable of. What he's done."

"I do." I also know that Austin would never deliberately hurt me. Not now.

"I knew it." Blake punches a pillow. "You always wanted him. I could feel it when we were bonded."

Austin raises his eyebrows at me as if this is news to him.

"It's not like that." It sounds half-hearted, even to me. I wanted Austin the other night. No matter how I try to justify it.

Blake reaches for my wrist, sending a shock of heat up my arm before I can break the contact. "So you're on his side now?"

Austin closes the distance between himself and Blake. "You're such a bloody idiot."

"For trying to help someone who would jump into bed with the guy who orchestrated my death the first time we had a fight?" Blake snaps.

"For shitting on everything that Brianna has given you."

155

Blake lifts his chin. "I could take her back. Maybe you haven't noticed, but our souls can't leave each other alone."

"Speak for yourself," I say. We both know that yesterday, I was the one to walk away. "Go back to Portia. See if you can find out which side she's planning to stand with at the Gathering." I don't tell him that I intend to do some digging on my own.

"The Gathering?" Blake looks confused.

"The god of the underworld has opened the gateway here," I say. "He'll call the Sons and the bandia, bringing them all together in one place."

"How can you trust him?" Blake points at Austin. "There's only one reason to bring all the Sons and Seventh Daughters to one place. He's trying to start a war."

"It isn't me," Austin says.

"There's a new god of the underworld," I say quickly. I finger the horseshoe charm on my bracelet.

"How?" Blake asks.

"That's none of your concern," Austin says. "The better question is, who."

"Who then?"

"A twisted, untrustworthy prick who's not as patient as I was."

"His name is Liam," I add. "He's putting together an army to take out the Sons."

"An army of two?" Blake looks from me to Austin.

I should be used to Blake's distrust by now, but it still feels like a noose tightening around my throat. It's hard to breathe.

Blake has no idea how ineffectual our little army is, and

I'm not about to share the fact that Austin's power is diminishing every day—or, in my case, just gone. I straighten my shoulders. "Joe's going to arrange a meeting with Rush. We'll tell you everything then. For now, it's enough to know that Liam is recruiting, and we're trying to stop him."

"You can't tell Rush about Portia," Blake says. "He'll freak."

"What about Portia?" Austin repeats the question.

"She's a Seventh Daughter," I say. It's not only Blake's secret to share.

Blake glares at me with eyes that glow silver.

"Someone has to tell Rush." Austin's voice is quiet. "He needs to be prepared for the possibility that he'll have to fight his own daughter."

"Maybe not." Blake looks past me now, at the wall. "I could convince her to fight with us."

My knees shake. This is too close to what Blake told Rush about me, not so long ago.

She's in love with me.

She'll lead us to the others.

I finally feel the anger I should have felt when I saw Portia and Blake together this morning. Only I'm not angry at Portia. I'm angry for her. I bite down on the inside of my cheek, fighting to keep a tirade from spilling out.

Austin just nods. "Do what you have to. We'll need all the help we can get."

He's right about that. We need a bandia on our side. And I no longer qualify.

TWENTY-FOUR

After Blake leaves, I go down to the stable and ask Malcolm for a brush. I climb into Molly's stall and groom her until she gleams.

"Going for a ride?" Austin hangs over the stall. "I could join you."

"You ride?"

"Autos are still a relatively new invention." He reaches out to stroke Molly's neck. "I've spent centuries in the saddle. After thousands of years of service, the horse is obsolete to many."

"Kind of like you. A creature that has lost its purpose."

Austin studies my face. "Or found it."

I feel myself blush. I concentrate on combing a cowlick below Molly's mane. "A ride would be nice."

Austin takes out a bay gelding named Samson. Molly has

to lengthen her stride to keep up, but seems to enjoy the challenge. At the end of the field, Austin turns Samson up the trail through the trees on the opposite side from the ocean.

"If we stay on the trail, we'll find the ruin."

"The ruin?" My breathing speeds up a little. Does he know I saw him in the past? With Gwyn?

"It's not as exciting as it sounds," he says. "A pile of rocks, really."

We ride in silence until we crest the small hill. The stack of large stones looks smaller in the sunlight, some crumbling, others still clinging to their shape.

"What was it?"

Austin shrugs. "A castle, maybe. Or, at least, one of the buildings surrounding a castle. This is all that's left."

"You never saw the original?"

"I'm not that old."

"How old are you?" I might not want to know.

"Eighteen."

"I'm being serious."

"So am I. As a god, age is meaningless. Time means little when you have eternity. Now I find it matters more." Austin slides off of Samson and lets him wander toward grassy clearing. "Come on."

I dismount but stay back. "I've been here before."

"Have you?" Austin smiles.

"A couple times."

"And?"

I walk forward. "It's really old, isn't it?" I walk up to the wall, deliberately going to the side where the crude carvings *aren't* located. I run my hands along the smooth stones, trying to imagine the walls as part of something larger. "What was it like? To be a god on earth?"

"I hardly know."

I turn to face him. "But the gods were here. Before the Milesians sent them away?"

"I was the god of the underworld. I didn't rule topside."

"So your life didn't change when the gods were trapped in the underworld?"

He grins. "It changed. I went from monitoring the passage of souls from one realm to another—which, to be honest, requires very little—to ruling all the gods, which requires a bit more."

I hadn't thought of that. Austin ruled the underworld and controlled the gateway, so the gods who were trapped found themselves under his jurisdiction. "So your situation improved?"

Austin laughs. "Hardly. The gods are a fickle bunch. And as the sole god who could pass through the gateway, I was under a fair bit of pressure to right things up here."

No wonder Austin wanted to free the gods. He wanted to free himself.

"What was Liam's role? Before?"

"Pain in my arse."

I laugh. When I turn around, Austin is closer than I expect. I nearly bump into him.

His face turns serious. "Are you sure you're okay?"

I surprise myself with my answer. "I think I might be."

"Good. Have you tried your power today?"

"No." But I did see time stop with Portia, although I wonder if that was her or me. Or both. "There was a flash of magic at the pub. Like when Blake claimed me at your party, only it was with Portia."

"Portia claimed the right to kill you?"

"I think so. She called me a witch."

Austin's brow furrows in that way that makes him look so human. So something.

Before I can think about what I'm doing, I reach for the lock of brown hair that always hangs over one of his eyes and push it away. The gold flecks in his eyes reflect a beam of sunlight that stretches between the trees, gracing him with its warmth.

I don't move my hand away. My thumb traces the lines above the bridge of his nose, smoothing them out.

"What are you doing?" His voice is a whisper.

"Thinking about asking you to kiss me."

Austin sucks in a breath. "By all means, don't let me stop you."

I let my finger trail down his nose to his lips. I hold it there. "This is probably not a good idea."

"No second thoughts." I feel the vibration of his words against my fingertip, the warm blast of air that passes through his lips. I inhale, as if I could breathe him in through the pad of my finger.

He lowers his head until his lips are a breath away from mine. "Ask me," he whispers. "Please."

"No," I say.

I close the tiny distance between us and kiss him myself.

His lips are as soft as the kiss, sweet and searching. I feel more than hear him gasp, his mouth parting just enough for my tongue to sneak through and taste him. My fingers tangle in the mop of hair at the back of his neck. His hands are at my waist, moving in light circles along my side.

At the same moment, we open our mouths and take the kiss deeper, now on more equal footing. He tastes like warm cinnamon with a hint of smoke, dangerous and comforting at the same time.

I pull back from the kiss before I'm tempted to take things further. I keep my hands around his neck and rest my forehead on his shoulder.

Austin presses his lips to the top of my head.

I turn my head to see that the horses have wandered to a patch of grass farther away. "We should get Samson and Molly before they go back to the barn without us."

Austin brings his hands to my shoulders and rubs them lightly. "You are far too sensible for someone who has just been kissed."

I smile into his shirt. "Aren't you forgetting something?"

"What?"

"Technically, you're the one who has just been kissed."

He laughs into my hair. "Well, that explains why my thoughts are anything but sensible."

I laugh with him. It's the lightest I've felt in forever. Looking back at the ruin, I can almost imagine that it's another time. I wish I could freeze this moment, so that nothing came before and nothing will come after. So that we could live inside of one perfect kiss.

For the first time in a long while, my own emotions feel like enough.

TWENTY-FIVE

Austin offers to go with me into town to find Braden Finley. Insists. I don't argue. At least he can still access his power, however difficult it is. I could use the backup. If Braden is what Austin says, then I need to be cautious.

I try to reconcile Austin's description of the fuath with the Braden I knew at Rancho Domingo High. He never failed to flirt with Haley, but that wasn't anything unusual. Lots of guys did. I never saw him do anything mean or strange or magic. I even liked him a little when he asked me to lunch, that day I didn't have my bracelet on.

Crap.

Could Braden have seen what I was? Does he know I'm a bandia? I was stupid to think that the Sons were the only ones I needed to hide from. Even now, I know so little about my history. Of what any of this really means.

Austin hesitates at the entrance to the Naughty Baron.

"A fuath will stir up trouble just to watch people twist on the wind. They feed on emotions. He'll start by trying to open old wounds because it takes the least effort. If that fails, he won't hesitate to inflict new ones."

"Charming." I have plenty of fresh wounds, so I doubt that Braden will have to work too hard.

Then I remember. The day Braden "saw me" at school, he deliberately ignored Haley, after a whole year of flirting with her alone, to pay attention to me. Haley thought he was trying to make her jealous, and then it led to our worst fight ever. Did Braden do that on purpose?

I spot Braden right away. He's sitting at the same table, with the same group of boys. Greenpeace II sits up in his chair when he sees Austin walk in behind me. He leans forward and whispers something in Braden's ear.

Braden smiles at me through clenched teeth. "You should've called."

Interesting. He doesn't sound happy to see me. Or is he trying to make me feel like I'm intruding so I'll be irritated?

Strike one for Braden. I couldn't care less. I know I'm intruding, and it's quite deliberate. "You know Austin Montgomery, right?"

Braden crinkles his nose before turning to Austin. "Hello."

"Hello, fuath." Austin flashes his trademark crooked smile.

Braden's eyebrows shoot up and his jaw drops. "Excuse me?" But it's too late; his face has given him away. He shakes his head. "Listen. I'm meeting some people here. Maybe we can hang out some other time?"

"Now would be good. We have much to discuss." Austin gestures for Braden to follow us.

Braden stands, but he looks toward the door. "This really isn't a good time."

"Nonsense." Austin's eyes darken.

Braden stares at Austin's eyes, and follows us to an empty table.

————

"You're no one now," he says under his breath. "Liam will enslave you and I'll enjoy watching you suffer."

"Have the fuath sunk so low that they're reduced to sniffing around pain inflicted by others?" Austin shakes his head. "Sad."

Braden seethes in his chair, grinding his teeth and cursing under his breath. He glances at me and his face changes as he flashes me that easy smile. "It's so crazy to run in to you like this. Twice now. I think fate is trying to tell us something." He leans close enough that I catch a whiff of musky cologne. It settles in my throat and threatens to gag me.

I flash him what I hope passes for a flirtatious smile. "I know, right?"

Braden flashes Austin a smug sneer.

I lean into Braden's shoulder. "I don't know if you've heard, but I broke up with my boyfriend recently."

Braden's sneer gets wider as he puts his arm around me. "And I am momentarily single."

"Perfect timing." I giggle into his shoulder.

Austin raises both eyebrows. I think I hear him stifle a laugh.

I bat my eyelashes up at Braden. "Are you really going to fight him for me?"

Austin raises his hand to his mouth. He's definitely laughing.

"Fight who?" Braden pulls his arm from around me.

"My ex. He's a Son. I thought that's why you were here."

Braden's gaze drifts to my wrist, watching the charms that dangle from my bracelet. "I'm not here to fight your boyfriend for you. I barely know you."

I wonder if Braden can feed off of his own dark emotions, because he seems to have a lot of them.

"Not just him. All the Sons." I punch him lightly in the arm.

Braden looks at me with new consideration. "Why don't you just do it yourself, bandia?"

"It's kind of complicated," I say. "I mean, he was my first love, so a part of me will always love him." I wonder if it's true. I hope not. It would be so much easier to hate him.

Austin isn't laughing now.

"Besides, we're outnumbered," I add. "Hasn't Liam told you anything?" I bat my eyelashes again. I'm a one-trick pony when it comes to playing dumb.

Braden sighs. "I don't know what our role will be yet. Liam hasn't told us anything other than the date of the Gathering."

I try to contain my excitement, but a small gasp escapes

my lips before I can stop it. Liam has set a date. How do I pry this out of Braden?

"So you know we don't have much time," I say.

"Six weeks is plenty of time for what I have in mind." Braden picks up a curl of my hair and wraps it around his finger.

I bite my lower lip. "I don't think that's a good idea."

Braden pulls on the strand of hair. Hard.

"Ow!"

Austin lunges across the table. He clamps a hand around Braden's throat. "Give me one good reason I shouldn't kill you right now, fuath."

Braden coughs, gasping for air.

Greenpeace II lays a hand on Austin's shoulder. "I've got this."

Austin lets go of Braden's neck abruptly. "So you do."

Braden gulps in oxygen. He glares at Austin and me. "We're on the same side of this," he rasps.

Austin shakes his head. "Make no mistake about it. I am on one side and one side alone." He takes my hand in his. "Hers."

We're nearly out of the pub when I see that woman I met the train. Corporate Tink, dressed up in a red velvet blazer and black pants. She's sitting at the end of the bar, sipping a drink the color of blood. Her eyes follow us as we walk into the street.

I shiver as we step into the cold.

TWENTY-SIX

Austin smiles when we get back in his car. "Do that eyelash thing again."

"This?" I blink my eyes.

He laughs. "You're a terrible flirt. Truly awful."

"Thanks."

"It's a compliment. No one who knows you would ever think of you that way. You're a brilliant warrior. Smart, strong, and sexy as hell."

I want to laugh. "Tell me more."

"Do you really want to hear how I fell in love the night we first met, the moment you spun that quarter into my lap?"

"Right." Austin had wanted to use me as much as anyone else did. "All you cared about was that I was a bandia. You only wanted me for your army."

Austin raises his eyebrows. "Which explains why I took you directly to my bedroom."

"You also told me we would end badly. Not exactly romantic."

"We will."

"We already did." I try to keep things light, but Austin's face is dark now. "I banished you for a thousand years, remember?"

"I remember well enough." He frowns and starts the car, then drives in silence until we're almost to the gate of Lorcan Hall. Concentrating on the narrow lane winding down to his house, he doesn't turn to look at me until the car is parked. "Truthfully, I didn't know how it would end. I only knew it would. I assumed it would end in death. That's why I pushed you so hard to kill Blake before he killed you."

A chill starts at the back of my neck and slides down my spine. "You saw my death?"

"I didn't see anything. Blake claimed the right to kill you. It was only logical. You believe in logic, right?" His eyes are dark. "I knew I would never give up on you. Not as long as you were alive. Death is the only thing that could keep me from you."

My blood flows with ice, almost as if my magic is there. I reach for water, but it's not magic. It's just the cold certainty that my fate is coming for me whether I fight against it or not.

Austin doesn't move to get out of the car. "We can't change our fate. Just how we get there."

"So, you tried to save me by making sure I killed Blake?"

"I thought I could prolong things. And that worked out well, didn't it? It's because of me that you've lost your power. I've only made you defenseless. By trying to keep you alive longer, I may have hastened your death."

"A different path to the same place."

"Exactly."

I pull my shoulders back, trying to manufacture a strength I don't feel. It's what I've known for a while now. I can't run. I can't avoid the confrontation that's coming. I need to be ready to fight. "Let's go down to the beach."

"Now? It's late."

"You heard Braden. We have six weeks. Liam still thinks I'm going to be part of his army. We need to know exactly what he's planning. We have to know what we're up against."

Austin watches me closely. "It's too dangerous. If he learns the truth about your power, he'll—"

"He won't."

"Liam will test you. He trusts no one."

"I'm doing this." I let myself out of the car and start walking toward the path that will take me down to the beach.

A few minutes later, Austin jogs up beside me. He reaches for my hand, and I let him take it.

"It's getting harder for me," he says quietly. "Soon I won't be able to access my power at all. In six weeks I'll be as defenseless as any human."

"I'm sorry." I squeeze his hand.

"Whatever for?"

I don't know how to put it words. Austin gave up his immortality, his power, everything when he saved my horse. As much as it was his own fault for killing Dart in the first place, in a misguided attempt to get me to fight the Sons, he didn't know what it would cost him when he brought Dart back to life.

"You've lost everything," I finally say.

He stops me on the path and looks down at where our hands are clasped together. In the moonlight, I can just make out his crooked smile. "That is where you are wrong."

The wind blows cold, still damp from an afternoon downpour, but my body is warm.

This is Austin—a vindictive god who killed Danu to spark a war between the Seventh Daughters and the Sons of Killian. Who killed Dart. Who nearly killed Haley. Who made me kill Blake. He's helping me now, but still, I can't let myself forget.

Have I learned nothing from Blake? Physical attraction is not the same thing as love.

I pull my hand away and walk the rest of the way to the trail at the edge of the bluff. Austin walks behind me, but I don't look back. I've already let myself rely on him too much. I let myself believe I could trust him. How could I let myself forget what he's capable of? What he's already done.

But part of me understands how Austin could do the things he did. I'm as much a killer as he is. I will fight for what I believe in. Kill for it.

The killer in me understands him completely.

The tide is in, and the waves crash against the two large boulders that lead to the cove with the gateway, filling the path with water. There's only a small patch of gravel at the base of the cliff, with just enough room for the two of us. Austin stands behind me, so close I can feel his body heat and the puff of his breath on my neck.

I cross my arms over my chest, shivering in the ocean air. It's strange to be so close to the air and sea, to witness its power, without being able to access it. A gust of wind blows me off balance, mocking me. I struggle to find my footing on the rocks.

Austin's arms come around my waist, holding me steady. "We're stronger together," he whispers.

"Maybe that's what I'm afraid of."

It only takes a few minutes for Liam to appear in a burst of white light. There's not enough room for three of us on the sliver of beach, but it doesn't matter. Liam hovers in the air above the water. His godliness is a sight to behold, glorious and gorgeous, but it's cold. One look is all it takes to know that Liam is not a merciful god. The awe he inspires is tinged with fear.

"Come to pay your respects?" He says the words to both of us, but he's glaring at Austin.

"I've come to invite you to stay."

Liam smiles, and it's unclear whether he notices the barely contained venom in Austin's voice. "You finally realize your place? Prepare your best room. I'll be by in the morning." He vanishes, leaving only a dark shadow where he'd been.

"You invited him to stay with us?" I shudder.

"You want to keep an eye on him, don't you?"

Austin's right. It will be easier to learn Liam's plans this way. Still, the guy freaks me out a little.

I don't hesitate when Austin offers his hand to help me

back up the path to the house. I don't let go until we step inside the warm entryway.

"It's late," he says, his gaze drifting to my lips.

I nod, but I don't move toward the stairs. "What happens before?"

Austin's brow furrows into those little lines I'm starting to love. "Before what?"

"Before this ends badly."

"I don't know."

"If it ends, does that mean that we're together?"

Austin closes his eyes. "God, I hope so."

"What if I'm just using you to get over Blake?"

"Is that what you're doing?"

Is it? It's exactly what I had in mind a few nights ago. Now I'm less certain. "I don't know."

Austin's jaw tightens, but his hand is gentle when he rests it lightly against my cheek. "I wasn't a patient god. I find I'm a much less patient man. But I will wait for you to find your way to me."

"What if this is all there is?"

"It's not."

I let myself wish that everything was different. That I hadn't let Blake take me out of Austin's room that first night. That I hadn't sent Haley back in to take my place. That I never let myself bond with Blake. That I never loved him. That I never killed him.

It's pointless. There's no going back. Not really.

"I can't forget what you did," I say. What I did.

Austin steps away, moving toward the stairs. He places a

hand on the banister and turns to look at me. "I don't expect you to forget, Brianna. But, maybe, you will be able to forgive me?"

I watch him disappear up the stairs.

Too bad he no longer has an eternity. The bandia aren't exactly known for forgiveness.

TWENTY-SEVEN

Mick announces Liam's arrival with all the enthusiasm of a cat eyeing a bath.

Austin barely glances up from his cup of tea, but I turn to watch Liam's grand entrance. The god stops and places his hands on his hips, surveying the large living room almost as if he's already mentally redecorating. Then there's a flicker of movement behind him and a gorgeous young woman steps forward.

Sherri Milliken's dark hair shines in the light from the large picture window. It's still a shock to see someone who seemed so mousy before her seventeenth birthday looking every inch the gorgeous descendant of a goddess. She runs over and gives me a hug, squealing like a sorority girl. "Thank God you're alive!"

Sherri ran away the night our friend Sasha was killed by the Sons, but it's no surprise that she's here now. Looks like

Liam found her before I did. She curls up next to him, wrapping an arm around his waist. "Have you met Liam?"

He smiles down at her. "You two know each other? Excellent."

Sherri presses closer to Liam and mouths, "Isn't he hot?"

"Hot" is not the word I'd use. He's cold. Icy. Liam's beauty is hard, more like a marble statue than a flesh-and-blood person. I nod my head, more to avoid an argument than anything else. Liam pulls Sherri tighter against him and starts making out with her, right in front of us. I stare down at my hands.

Austin sets down his tea. "Mikel, perhaps you should show Liam to his room."

"My lord."

Mick was addressing Austin, but it's Liam who comes up for air to respond. "Yes, Mikel, show me the way."

Mick scrunches up his face as Liam walks out of the living room in front of him.

Sherri runs over to the couch and sits next to me. "So, tell me everything. How did you get away? Did you kill any of them?"

In a manner of speaking. I don't want to explain any of this to Sherri. So I don't. "No."

She looks over at Austin and back at me. She lowers her voice to a whisper. "He's not one of them, is he?"

Austin leans forward. "I can hear you perfectly."

Sherri straightens her spine.

Austin laughs. "I remember you, bandia."

Sherri's eyes narrow. I can almost see the magic bubbling up.

"It's okay, Sherri. Austin is here to help us. Like Liam."

Sherri looks him up and down. "How? Liam opened the gateway. He's the only one who can cross over."

Where does Sherri get her information? I need to see what I can find out from her.

"I am Liam's predecessor." Austin uses his haughtiest tone.

Sherri still looks skeptical, but she settles into the couch.

"Where have you been?" I ask.

"Here, mostly. I figured the last place they'd expect me to go is back home."

"You didn't answer the call to arms." If Sherri was here, why didn't she go to the gateway?

"What's that supposed to mean? I'm not the one who bonded with a Son and got Sasha killed."

She blames me for Sasha's death? "You're the one who decided to attack the Sons without knowing exactly who and what you were up against. And if I recall right, I saved your life."

Sherri rolls her eyes. "Fine. We'll call it even." Her eyes drift to the doorway. "Is Liam amazing or what?"

"How did you meet him?"

She laughs. "I answered the call."

"But you weren't there."

Sherri stands up and stretches. She glances over at Austin, but he doesn't look up. "You weren't there," she mocks my voice. "Really, Brianna, are you still so clueless?" She walks to the doorway. "You were the one who missed the call. Even the hybrid was there."

Then she disappears down the hall.

I turn to Austin. "What does she mean? I didn't miss the call. I was there, on the beach, when the gateway opened. I was the only one."

"Maybe he called them again? After your power disappeared?" Austin leans forward. "She's a bit of a true believer, that one."

"A bit? You missed out on that one. She would've fought like the devil for you."

"I might've killed her myself before she got that far." He's smiling, but I can't help thinking that Sherri is everything Austin wanted me to be.

"You say that now. But at the time, all you wanted was to find a bandia to fight for you. She's perfect for you."

"If I didn't know better, I'd think you were jealous."

Am I? I freeze in place.

"Brianna, I did find Sherri. I was at Rush's restaurant the night she attacked the Sons. But I didn't go after her. Not even when it was clear that you would never fight." Austin reaches across the couch and lifts a strand of hair from my shoulder. "You thought I was looking for a bandia, any bandia, to carry on the cause. As it turns out, I was only looking for you." He twists the lock of hair around his finger. "My fate is tied to yours, and yours alone."

I throw my arms around his neck and pull him to me, crushing my mouth against his. He answers with a kiss so deep it fills me with an ache for more. He pushes me down on the couch, letting his weight settle in all the right places. My hands find his hair, then his shirt, then his waistband, until my fingers brush the warm skin underneath. His hands are on me too, drawing circles that make my heart race and my breath come in hard gasps.

I want, I want, I want. It's the only thought I can manage in the flood of sensation. I want to feel every part of Austin. I want him to feel every part of me.

"God," Austin says, his lips tracing the line of my bra. "Please say you want this as much as I do."

I smile into his gold-brown eyes. "I want this, Austin. I want you."

His lips find mine. As he kisses me, I can feel the emotion behind it. Whatever Austin's done, I want him to love me. I want him to show me everything.

I can give him this. I can give him this part of me at least.

Austin stops kissing me. "What?" His breath is coming fast, but his eyes are serious.

I try to read the question there. "Don't stop."

"You hesitated."

"I didn't." I lean up and nip his neck.

"Damn it." He sits up and straightens his shirt.

I push a tangle of hair away from my face. "What's wrong?"

"Can you tell me you love me?" He closes his eyes and opens them again.

"What?"

"That sounds like a no."

"Austin, please."

"Definitely a no." He stands up. The little furrow at the top of his nose is back. "I know I'm asking too much. You can't forget what I've done, and I'm going to waste whatever time I have with you because of these stupid human emotions."

"They're not stupid. They're kind of sweet."

"I'm pretty sure no one has ever called me sweet."

"In how many thousand years?"

"Watch yourself." His eyes find mine.

I can see the barely contained desire in them. Oh yes, I want him. But love? I thought I loved Blake. I did love Blake. But now I wonder if I was confusing lust with love. In the end, neither of us fought very hard to be together. I threatened his sister and ran off to Ireland without even trying to stay and make him understand. Blake may have kept the Sons from killing me, but there was no question that he expected me to help the Sons find Sherri Milliken. Without the bond, we were quick to challenge each other's real motives.

There was no trust. That can't be love.

I trust Austin. Even after all he's done, I trust him with my secrets. That's not the same as loving him, but it's closer, maybe.

I stand up and close the distance between us, taking his hand. "Can you say you love me?"

"What?" He's caught off guard.

"I guess that's a no, then."

"I told you, I've loved you since you threw that quarter into my lap."

"You believe in love at first sight?"

"No, of course not. It wasn't the first time I saw you. And there were times I had my doubts. But fate will out."

"Doubts?"

"Let's see. You set me up with your best friend. Twice, I might add. Then you let me nearly get killed by Jonah before you finally stepped in. Oh, and there's the small matter of you falling in love with someone else."

"Okay, I get it."

"I'm not done. You tried to kill me with those damn fireballs. And when that didn't work, you lured me to the gateway and banished me for a thousand years." His lips curve into that crooked smile. "Perhaps I should rethink this."

"You're right. Why do you even like me?" I'm only half joking.

"Don't you know?" He kneels in front of me, bringing his hand to the back of my neck. His thumb strokes my throat. "You have the heart of a warrior, yet you long for peace. Even so, you fight fiercely for those you love, no matter what it costs you personally. You are, quite simply, a goddess."

I have to remember to breathe. "Okay. I might like you a little."

Austin kisses my forehead, before he stands up. "Let me know when you're sure."

TWENTY-EIGHT

Something Austin said stays with me all night. When I wake up, it's still there, a niggling thought that won't let me go:

It wasn't the first time I saw you.

The night I met him, at the party, wasn't the first time he saw me. Had he come into Magic Beans at some point, with Blake and the crowd from McMillan Prep? I don't think so. The magic in my bracelet made me invisible to guys then, and no one looked at me, so I definitely would have noticed if he'd seen me.

Does he remember meeting me in the past, as Aaron? Is that why he took me to the ruin?

I storm through the house, past the living room and down the hall to Austin's office. I barge in without knocking.

But it's not Austin hunched over the antique desk. It's Liam.

"Well that's more like it," he says, taking in my wild hair and fury. "Perhaps you're a fighter after all."

"What are you doing here?"

"Planning the new world order. Would you like to help?"

I can't stop the eye roll.

Liam raises his eyebrows. "I see you'll have to learn your place the hard way." He lifts a finger and a shock of lightning arcs in the air.

I reach for my power, but there's nothing. I can only duck behind a chair as the lightning flies at my head. It barely misses, exploding with a crack into the floor beside me.

"I'm disappointed." Liam stands. "I thought you'd put up more of a fight."

I'm helpless, crouched on the floor while Liam walks toward me, electric currents pulsing around him. I scramble for a small statue of a rearing horse on the table next to the chair. It's heavy, probably brass. I lob it at Liam's head.

He laughs as it glances off his shoulder. The room goes bright white and a loud crack reverberates in my ears. I barely feel the hard floor as my head hits it.

The next thing I'm aware of is a prickly numbness, like my entire body has fallen asleep. The pins and needles jab at the surface, pain cutting through as my nerves come back to life.

"Brianna." Austin's voice sounds far away. A damp cloth presses against my forehead.

I blink. The flash of daylight is enough to trigger a throbbing pain in my head. I grit my teeth against the metallic taste in my mouth, biting back a scream. I try opening my eyes again. I'm still on the floor of the office, propped up against Austin, who sits on the floor behind me.

"What happened?"

I try to remember. "I'm not sure." At first it's all a blurry dream. Liam. Lightning. Why I came here in the first place. "You used to go by Aaron."

"There have been many Lord Lorcans."

"But Aaron was the last one. Before you were banished."

"True enough."

"You were with Gwyn."

His whole body tenses beside me.

"I saw you with her."

"Ah." Austin leans his head back against the wall so hard it makes a loud smack that makes my head hurt even more. "A thousand years ago."

"She was Danu's daughter. A first-generation, right? She had no power." Which means Austin didn't need her to fight for the gods. He wasn't using her. I know I shouldn't care about something that happened so long ago, but I do. And then a sick thought pops into my head that I can't quite shake. What if he married her? What if they had children?

"Gwyn was my grandmother. To the hundredth power, but still." I can't hide the panic in my voice.

Austin shakes his head. "We weren't together, Brianna. We never even—" He stops himself. "Why am I telling you this?"

"This is what humans do. We tell each other about our pasts. It's how we get to know each other."

He wraps his arms around me. "You want to know about Gwyn?"

I nod.

"A harmless flirtation. Nothing to speak of, really. I kissed her once."

"That's it?"

He sighs. "I met someone else."

Oh, God. It wasn't just Gwyn. I shouldn't need to know about girls he was with a thousand years ago. I shouldn't care, period. "Oh."

"Are you jealous?"

"A little." The admission scares me. The possessive bandia in me is alive and well, powers or not.

He laughs.

"It's not funny."

Austin kisses my hair. "If you saw me with Gwyn, then you already know what happened."

I shake my head.

"The girl I met was you."

TWENTY-NINE

I can't stop thinking about what Austin said. I know that we met a thousand years ago—I was there, twice, and we talked. But why would that have changed things between Austin and Gwyn? And why didn't Austin tell me this before?

I take the car keys without asking. The Sons should be in Cath now, so I keep to the outskirts of town. I pass an old church with blackened stones, then make a U-turn and park across the street.

I stare at the dark wall.

In seven generations, Cath has recovered. The fire that nearly destroyed it is nothing more than a scar that's so old, it's woven into the fabric of the town. Still, the evidence is there. The rectory next to the church boasts charred stones along the entire east wall. I get out of my car and walk up to it, running my hands along the stones, the remnants of my grandmother's great-grandmother's grandmother's revenge.

I don't need proof that my power is dangerous, but it's sobering to see the lingering effects of a moment's rage from so long ago. The world is safe from me, now that my power is gone, but what of the other bandia? And what if Liam succeeds in bringing the gods back from the underworld? Austin has already said that they aren't happy, that they plan to put the humans in their place. How many people will suffer if we don't stop them?

"Brianna?" I turn to see Shannon standing just behind me. Her blond hair is plaited in two French braids that meet in the back, but she's dressed casually, in jeans and a fisherman's sweater that hangs on her thin frame.

"Hey." I drop my hand from the wall. "Just doing a little sightseeing."

"Interesting choice of sights. Most people go into town." Shannon places her hand in the front pocket of her jeans. "Are you what my mum says?"

"A witch?" I shake my head. "No." Not anymore.

"I don't care if you are. I'm not afraid of witches."

I glance back at the charred stone. "Maybe you should be."

"You sound like my mum."

"I'm sorry I haven't stopped by your shop. I don't get into town much."

Shannon shrugs. "It's okay. I heard that Lord Lorcan's in residence for a change. Is he as much of a bob as they claim?"

"A bob?"

"Is he hot?"

I smile and maybe blush. "He's cute."

"Is he now? No wonder you're not spending much time in Cath." She walks up next to me, running her hand along the charred wall. "You've heard about the fire?"

"Hell hath no fury like a woman scorned."

"Unless it's a man."

I laugh. "Are there more? Stories, I mean."

"We have many."

I try not to get too excited, but it occurs to me that Shannon might know everything that my family failed to preserve. My stories. My history. I run my hand along the wall too. "What happened to the woman who did it?"

"She fled. She had to. They would've killed her otherwise. But justice was done a few years later. Her body was found in a field near Dunfield Abbey. Knife to the heart."

"Did they know who killed her?" A Son, of course, but I need to know if my foremother knew her killer. If she was bonded to him.

Shannon shakes her head. "They never did catch him. Not that anyone tried too hard."

"Have you heard of a god called Pwil?"

"Friend to Arawn."

"What's his story?"

"He was Arawn's second, lording over the underworld in Arawn's place whenever Arawn passed between the worlds. Arawn gave him a special place when he learned that Pwil was protecting Arawn's lover in his absence."

"Arawn's lover?" I can't ignore the dark feeling that starts in the pit of my stomach and spreads in a black wave. Austin never mentioned that he had a lover in the underworld. A goddess?

"Little is known about her."

My stomach clenches. Austin has been holding back on me.

Shannon touches a dark stone. "If you believe my mother, we still live history, every day. We are tomorrow's past."

"Can we change it? Tomorrow's history?"

Shannon doesn't take her hand off the wall. "It is already written. We're just the players."

"Yes, but do we win?"

"Of course." Shannon smiles. "Why else are we here?"

I think of my seventh-generation grandmother, bleeding to death alone in a field. Some of us are here to lose.

THIRTY

I don't go back to Lorcan Hall. I'm not about to sit around the lunch table with Sherri Milliken and Liam after what Liam did to me this morning. And I'm not ready to talk to Austin about his girlfriend in the underworld.

I head for the Naughty Baron, not wanting to chance running into Blake or the other Sons at the Ornery Knight. Too bad there's not a third pub, named for the Dastardly Duke or the Wretched Queen or some other obnoxious royal, where I could eat alone.

Even in the dark hall, I spot Braden immediately. He's seated at a table in the back with his giolla, downing pints and laughing. He glances at me and winks.

I head toward them. "Hey, Braden." At least I can try to learn more about the Gathering.

He looks past me like he's expecting someone else. When

he sees I'm alone, he breaks into a huge grin. "Finally ditched the excess baggage, I see."

"Something like that."

He scoots into the booth so there's a small spot next to him. "By all means, join us."

Having spent most of my teens being invisible to guys, I don't miss the way Braden's eyes stay with mine as I sit down next to him. It's so much more meaningless than I expected it to be. It turns out I don't necessarily want guys to look at me like I'm a present to be unwrapped.

Braden slides a full pint over to me and I take a long sip. It's warm and heavy and dark. It fits my mood perfectly. I drink it faster than I should. Braden watches me drink, but his eyes keep darting to the bracelet around my wrist. As soon as my pint is empty, he orders me another.

The giolla goes by Sam. He raises his glass in a toast. "To the drinking age in Ireland!"

Other than the Greenpeace tattoo on his left forearm, Sam looks surprisingly modern for a giolla. While Joe still dresses like a fifties retro greaser, and Mikel's mutton chops make him look at least a hundred years behind the times, Sam's spiky hair is fairly current, even if his guyliner is a decade or so off. He could easily pass for a modern teen.

Braden sips his drink and watches me. "You're too pretty for your own good."

"What's that supposed to mean?"

"It means I'm tempted to take you to the bottom of the sea and keep you there forever."

I laugh, even though I know he's only partly joking. "Well, there's a fuath for you," I say.

Our table goes deathly silent.

Sam looks from me to Braden and back again.

"What?" My voice comes out too loud. "He doesn't know?"

Braden leans into my ear. "He knows. But we don't want the whole pub hearing. These people are superstitious enough as it is."

I lower my voice. "Sorry. It's not like they like me either."

"Their loss."

The hair on the back of my neck rises. I look toward the door instinctively. Jonah Timken has walked into the pub, his arm slung around Sierra Woodbridge. No one pays any attention to them as they talk to the guy behind the bar. They're just a couple of tourists.

A couple of tourists who want me dead.

"What's the matter?" Braden looks around the room.

"I need to get out of here," I say, keeping my eyes on Jonah's back.

Braden follows my gaze. "Is he a Son?" He whispers something to Sam, and Sam heads for the bar.

"We should be able to get out through the kitchen." Braden stands in front of me.

I hesitate. Austin doesn't trust the fuath, and there has to be a reason for that. But Jonah is one hundred percent bad news. I have to play the odds and go with Braden.

Jonah turns his head just as I stand up. His eyes widen when he sees me, and then a sick smile lights up his face.

He abandons Sierra and Sam, crossing the room in a few smooth steps. He looks from Braden to me and back again. "Who's the new boyfriend?"

Braden's nostrils flare as he takes a deep breath. "Seriously? You think this is the time or place?"

"Sorry, buddy. I hate to break up your little party, but Brianna and I have some unfinished business." Jonah grabs my elbow and jerks me away from Braden.

"Don't touch me." I wrench my arm away and shrink back against the wall.

"Sucks for you we can't be friends." Jonah tilts his head to the side, a dark look crossing his face.

Braden steps in between us. "Go."

I run toward the kitchen, ducking through the door just as the pub lights up with silver. Crap. I nearly knock over a petite woman chopping celery at the counter, but I don't stop. I hear footsteps chasing from behind. I get to the back door and glance over my shoulder.

"Get outside!" Braden runs up beside me and pushes the door open, ignoring the alarm that blares as we duck out into an alley just as silver fills the room behind us.

"This way." He points to the left and grabs my wrist, pulling me as he runs around another corner.

The rain is back, coming down in a cold drizzle. Braden pulls me down another alley, and then another, stopping only when we're confident that we've put enough walls between us and Jonah.

"That guy is an idiot. He didn't care about revealing himself. He just wanted you dead."

"Sorry for dragging you into it."

"You think I'm not in this already?" Braden laughs.

"I don't know anything about you. You were kidding about dragging me to the bottom of the ocean, right?"

"It's tempting, but we need you for the Gathering." Braden's face is hidden in shadow, so it's impossible to tell if he's being serious. He pulls me under an awning. "What about you? What kind of game are you playing?"

"What do you mean?"

"Lose the innocent act. You show up with your boyfriend and ask me a bunch of questions about the Gathering. I know you're not interested in me. And you're a lot smarter than you pretended to be."

"How do you know I'm not interested?" My brain is still fuzzy from the beer. I'm having a hard time following his logic.

"I absorb other people's emotions. I know what you're feeling."

"Negative emotions, right?"

"All of them. Negative ones are just the easiest to access."

"So what am I feeling now?"

Braden raises his eyebrows. "Don't you know?"

"Of course. I just want to see if you do."

"Fear. Relief. But those are the obvious ones. You're more complicated than that. When you came in there was confusion, disappointment, and jealousy."

"Not bad." I felt all of those things. Austin and some goddess? A real one. I can't even think about it.

"And you were afraid even before that bastard showed up."

"I'm not afraid of you," I say. I probably should be. But I'm not.

"I didn't say you were afraid of me."

"What am I afraid of, then?"

"I only get the emotions, not necessarily the reasons behind them. But if I had to guess, I'd say you're afraid of falling in love."

"Not even close. You're not as good as I thought."

"And that, right there, is denial." He sniffs the air. "Tastes like chicken."

I laugh with him. "You know, for an evil killer, you're kind of fun to hang out with."

"I could say the same thing about you."

"Why would you think I'm afraid of falling in love?"

"When you were here with your boyfriend, you kept pushing your feelings away."

"Maybe I don't want a relationship right now. That doesn't mean I'm afraid."

"Tell yourself whatever you need to." Braden shakes some water out of his hair. His eyes flit back to my wrist.

"Stop staring at my bracelet."

He looks up quickly. "Sorry. It's a fuath thing. I'm drawn to shiny, pretty things. They're like magnets for people's emotions. Yours seems particularly potent, which means it's probably very old, and maybe even magic."

"Do you want to see it?" I lift my wrist toward him.

He backs up. "Don't tempt me. I might be able to stop

myself from taking you to the bottom of the sea, but I make no promises where that thing is concerned."

"You want to steal it?"

He smiles. "You really have no idea what I am, do you?"

The sky lights up with silver. Braden looks over his shoulder. "Wait here." He darts around the corner. I blink toward where the light came from, searching the ground for something I can use as a weapon.

A clacking sound, hoofbeats on stone, comes from where Braden disappeared. I peer around the corner. A horse emerges from the shadows in the alley, shaking its mane at me. Calling it a horse is not exactly right, though. It's an unearthly white, almost glowing, with black eyes that blink under white lashes. Long feathers of fur flow from its fetlocks. It's the most beautiful creature I've ever seen.

I step toward him. "Braden?"

The horse shakes his mane again and lowers his head to the ground.

I reach for his neck, stroking the soft fur. His coat is gorgeous, more mink than horse hair. I want to bury my hands in it.

Jonah appears a few feet away in a bright blast. I don't have time to think.

The horse drops to his knees, and I put my hands on his withers and swing my leg over his back, grabbing a handful of the thick mane.

Jonah lunges at me with his knife, but Braden is faster. He takes off in a canter down the street, rounding a corner and then another before Jonah can dematerialize. Braden's hooves clop along the stone as we emerge onto the main road, out in the open. The flash of silver light behind us is the only warning I get that we haven't lost Jonah. Braden turns toward the harbor, racing for the pier. As we gallop onto the dock, Jonah appears directly in front of us. Braden's pace doesn't slow. If anything, he speeds up, lengthening his stride.

Jonah raises his knife just as Braden leaps into the air. All I can do is lean forward and stay with him as we sail over Jonah, high into the night sky, barely missing the blade in Jonah's outstretched hand. At first it feels like we're flying, and I'm sure I must be smiling from ear to ear. Then Braden drops his head and we dive straight into the black sea.

Oh my God.

I try to push off his back as we go deeper into the freezing water, but it's like my legs are glued there. I can't get away. I hold my breath, desperately searching for some connection to the water as Braden swims. But the water is silent. It does nothing but close in on me as I struggle to keep from breathing it in.

I feel a swish behind me and we're rising again. We break the surface and I gulp in a breath. Braden tilts his head to check on me and then glances back at the pier, far in the distance. There's no sign of Jonah's glowing demigod form.

Braden moves along the surface of the water, making no move to take me under again, and I let myself relax.

I'm drenched, but somehow warm and comfortable as we swim along the shoreline. The rain stops, and from here I can see the lights of the small town flicker. It's beautiful. Peaceful. Perfect.

We swim to the other side of the harbor before Braden

turns for shore and walks us in. I slide off his back easily when we reach the beach, grateful to be on solid ground. I turn to pat the animal's neck.

Braden stands in the horse's place, grinning. "You were really scared there for a minute."

"I'm pretty sure that's what you were going for."

He laughs. "Maybe. There were some pretty sweet emotions in there, too."

"A couple."

"I like those better."

"Me too." I shiver in the cold. I'm soaked.

Braden takes off his coat and sets it on my shoulders. "Come on. We'll get a cab back to your car. You should probably lay low for a little while."

"So everyone keeps telling me."

We walk to the taxi stand on the corner, the one right in front of the Ornery Knight. "You're nervous." Braden picks up on the change in my emotions immediately.

"Stop doing that. It's intrusive."

"Sorry. It's not like I can turn it off. What's the matter?"

I nod to the pub. "I think the Sons are staying there."

"Since when are you nervous about seeing the Sons?"

"Not all the Sons. Just one in particular."

"I think we've ditched him for a while." His nostrils flare and I know he's reading something else in my emotions, since it's not Jonah I'm nervous about seeing. It's Blake.

"Ahh, no wonder I can't make a dent," he observes. "Your dance card is pretty full."

"If you mean my love life is already a train wreck with

its fill of evil creatures who will only break my heart, then yep, got it covered."

Fortunately, a cab pulls up almost as soon as we get to the curb. Braden opens the door for the couple inside, and it's Portia who takes his hand and steps out. Braden glances at me with raised eyebrows as my nerves morph into heartache and betrayal.

Portia flashes a pretty smile at him, but it lasts only as long as it takes for her to shift her head in my direction. "Oh my God. You *are* stalking us."

Blake steps out of the cab behind Portia, his face nearly as dark as hers. Then he takes in my wet clothes and sees Braden and his expression changes to something more lethal. "What happened? Are you okay?"

Portia's eyes narrow, but it's not me she turns on. It's Blake. "Don't. Please. Do not tell me that you still give a shit what happens to her. Not now."

The vein on Blake's neck throbs, his tell that he's furious. Why? I'm obviously perfectly fine, aside from the fact that I'm soaking wet. Blake closes his eyes. When he opens them again, he looks concerned. "You sure you're okay?"

"Fine." I push past him into the waiting taxi.

Braden climbs in beside me. "Wow. What was that about?"

"You mean the uber-jealous new girlfriend of my ex?"

"That, and the fact that she was pushing her emotions into him."

"What?"

"I could feel her emotions in him. And his in her, for that matter, but hers were stronger."

And now my day is perfect.

Blake and Portia are bound.

THIRTY-ONE

Austin is waiting for me when I get home. He barely lets me get in the door before he starts giving me the third degree about going into town alone.

I walk past him, water dripping off me, ignoring his questions. He's right, of course, but the last thing I want is to have to tell him about Jonah. Or Braden. Or Blake.

I'm cold and I'm wet and I just want a hot shower and a long, long sleep.

"We need to talk," he says. "I really need to know what happened to you this morning."

I'd left the library as soon as he mentioned that I was the girl he'd met a thousand years ago. I didn't even tell him about Liam's attack. "I'm not ready to talk about it," I mutter. He would just throw Liam out, and we need to know more about the Gathering.

Keep your enemies closer.

I'm letting my enemies get much too close.

I move past him and up the stairs to my room.

Everything is changing too fast.

Braden is definitely a fuath. But he doesn't seem nearly as evil as Austin made him out to be. Blake and Portia definitely slept together, and now he's bound to her. And Austin? Austin has definitely been keeping secrets.

The only thing I know for certain is that I have to stop Liam. No way can I let that sadistic bastard take over the world.

So I fight.

I just have to figure out how. My options are pretty limited at the moment.

My mind keeps going back to the idea that I can stop everything before it starts. So, the next morning, I take Molly back to the ruin.

I rub the little horse charm between my fingers. All three carvings in the stone wall look softer somehow—are they fading? That doesn't make sense. They've been here for hundreds of years. The last few weeks would barely register on a timeline. Unless I'm the one who is running out of time.

The charm still fits into the carving perfectly.

The sun gives way to clouds. The fog is less disorienting now that I know what's on the other side. I close my eyes and wait until I feel the grass beneath my feet. The wind is quiet.

There's a rustling to my right. I open my eyes, expecting to see Austin. But it's Gwyn who meets my gaze. She strides toward me, holding the wide skirts of a dress that's a shade deeper than the blue sky overhead.

"Who are you?" she asks, more accusation than question.

"Your heir."

"Is that so?" Her accent is thick, and I have to strain to understand her. "You believe you can just appear out of nowhere and claim my birthright?"

"I don't know why I'm here."

Gwyn puts her hands on her waist. I notice the silver chain around her neck again, with the charms identical to the three on my bracelet.

"Look." I hold out my wrist.

Gwyn's fingers fly to her neck. "A good replica."

I shake my head. "It's the same. A thousand years from now."

Gwyn moves closer, examining the small objects that dangle from my wrist. She wrinkles her forehead, her eyes narrowing. "Why are you here then?"

"I don't know. To change things, I think."

"Perhaps it is so you can follow through with your plot to kill my mother."

"My plot? I don't want anything to happen to your mother. I'm trying to stop it."

She waves me back. "False modesty flatters no one. We have avoided the inevitable for too long. If we are to rise to power and take our place among the gods, we must act."

"You're not making sense." She can't possibly think that I'm here to kill her mother. She's much too calm.

"I said we must act. You were right to come and shake things up. The path we are headed on will assure our destruction. My mother has forgotten our purpose. But she may still be of use. Her death will ensure a war with the Sons, will it not?"

Can Gwyn seriously think that killing her mother is a good idea? "No. I mean, yes. But it won't work."

"Of course it will. Her death will be blamed on Killian. We will spark a war. That's what you told Aaron, isn't it?"

"She's your *mother*."

Gwyn takes another step, invading my personal space. "She is a pawn when she should be a knight. When she could be a queen."

"A war won't change anything. Killian's Sons are winning."

"His sons claim victory now." Gwyn practically spits out the words. "My mother is married to one of them."

Austin—Aaron in this century—rides into the clearing on a huge bay warmblood. He brings the horse to a halt in front of the ruin, dismounting with the ease of someone who has been riding all his life. "I see you two have met."

Gwyn grins at Austin. "We were just discussing the reason she might be here."

"And what wicked ideas have you concocted in my absence?" Austin looks from Gwyn to me with a gleam in his eyes. I want to hit him.

Gwyn just laughs. "We can't share our secrets with every handsome boy who wanders up the trail." She puts a hand on his arm, claiming him. "But for you I might make an exception."

Austin lowers his eyes, his lashes nearly brushing his cheek. "Is that so?"

I look out at the trees, doing my best to curb the tide of

envy rising in my chest. I have no claim on Austin here. I'm not even sure I have any claim on him in the present.

Gwyn glares at me over her shoulder. "She dresses to provoke. Perhaps you should see how far she means to push it."

"What's that supposed to mean?" I stare down at my jeans and bulky sweater. I'm dressed for comfort, not seduction.

Gwyn's smile is smug. "The daughters of Danu are indebted to you. I'm sure the gods will reward you." She winks at Austin and walks away.

Austin doesn't say anything until Gwyn disappears down the trail. "What was that about?" he asks.

"She knows about me?"

"She heard us talking. Don't worry about her. She is a bit of a gossip. And it is not every day you meet a girl from the future who accuses you of murder."

"Did she tell you that she thinks that killing her mother is not necessarily a bad idea?"

"No. Is that what she told you?"

"That girl has some serious issues." I still can't believe Gwyn would really consider killing her own mother.

"I'm sure she was just trying to get your dander up. She is less than pleased that my attention has been diverted."

"What's that supposed to mean?"

Austin moves a step closer, so close I can feel his body heat. "It means that since you appeared, I have been preoccupied."

"With what?" The words are strangled in my throat.

Austin lifts a hand to my cheek. "With a beautiful lass from another time who is not meant for me."

"Remember that last part when you see me a few centuries from now."

"Do you know me, then? In the future?" The gold flecks in Austin's eyes radiate light.

I nod.

His hand slides to my throat, gently, his thumb stroking the sensitive spot where my pulse beats. His lips curve into a crooked smile. "Ah. But do you *know* me?" His voice is laced with innuendo.

My pulse races against his thumb. My lips part but no words come.

He leans closer, so that if I stretched onto my toes our lips would touch. "I would very much like to know you now," he says.

I freeze. On the one hand, this is Austin. It's not like we've never kissed. On the other hand, we're strangers to each other in this place. I wish I knew the protocol for meeting the guy you're kind of seeing a thousand years in the past. Is this cheating?

What about the girl in the underworld? I step back.

He brings his hand to his side. "Forgive me."

"It's okay." I take another step away. "What are you doing here? At the ruin?"

"Exercising my horse."

"Oh." I don't know what I expected him to say. That he was looking for me? It shouldn't matter.

He raises an eyebrow, mocking me. Am I that obvious? Or does he just expect girls to throw themselves at his feet and worship?

I turn toward the little wall. "I shouldn't be here."

Austin steps up behind me. "Yet you are." His breath whispers along my neck.

I spin to face him. "I think I'm supposed to stop you from killing Danu."

He holds up his hands, palms out. "You have succeeded then. I have no intention of killing anyone."

It can't be that easy, can it? And what does that mean for the future? "Just like that?"

"Just so." His eyes drop to my mouth.

I feel dizzy. Mist starts to curl around my feet. "I think I need to go."

"Perhaps you can give me just a little hope for the future?"

I reach for his hand, lacing our fingers together. "I know you," I say, and I wonder if it's true.

Austin blushes, and my heart melts with the blue sky as it turns to mist.

THIRTY-TWO

"Just in time to practice," Sherri says from behind me.

I gather Molly's reins and turn around to see Sherri and Liam riding up the trail on horseback. "Practice for what?"

Sherri swings off a large bay. "Liam wanted to run through some drills." She holds out her palm. A ball of blue fire dances along her fingers.

Great. Just what we need—Sherri burning down another hundred homes like she did in Rancho Domingo. "Easy on the fire."

Sherri laughs and hurls the fireball at a bush. It ignites and goes out just as quickly. "Everything here is soaking wet. It's perfectly safe. Come on, try it. It's fun."

I put my foot in the stirrup and lift myself into the saddle. "Maybe next time."

Liam watches me from atop a dapple-gray mare. "You need to be prepared to fight. You were useless yesterday."

I clutch the reins, trying to hide my shaking fingers. "I'll be ready when the time comes." *And you'll be the first one in my sights.*

I ride past them, urging Molly into a trot. It's not until we get back to the barn that I let myself breathe.

I find Austin in a wood-paneled room on the first floor, stretched out on a plush leather recliner that looks far too modern for the house. He looks up from a soccer game on the flat screen, removing his black-rimmed glasses. With a smile, he takes in my riding clothes. "Are you ready to talk?"

"I just saw you again. A thousand years ago."

"And?" He looks expectant.

"And what?"

"I hope I was a gentleman."

"You remember it. All of it. You knew exactly who I was when we met at the party. How come you never told me before?"

"This from the girl who told me absolutely nothing about what was going to happen in the future."

"You said you didn't think we could change anything."

"We can't."

I let out a growl of frustration. "What's the point of any of this, then? So many people die."

"Everyone dies, Brianna. You want to know the meaning of it? It's love and heartache, art and science, dreams and sacrifice, all rolled up into one messy, tangled package." He walks over to me. "Take it from someone who was alive for thousands of years, yet never lived. Death is what makes life matter. Perhaps life can only be appreciated *because* it ends."

"You still don't know what to do with these human emotions, do you?"

He laughs. "Too much?"

"A little." It's all too much. Seeing Austin all those years ago. Before he became a killer. Before he made me one. "Tell me what happened."

He glances up at the screen. "Manchester tied it up just before the half."

"With Danu."

"Ah."

I wait, but Austin doesn't say anything. "Why won't you tell me?" I ask.

"You already know how it ends."

"That's not the same thing, and you know it. You told me you weren't going to kill her, and I believed you. Did I stop you? Is everything different now?"

Austin shakes his head. "Everything is as it should be."

"But I went back. I could change it."

"You tried."

"*What* did I try? Maybe there's still time for me to change it. To try something else."

Austin gets up and walks over to me. "Knowing doesn't help, Brianna. It's just another burden to carry. No one wants to know how or when things end. It changes nothing, and steals something even more precious. Hope."

"What's the point of my being there, then?"

"Must you always have an answer?"

"Quantum theory allows for someone to change the

past. For there to be paradoxes in alternate universes. I could change it."

"The past has already happened. Your part in it has been written, whether you've experienced it yet or not. Your energies might be better served planning for the future."

"You know what happened."

He smiles. "I was there, remember?"

"Like it was this afternoon." I close my eyes. "You wanted to kiss me."

"I always want to kiss you."

"Not now." I open my eyes to find Austin standing in front of me. "A thousand years ago."

"And did we kiss?"

I shake my head. "It was weird. It was you, but not you."

Austin leans toward me. "It was most definitely me."

"So you wouldn't be upset if I kissed you, back then?"

"Did you want to?"

"Yes."

He takes my wrist and pulls me the rest of the way to him, until our chests are touching. "When I found you talking with Gwyn, you mean?"

"You remember that?"

"God, you looked just as you do now, beautiful and wild." He raises his hand to my cheek. "I touched you here." He lets his hand slide down to my neck. "And here." He lowers his face until his lips nearly touch mine. "I wanted you nearly as much as I want you right now."

"Nearly?"

"Very, very nearly." His breath mixes with mine, warm apples and spice. "Promise me something."

"What?" My stomach tightens into a ball of string.

"Next time, let me kiss you. Please."

"Are you sure?"

"God, yes." He smiles and steps away. "If you must know, your visits did have a purpose." He looks down at the floor and rubs his eyes. When he looks up, there are traces of tears at the corners of them. "Those moments at the ruin?"

"Yes?"

"Made the next thousand years bearable." Austin walks back over to the couch and puts on his reading glasses.

It's all I'm going to get.

THIRTY-THREE

It's another week before I make my way to the ruin again. I walk past the stable and through the field, ignoring the dampness that clings to the bottom of my jeans where the grass brushes against it. It's a long walk on foot, but I press forward.

A blue flash lights up the trees in front of me. Sherri is still practicing the fine art of warfare. I step into the trees and move forward for a closer look. If I can't go to the ruin, I may as well get in a little recon.

"Nice one," Sherri says, grinning at Portia.

Portia's here. I don't know why I'm surprised. She's a Seventh Daughter... and Sherri did say that "the hybrid" had answered the call. Still, Portia is the daughter of a Son. She's a breeder through and through. Using her power to cause trouble for me is one thing. It's harder to imagine her really taking up arms against her own family.

Liam comes up behind Sherri and wraps his arms around

her. She spins to greet him and they kiss, mouths open. Little smacking noises echo through the trees.

"Eew," Portia says, and I have to agree with her. "Get a room, or at least wait until my back is turned."

Liam stops kissing Sherri long enough to flash Portia a warning glare. "Insolence is a luxury you cannot afford to indulge."

Portia's left hand erupts in blue flame. "Last time I checked, we were doing you the favor."

"That remains to be seen." Liam stops the grabby-hands with Sherri long enough to point out a large tree branch hanging over the edge of the meadow. "Try that one."

Portia smiles and raises her arm to throw overhand. She sends a fireball flying through the air. It skews left, only brushing a few leaves on the outermost end of the branch before fizzling out in a smoldering pile of ash in the damp grass below.

Sherri steps next to Portia and calls fire to her hands in a heartbeat. She throws it almost carelessly, but the arc is perfect and it hits solidly in the heart of the branch, igniting a large group of leaves.

"Show off," Portia says. Then she turns her back on them both and starts walking toward the trail.

"You'll come again tomorrow," Liam calls after her.

"Yeah, fine."

I crouch behind a tree, letting Portia pass on her way down the path.

I wait for her to disappear around a bend before I head down the path after her. When I'm sure we're out of earshot of the others, I pick up my pace.

She hears my footsteps and spins around, her hands already lit with blue flame. She laughs when she sees me, but the fireballs still dance in her palms. "You missed practice."

"Oh, darn. Does this mean I'm off the team? Because I was really looking forward to dying for a bunch of selfish gods who want to destroy the human race."

Portia sends a fireball at a tree a few feet to my right. It's close enough that I jump. The tree catches fire for an instant before the flames turn to damp smoke. "Get your facts straight. They only plan on enslaving them."

"And you're okay with that?"

Portia shrugs. "It beats the alternative."

"Which is?"

"Let's see. I could spend the rest of my life letting the Sons walk all over me like they own me, treating me like crap. I could stand in the corner and hide my power while the lowest breeders look down their noses at me. That sounds so much better than ruling their asses."

"You're the daughter of the Sons' leader. That has to count for something."

Portia laughs. "You should know better. The only thing that matters to them is where you fall on the genetic ladder." She stares at the other fireball in her hand. I know she's itching to throw it. She's got to be burning up on the inside by now. It's hard to contain fire for long.

I glance over my shoulder. There's no sign of Sherri or Liam or anyone who might care if I survive this day. "You have power. They'll want it for their side." *They'll want to use you the way they did me.*

"Easy for you to say. You come in and announce to the entire tribe that you're a bandia, and not only do they not kill you, they let you into the Circle. They let you into the family."

"Hardly."

Portia walks back up the trail, closing the distance between us. She waves the blue flame in her left hand in front of my face. "You think you had it bad? No one hurt you. They feared you. They wanted what you had." Sweat beads on her forehead but she doesn't look away from me. "I hope you enjoyed ruining my life."

She's going to pass out if she doesn't let the fireball go soon. "I ruined your life? I hardly know you."

Her breath comes faster but she hangs on to the fire. "I was finally getting somewhere. Dad pushed Blake on Sierra as a potential pairing—he wouldn't shut up about how her kids would be sixth-generation. Like it was the holy effing grail."

"What does Rush pairing Blake and Sierra have to do with me?"

"Blake didn't want the match. He asked me out instead. The lowest member of the Circle. A first-generation carrier with no value as a breeder. Blake wanted me." Her voice gets tight. "Me."

Her words stab at my throat, depriving me of air. Blake picked Portia. Not because of some sick and twisted bond. Not because the Sons were forcing him to pair with a good genetic match. Because he liked her.

"I still don't see what this has to do with me." Even as I say the words, I know I'm wrong. This has everything to do with me. Blake was dating Portia when he first recognized what I was and claimed the right to kill me. Then we bonded and our souls were tied to each other. Portia never had a chance.

She levels her dark eyes at me. "You ruined everything. You ruined my life. You ruined Blake."

She has it backward. Blake ruined me. He used me.

Portia raises her left hand and thrusts the fireball in my direction. I jump to the right, throwing myself to the ground behind a thick tree trunk. I wait for the burning pain of fire but it never comes. I prop myself up on my elbows and risk a glance around the tree. Portia lies slumped in the path where she fainted, her fire extinguished.

Wow. Portia holds a grudge. I make my way to where she's curled next to a bush. "Portia?"

She doesn't move. I find a pulse just below the line of her jaw. Her chest rises and falls with shallow breaths. She's alive, at least.

She stirs and blinks up at me. "Why are you still here?" Whether she thinks I should be dead or just have run home in a panic is unclear.

"Did you just try to kill me?" I help her into a sitting position.

"It's not like you can't defend yourself."

Yeah, that. "I know you don't like me, and I get it," I say. "I just need for you to understand something. Maybe you can conjure fire—that's the easy part. It's not the same as seeing someone you care about reduced to a charred shell, a lifeless body that isn't coming back."

"And you would know this, how?"

I picture Blake lying on the beach with a black ring around his heart. It's awful to know that someone you love is gone forever. It is a million times worse to know that you killed him. I close my eyes, forcing the image away. It doesn't budge. "I just know."

"It's my problem, not yours."

"You really think you could kill your family?"

"It's nothing less than they deserve." Portia shakes the leaves out of her chestnut hair.

"What about Blake? Will you kill him too?"

Her eyes narrow. "Thou shalt not covet thy sister's boyfriend."

"We're not sisters."

"Aren't we?"

"Think this through. You and Sherri will be outnumbered. Even if you could win, what then? You really think the gods are going to care about you when they don't need you anymore?"

"You mean, me and Sherri and *you* will be outnumbered, don't you? Oh, right. I almost forgot. You don't want to kill people. You prefer to drain them of everything that's beautiful and happy and then throw them to the wind. That's so humane."

"What?"

"You ruined him, Brianna. If Blake dies, it will be a mercy killing."

I scramble to my feet, backing away from her. "You can't mean that."

Portia laughs. "My dad was right about you. You're a pathetic excuse for a bandia."

The words sting more than they should. I never asked to be a Seventh Daughter. I shouldn't care. I turn down the trail, walking as quickly as I can without losing my footing in the sharp rocks that dot the ground. I can still hear Portia's laughter in the distance.

I hear it well enough to know when the laughter turns to crying.

THIRTY-FOUR

Austin and I spend the next week avoiding each other. He's perfectly polite when I run into him in the giant house, but we don't talk about anything that matters. He's giving me space. It's exactly what I wanted when we first arrived, but now I'm not so sure.

It's harder to avoid Sherri and Liam. It's both a blessing and a curse that they're usually so busy making out they hardly pay attention to me. Still, with the Gathering only weeks away, I know I can't escape Liam's notice for much longer. They've been up at the ruin every day, training.

My phone buzzes with a text message. I glance down, expecting some pithy joke from Braden, but it's from Joe. Finally. *Meet at the Ornery Knight at 3. No fire.*

That last part will be easier than Joe realizes.

I don't find Austin in his office or the library. I make my way to his room and knock lightly on the door.

He opens the door halfway.

I hold up my phone up wordlessly as he leans against the doorframe. "I don't suppose there's any hope of your letting me go alone?"

"None."

"Didn't think so." When he flashes that crooked smile, I melt a little. "Are you going to invite me in?"

He doesn't move from where he's standing, between the half-closed door and the frame. "Are you asking to come inside my bedroom?"

Heat rises in my cheeks. "We need to talk."

"We can do that downstairs."

He's right, but neither one of us moves. I stand frozen in the hallway, watching the way his hand absently strokes the wood of the frame.

I take a breath. "But I'm asking to come into your bedroom."

His sigh is so soft, I would miss it if I weren't listening so intently. He swings the door open all the way and steps back, ushering me inside.

I make my way over to the large leather sofa, but I don't sit down. I concentrate on Austin as he shuts the door behind him, doing my best to ignore the giant bed in my peripheral vision.

He approaches me with something close to trepidation, his eyes wary. "Do you not hate me then?"

"I don't know what I feel." I close my eyes, searching for some inescapable truth. Part of me still wants to hate him, but it's fighting with other, stronger emotions that I'm too afraid to name.

"I never meant to hurt you. I just wanted you to live."

I step toward him, stopping when I'm close enough to take his hand in mine. "It doesn't make it right."

He stares at our interlaced fingers. "Maybe not. But there's nothing I wouldn't do to protect you."

"Then trust me to protect myself."

"What?"

"I'm asking you to trust me."

He smiles. "Okay."

"Just like that? Why?"

"What kind of question is that?"

"Why would you trust me?" God knows he has no reason to.

"Because I want to."

"That's it?" He makes it sound so simple. Like trusting someone is just a matter of will.

"That's it. I would follow you to the ends of the earth. I have."

"And I betrayed you. I sent you back to the underworld."

"A chance I was willing to take."

"Even now?"

He pulls me the rest of the way to him, brushing my lips with a feathery kiss. "Especially now. Do you think I'm a bloody fool?"

I lean forward so I can whisper in his ear. "What do you think?"

His low laugh resonates in the base of my spine. "I think you're playing a dangerous game."

I bring my hands behind his neck, pulling him the rest of the way to me. "If this meeting with the Sons turns out to be a trap, I don't want to waste today." Whatever else I'm feeling, if I only have these few hours left, I want to feel alive.

I stretch up to kiss Austin. He meets my kiss with an intensity that floods me with shivery heat. I press closer to him until he falls back on the leather couch, pulling me into his lap. His fingers move under my shirt, dancing along the edge of my bra and dipping underneath. He groans into my mouth as I move against his hand.

I sit up and pull my tee shirt over my head. Austin reaches for a lacy bra strap, sliding it along my shoulder until it falls to the side. His eyes are dark, and his smile takes my breath away.

He kisses my bare shoulder and then moves to the base of my neck, licking the sensitive skin where my pulse beats. He brings his arms around me, holding me to him while he stands up. I wrap my legs around his waist as he carries me across the room and lays me across his giant bed.

Lying on his side next to me, he trails a finger from my chin to my belly button. "I can't believe you're really here."

My skin aches for more contact. I brush away the bit of hair that hangs in front of his eyes. "Are you just going to lie there staring, or are you going to touch me?"

"I'm definitely going to touch you." His voice is laced with laughter. "But it's not a race to the finish. I want to savor every moment."

I run a hand from his shoulder to his wrist and back again. "Take off your shirt."

"As you wish." He sits up and brings his long-sleeved tee over his head in one smooth pull. I reach for the soft skin above his heart. When he kisses me, I feel his pulse race beneath my palm.

He moves his hand along the inside of my thigh, tracing invisible lines on my jeans. It's not enough. I want his hands on my skin. I want his skin on my skin. I want everything that his kiss promises. More.

I pull him down to me until his body covers mine, running my hands down his back and under the waist of his jeans, dragging him closer.

"God, Brianna," he breathes into my neck. "You are determined to rush this."

I smile into his hair. "I want this."

"Ah." He thrusts against me, so that even through our clothes, I can feel how much he wants this too. "I'm no match for a goddess."

He rolls on his back and pulls off his clothes, grinning at me in a way that melts me from the inside out.

I can't not stare. Austin may not be immortal anymore, but every part of his body is sculpted to perfection, sinew carved in perfect balance with his lean frame. My eyes drop of their own accord, and I can feel them widen despite my best efforts.

He reaches for the button at the top of my jeans. "Your turn."

I nod and let Austin peel away what remains of my

clothes. Before I can feel too self-conscious, he covers me with his chest, holding himself above me as his lips crush mine. He lets his weight shift gradually, lowering his chest to mine. When he brings his bare leg between my own, his skin is warmer and smoother than I expect.

I bring my hands between his shoulder blades, urging him closer.

This time, when his hand reaches my thigh, I can feel every bit of the soft pressure of his fingers as they graze my skin. When his hips press into mine, I feel the full length of him.

"Is this okay?" he asks, pressing closer.

"Just okay? Don't you think you should be aiming a little higher?"

He laughs and reaches for a drawer in the wood frame of the bed. "Perhaps. To be honest, I'm hovering somewhere between a sliver of control and complete abandon. I'm just aiming to get through this without embarrassing myself." He takes a square wrapper from the drawer and tears it open with his teeth. "I don't know how much longer I can keep it together."

"Who said anything about wanting you to keep it together?"

He moves between my legs and sighs into my ear. "Indeed."

It hurts a bit. I'm not technically a virgin, so the pain catches me by surprise, and I cry out before I can stop myself.

Austin freezes. "Did I hurt you?"

"A little." I feel myself softening around him. "Try it

again." This time when he moves into me, I feel nothing but sweet pressure. "Again."

"Like this?" He thrusts forward.

"Yes," I whisper. "Like that. Again."

He kisses me as he moves inside of me, and I kiss him back, pushing against him, urging him forward, faster, further. I don't know what I expected, but it wasn't this pure joy that starts at my toes and fills me completely.

The rush of endorphins stays with me long after it's over, and I lie with my head cradled on Austin's chest. I'm treading water in the middle of the ocean. Austin was right about one thing: this can only end badly.

THIRTY-FIVE

The pub is busy this afternoon. A crowd gathers around a large television, cheering and shouting at a soccer game.

The Sons sit at a table in the back corner, not glancing at the television at all. Instead, their eyes watch me, flashing with silvery venom. I should be used to it, but the hair on the back of my neck rises in response. Austin's hand rests in the middle of my back, propelling me forward.

Blake is sitting at the end of the table. Though his gaze follows us, he doesn't watch me like the others do. He watches Austin. There's no trace of Blake's signature dimples. His face is dark, his eyes ringed with black circles, his lips set in a thin line. My heart breaks a little. Not for me, but for Blake. Where is the Blake who could win over an entire room with a smile? I spent months watching him before we got together, and this bitter boy who snaps a straw in half at the end of the table is someone else entirely.

Jonah winks at me from his seat next to Rush. Dr. McKay sits on Rush's other side, and Levi and the twins sit next to him. Jeremy is playing with a long strand of his hair, winding it around his finger; his brother Micah tries to smile at me, but his lips twitch. Either these two missed their dose of medicinal this morning or, more likely, peace is not in the cards for us.

Two seats are vacant across the table from the seven of them. Austin and I are meant to feel intimidated.

It works.

Facing seven demigods, the majority of whom want me dead, falls somewhere on the extremely stupid side of the continuum of good and bad ideas. I take the seat across from Rush. Austin takes my hand as he sits down next to me.

Rush narrows his eyes at Austin. He's a big man, with dark eyes and long hair that makes him look as wild as the animals he hunts. "And you would be?"

So Blake hasn't told the Sons about Austin. I try not to think too hard about what that might mean. Is he going to help us?

"I am Arawn." It's the first time I've heard Austin use his true name. He looks every bit the god when he says it.

Rush blinks. "Impossible."

Austin squeezes my hand under the table. "Apparently not."

Rush turns his hard gaze on me. "You couldn't hide your true sympathies for long, bandia."

Blake looks down at the floor. He'd convinced the Sons to

accept a truce with me once already. Rush isn't the type to let him forget it.

Dr. McKay is still staring at Austin, clearly fascinated. "We tested you. You didn't have any sign of the Killian gene."

"You forget that you were created by the gods, not the other way around."

I squeeze Austin's hand tighter. He may not be a god anymore, but I believe in him.

Rush leans forward and addresses me. "You asked for this meeting."

"Yes. We've all been called here for the Gathering."

Rush doesn't look surprised. Blake must have already told him. He sits up straight and glares at Austin. "So, are you responsible for this?"

"My successor."

"The other bandia are here," I continue. "They plan to ignite a war."

"Then we'll fight." Rush makes it sound so simple. If Liam wants a war, they'll give him one. It's what the Sons want too. All the bandia in one place.

Jonah makes a kissy motion with his lips across the table. It's a good thing I don't have my power. Even without it, it's hard to resist the urge to knock Jonah off his stool.

Blake finally looks up from the floor. He stares at the table between Austin and me as if he's trying to see through the wood to where our hands are laced together. "Whose side are you on?" Blake directs the question to both of us, but it's meant for me.

"My own," I say. "But I intend to fight with the Sons."

Rush leans forward. "You said the bandia are here. More than one?"

"Two besides me."

Blake visibly pales. Is he worried I'll give up Portia? Doesn't he want them to know? It occurs to me that I have no idea what he wants where Portia is concerned. They bonded. I know how that can screw with your own emotions.

A cheer rises from the crowd watching television.

Rush ignores the noise. "We have them outnumbered, then. The battle will be short."

I shake my head. "Maybe not. The new god of the underworld wants to win. He's been talking to the fuath."

Rush smiles slowly. "As have I."

Jeremy looks sick. The lock of hair in his hand is a gnarled tangle. Micah mouths the word "sorry." They're not fighters, but they won't stand against the Circle of Sons either.

Blake's sister walks down the stairs from the rooms above. Her face changes when we make eye contact, transforming to fear and then to anger. She marches up to the table, her eyes darting from Blake to Rush to me. "What's she doing here? Why is she even alive?"

Rush stands up. "Her fate is not your concern."

Mallory shrinks away from Rush, but she turns her cold green eyes on me. "I'll kill you myself if they won't do it."

Joe appears behind Mallory, from a table behind the wall near the kitchen. "This is a private meeting." He presses a hand on Mallory's shoulder.

"Does Portia know you're meeting with her?" Mallory glares at her brother, ignoring Joe.

"Let's go outside, Mal." Joe's hand curls around her arm. "Now."

Several of the people crowded around the TV turn to watch us.

"Stop acting like a child," Rush says. "Your brother claimed the right to kill this one, and he'll carry out his promise to the Circle."

Blake stares at the floor again. Like the scratches in the hardwood form the most fascinating patterns known to man.

Mallory rolls her eyes. "Like he did at home? She's got him wrapped around her little finger, or at least she's got her fingers wrapped around his—"

"Enough!" Rush's voice carries through the pub.

Everyone in the room stops talking. All eyes are on Rush. Even Mallory looks chastened.

Austin squeezes my hand.

A gust of wind comes from behind us. The wind whips across the table, sending glasses and pitchers scattering. A glass of ale lands in Rush's lap.

Levi and Jonah both stand at the same time.

"We need to go." Austin pulls me to my feet.

There's a flash of silver. It's bright enough to be disorienting, but I can't afford to wait until my eyes adjust. I point myself in the general direction of the entrance and run.

I skid to a halt, stepping away from the demigod that materializes in front of me. It's Blake. He holds his broadsword at his side and takes my hand, pulling me off my feet. I fall into the solid wall of his chest as he shields me from a flash of light to my right. He turns us around just as Jonah draws his serrated knife.

Blake pushes me toward the entrance as the knife hits him in the shoulder. "Go!"

I don't stop to help him. I run as fast as I can, trying to put walls between me and the rest of the Sons.

Austin is waiting at the door, holding it open. He slams it behind us. We run around the corner and duck into a gift shop. With a nod to the short woman at the register, Austin pulls me to a rear door used for deliveries. We come out in an alley not far from where we left the Porsche.

We run the rest of the way to the car, but there don't appear to be any Sons giving chase. Austin drives the Porsche the way it was designed to be driven, hard and fast. We don't speak until we're safely though the gates of Lorcan Hall.

"Portia?" He's referring to the wind that took out the Sons' table.

"That's my guess."

Austin puts his head in his hands.

"What?"

"I was supposed to look out for you."

"You did. You got me out."

"Blake got you out."

"You were there too."

"But I couldn't help, Brianna."

"What do you mean?"

Austin's brows furrow, creating that little crease I ache to smooth away. "My power. It's gone."

THIRTY-SIX

Mick has a tea service set up in the sitting room with the giant fireplace. I want to hug him. I almost do, but he waves me away. Apparently, hugs are not his thing. I sip from a warm cup, savoring the brisk peppermint flavor. "At least the Sons know that the Gathering is a set-up."

"Liam might not wait for the Gathering now. He won't want to lose his advantage." Austin throws himself onto the couch and rests his feet on the table.

Mick glowers and waits for Austin to set his feet back on the floor before he leaves the room.

"You're assuming he'll find out that the Sons know what's going on," I say. "And that he even knows who they are."

"We have to assume Portia will tell Liam about the meeting today," Austin says. "Half the town probably knows about it after that display."

"Joe will compel the people who were there to forget

what they saw. Like he did the night Sasha was killed at the poker game."

"Which will only fuel the rumors," Austin counters. "The people here don't need to trust their memories to know when something isn't right."

"How can they suspect something they don't remember?"

"Remembering and knowing are two different things. Memories can't always be trusted, colored as they are by perception and time. Knowledge is something that lives in our hearts. It is not so easily shaken."

"I don't get it."

Austin sets down his cup of tea and looks at me. Right into me. "I could be stripped of a thousand years of memories, and I would always know, in my heart, that I love you."

Okay, wow. My cheeks flush with heat that doesn't come from the tea. "What does that have to do with the townspeople?"

"You can take away what they saw, but their feelings will linger. They'll know something isn't right."

Mick returns to the doorway. "Brianna has a visitor."

I stand up. Whoever it is, I want to be in a position to fight if I have to. Or run.

Shannon walks into the room, her eyes downcast. She's undoubtedly not used to coming into Lorcan Hall as a guest.

Austin nods at me and follows Mick out of the room.

"You were right about that one." Shannon looks up and grins. "He *is* a bob."

I feel my cheeks get warm.

"I've come to help you," she says.

"Help me what?"

"Fight the witch's black magic."

"I'm listening." I sit down on the couch and pat the space next to me.

She pulls a handful of twigs from her pocket. They're cut into identical three-inch pieces and bound with a green ribbon. She holds it out to me.

I take the little bundle of sticks. "What's this?"

"Broomstraw. A ward against dark magic."

"I don't understand."

"It's not our place to understand."

"Why are you giving this to me?" I turn the sticks over in my hands.

"I was at the Ornery Knight this afternoon. I know you're not a witch. She just wants them to think you are. This will help you." Shannon crosses herself.

Did she see what Portia did? Joe should have replaced her memory; she shouldn't recall the details. "You remember what happened?"

"I was behind her on the stairway. She called the wind to her before she sent it to the table."

If Shannon remembers Portia, she probably also remembers the Sons in their demigod forms. "You saw the Milesians, too?"

Shannon looks confused. "Of course. I'm one of them."

"You're a Milesian?" I'm confused for a moment. But I shouldn't be—Mick told me that the human Milesians were still here.

"As long as there's magic in this world, we will be here to defeat it."

"But I thought that Killian rid Ireland of magic a long time ago."

She laughs. "Only an American would say that."

"And the Seventh Sons? Will you defeat them too?" Killian may have started out as a Milesian, but I suspect the Milesians in Cath no longer claim his heirs as their own.

"And others as well," Shannon says. "It's been generations since the Sons fled our country, but we always knew they would return. Home calls to even those who forsake it."

"You shouldn't be helping me." If Shannon is this committed to the Milesians, I'm as much her enemy as Portia is. "Your mother will be upset."

Shannon looks past me. "I wasn't planning on telling her. Were you?"

"But what if I am what she says I am?"

"You're not. I saw you today when your life was in danger. If you had even an ounce of magic, you would have used it."

"Damn straight." But does my lack of power mean that I'm no longer a Seventh Daughter? I cling to this idea and all it could mean. A normal life.

Shannon glances up from the floor, a shy smile playing on her lips. "Keep the broomstraw close."

"Thank you."

She stands and walks to the door. "Call me if you have trouble with the witch."

The door opens as she reaches it, and Sherri and Liam

waltz past her without acknowledging her. They're too busy playing grab-ass with each other.

Sherri barely waits for Shannon to leave before she conjures some wind and slams the door shut from across the room. "We need to talk."

Liam curls his lip into a sneer that's more menace than smile. "Portia tells me you haven't been playing fair."

I clutch the pouch of bark in my fist. I have a feeling I'm going to need it.

THIRTY-SEVEN

Liam takes a seat in the largest chair, a wingback trimmed in delicate gold fabric that makes it look like a throne.

Sherri stays on her feet, pacing the length of the room. "You told the Sons about our strike. You still have a thing for one of them, don't you?"

"No." As I say the word, I realize it's finally true. "I have a thing for humanity."

Sherri waves her hand in the air, dismissing my words. "You think the Sons care about humanity? Why do you think they kept breeding for more Sons even after they thought we were all dead?"

I've asked myself the same question. The Sons covet their own magic. It's everyone else's that's a problem for them. No wonder the Milesians don't claim Killian's heirs as their own. "At least the Sons don't plan to enslave humans." I tuck the little bundle of twigs in the front pocket of my jeans.

"I'm running out of patience with you," Liam says from his throne. "You take your powers for granted, but you only have them by the grace of the gods. If you're not going to use them for the right reasons, you don't deserve them." The unspoken threat is in his eyes: *You don't deserve to live.*

"And you trust Portia?" I ask.

Sherri walks over to Liam and places a hand on his shoulder. "Portia has spent her whole life under the thumb of the Sons. She hates them more than I do."

It's what Portia told me herself, but I still can't believe that she could kill her own family so easily. That she could kill Blake. I still might be able to save her. Sherri, on the other hand, is a lost cause.

Liam clears his throat. "Portia will do as she's told. So will you."

I turn to face him. He looks almost like one of Braden's crew, dressed in jeans and a Dublin sweatshirt, a college kid on holiday. But he hasn't been on earth long enough to learn how to mask his otherworldliness. He doesn't take on any imperfections to offset the sculpted line of his jaw or perfect symmetry of his face. His voice, his movements—they're all too smooth. It makes everything about him seem fake.

"You don't own me."

"Another lesson in humility?" He turns to Sherri.

The corner of her lip quirks.

Wind whips around her hair, and I brace myself for her assault. I see the moment she sends the wind straight at me. It sails by with such force that a statue of a small dog is blown off the table next to me, crashing to the marble floor.

The wind doesn't touch me. I tighten my grip around the small pouch in my pocket.

"Come on, bandia." Sherri can't hide the shakiness in her voice. "Let's see what you've got."

Crap. Sherri wants to spar and I've got exactly nothing in my arsenal of magic. "I'm not fighting you."

Sherri shakes her head. "You're pathetic."

A blast of wind hits the back of the couch hard enough to knock it forward and send me flying from the seat. I put out my arms to brace my fall, barely keeping my head from striking the marble floor. Out of the corner of my eye, I see an iron fire poker next to the fireplace. As I roll to the side, I reach for it and lob it at Sherri's knee.

She's not expecting a physical fight. The poker lands with a crack against her leg. She falls to the floor with a shout and curls into a ball, a string of obscenities flying from her lips.

The door opens so fast it slams against the wall. Austin runs past Sherri to where I'm still pushing myself off the floor. He turns to Liam. "Get out!"

"That's no way to speak to your guests." Liam sets his chin in his palm and smiles.

"You are no longer my guest. Get out of my house. And don't touch Brianna again."

"This won't be your house for long." Sherri sits up, holding her knee.

Austin raises his eyebrows. "Your life is as fragile as mine. Perhaps you should refrain from throwing stones."

Sherri hobbles over to Liam. "I have the gods on my side."

Austin helps me to my feet before he looks at them again.

"You have ten minutes to pack up your things and go. You will stay away from Brianna between now and the Gathering."

Liam stands up and puts his arm around Sherri. "You cast out your betters at your own risk."

Austin glares at Liam. "You touch Brianna at yours."

We wait for them to leave before we make our way upstairs to Austin's bedroom. As soon as we're safely inside, Austin pulls me into a hug. "What was that about?"

"Training, I think."

"It looked like you got in a nice shot."

"I don't need magic to put up a good fight."

"You don't have to tell me." Austin presses his lips to my forehead.

"For a second there I almost believed you still had your power," I say.

"You're not the only one who's good at bluffing."

I stretch up to kiss him.

"Stay," he whispers against my lips. There's no magic behind his plea, no soul bond that brings us together. There's just him and me and a kiss that has a power all its own.

He doesn't have to ask me twice.

THIRTY-EIGHT

From across the breakfast table, Austin grins at me.

"What?"

"I think it's time you learned how to handle a broadsword."

"Okay. Wow. Tell me that's not a euphemism."

"It would certainly make the day more interesting if it were. But the thing with the fire poker got me thinking." Austin reaches across the table for my hand. "We might not be able to fight with magic, but we can still fight. It wouldn't hurt for you to learn a weapon."

"And the broadsword is so relevant."

"It is if you're fighting Sons."

"We're supposed to be fighting *with* the Sons, not against them." Although we can't exactly count on that. It seems the Sons still want me dead. "Wouldn't a gun be better?"

"The only way to kill a Son is at close range. Reduces

the likelihood of an unintentional hit." Austin doesn't need to explain; an unintentional hit was exactly how I killed Blake. "And I don't trust the Sons not to try to take you out if they can. Even if you help them win."

An hour later, Austin is waiting for me in the courtyard behind the house. The sun shines through fluffy white clouds, its golden rays casting Austin in a warm light. An echo of his godly form, but softer. More.

He twirls a large sword with one hand. "We'll make a warrior out of you yet."

I try to lift one of the giant swords, but it takes two hands and all my strength just to pick it up off the ground. "Shouldn't we go with something a little lighter?"

"You'll learn to appreciate the weight. It will give you the momentum you need to strike."

I try swinging it like a baseball bat. I nearly fall forward.

Austin laughs. "First you need to find a stance." He bends his knees slightly, spreading his feet to shoulder width. "Try it again."

Blake comes up the stone path from the house, Mick chasing at his heels. "Have you lost your mind, Montgomery?" Blake's left arm is in a sling, but otherwise he appears to have survived his run-in with Jonah just fine.

Austin stands up straight. "You would prefer Brianna lie down and wait to die?"

I let the tip of my sword fall to the ground. Even the sunshine can't mask Blake's pale complexion. His eyes are dark and sad.

"Of course not. You need to get her out of here before the

Gathering. Everyone could see that she's defenseless." Blake finally looks at me. "What happened? Did he do something to you?"

"No." I lift the sword again. I may not have magic, but I'm not defenseless.

Austin steps forward. "She paid a high price for your life."

"What's that supposed to mean?" Blake glares at Austin, much more comfortable in the role of aggressor. "You're the one who put my life in danger in the first place."

Austin rolls his eyes. "The bond put your life in danger. And hers. Emotions are closely linked to the soul, and being forced to feel someone else's blackest thoughts twenty-four/seven will take its toll. Eventually one soul will dominate the other. You would have grown to resent each other more than you cared for each other."

Is what Austin says true? Would I have started to feel Blake's emotions more than my own? Or vice versa? When we were bonded, there were times when our emotions bled together until I didn't know if what I was feeling was mine or his. Times when his emotions were stronger than mine, but that was usually when Blake believed in me and I didn't.

Blake believed in me.

I push the thought away. It doesn't matter now. Blake may have thought he believed in me once, but he didn't trust me. Not when it mattered. Somewhere along the way he stopped loving me. I set down the sword and put my hand on Austin's shoulder. "Can you give me a few minutes?"

Austin nods, but he throws his sword on the ground with more force than necessary. "I'll be just inside."

I wait until Austin is gone before I look at Blake again, taking in the shadows that ring his eyes. "Are you okay?"

I've caught him off guard. The vein on his neck throbs in response to my question. "Me?"

"You've looked better."

"I'm fine." Blake says the words like a petulant child. He lifts the arm in the sling. "Just a flesh wound. It's you I'm worried about. What happened to your power?"

"I guess there's a price for bringing someone back from the dead."

He stares back at the house. "He was right then. You paid a high price. This is his fault."

"Blake, it's not." Austin might have set me up to kill Blake, in the name of protecting me, but I let loose the ball of fire. "I'm the one who killed you."

When Blake finally turns back to me, his eyes are softer. "You shouldn't have saved me."

"Of course I should have. I'd do it again. Blake, I—" I stop myself from saying that I loved him. It doesn't matter now. "I would never let you die if I knew I could save you."

Neither one of us says anything for a few minutes. We stand a few feet apart, but there may as well be oceans separating us.

"We can't stop the war from coming," Blake finally says. "The Sons will fight the other bandia, and the fuath too if they have to."

"So we fight."

"You're bringing a knife to a magic fight?" It's Blake's first hint of a smile.

"I was pushing for automatic weapons, but Austin said that the broadsword is the weapon of choice when it comes to battling demigods. Go figure."

Blake's chuckle drifts away. "He's taking care of you?" He doesn't hide the pain behind his words.

Blake is upset? He left me. He bonded with Portia.

"We're taking care of each other." I don't say the words to hurt Blake. I just need for him to understand that I'm with Austin by choice. On my terms.

"Then leave. Get as far away as you can. If he loves you, he won't let you anywhere near the Gathering."

"If he loves me, he'll let me make my own decisions."

Blake picks up one of the broadswords with his good arm and throws it as far as he can. It sails across the grass, over the edge of the bluff, dropping into the sea. "The Sons don't trust you, Brianna."

"And you do?" Since when?

He ignores my question. "They'll kill you without a second thought. I won't be able to stop them."

I walk to where Austin's broadsword lies on the grass. I pick it up with both hands and slash at the air. "I won't go down without a fight."

"Either way, you end up dead."

"Why are you here?" I ask.

The shadows under Blake's eyes grow darker. "I wish I knew." He turns and walks back toward the house. He doesn't look back.

THIRTY-NINE

After Blake leaves, I walk to the barn. Malcolm automatically moves toward Molly, but I take the brush box from his hand and wave him away. The next half hour goes by peacefully, as I brush Molly until her dark coat gleams.

When I'm done, I ask Mick for the car keys. He looks skeptical, but I remind him that I'm not a prisoner here and he finally relents. I text Braden on the way. If Austin and I are going to survive, we need allies. Or at least fewer opponents.

Braden meets me at the little bakery with the layered tea cakes. "What happened to laying low?"

I don't bother with small talk—I need to make sure the fuath won't fight against us. "Is it true that the fuath are aligned with Liam?"

Braden wipes a yellow crumb from the corner of his lip with his thumb. "We're weighing our options."

"The Seventh Daughters are outnumbered. My money's on the Sons."

"Are you here to recruit me? 'Cause I was kind of enjoying the lack of strings in our friendship."

"I'm not recruiting you. I'm trying to convince you to stay out of it."

Braden grins. "Because you don't want to see me get hurt?"

"Because I don't want to have to hurt you."

"Aw, you actually mean that."

"Stop sucking on my emotions."

"It's not like I can turn it off. Wait—you're worrying about hurting me if I align with you? That doesn't even make sense."

I don't say anything.

Braden's eyes widen as he works out the answer himself. "You're not going to fight for Liam." The statement hangs in the air. He doesn't need me to affirm it. He can feel my conviction. "Well, well, aren't you the rebel?"

The fuath can't seriously be considering fighting alongside Liam. I choose my words carefully. "What did Liam promise you? Do you really trust him to keep his word?"

Braden shrugs. "Don't mistake our lack of involvement for weakness. We survived alongside the gods before, and we'll do so again if necessary."

"Why did you stay underground all this time?"

"We prefer not to be hunted."

I can't argue with his logic. "Liam doesn't seem like the

type to sit around and wait." Maybe Braden will say something about Liam's plans.

"Liam wouldn't wait at all if he thought he could win now. But he needs help. He's waiting for the day the sunset coincides with the changing of the tides. When the elements will be strongest." Braden takes a long sip of tea, as if it's no big deal that he's just given me the exact date and time of the Gathering. Even knowing that I don't intend to fight for Liam. Then Braden looks over his shoulder and smiles. "Your boyfriend's here."

Austin enters the bakery and slides into an empty seat at our table. He doesn't acknowledge Braden. "Have you talked to Joe?"

"No. Should I have?"

"He's looking for you." Austin reaches for one of the tea cakes in front of me. "You should've told me you were going to town. I would've come with you."

Braden takes the cake Austin had been reaching for, popping it in his mouth in one bite. "Well, isn't this interesting?"

"What?"

"The immortal god is afraid."

"I'm not a fool," Austin tells him. "You of all people should feel the rising storm."

"Oh, I feel it. But since when are you afraid of it? It's what you want, isn't it?"

I don't miss the way Austin looks at me. I have to remember to breathe.

"Priorities change," Austin says.

Braden laughs. "No way am I missing the Gathering now."

Someone waves from the sidewalk. It's Jeremy, who flashes me a goofy grin through the window. He pushes a long strand of hair from his face, looking more like himself than he did yesterday at the pub. Micah steps next to him and pulls Jeremy's wrist down to his side. Jeremy rolls his eyes at me, and I can't help smiling.

Austin looks out the window and stiffens.

"It's okay," I say. "They're friends."

Braden nods as the twins walk into the bakery. "Keep your cool, Arawn. These two aren't aggressive."

I stand up to greet them. Jeremy pulls me into a huge bear hug, lifting me off my feet and swinging me from side to side. "Looking babelicious as ever."

Micah nods his chin in my direction as Jeremy sets me back on my feet. "Dude."

I pull a couple more chairs over to our table while Micah orders about ten different cakes from the boy behind the counter.

Austin narrows his eyes as the twins sit down, but he keeps his mouth shut as Jeremy and Micah start shoving the little cakes into their mouths.

"You look like you're holding up okay," Micah says.

"Jonah's an ass, but don't worry." Jeremy eats a little yellow cake in one bite. "We made sure he won't be bothering you for a while."

"Okay." I can't stop smiling. "I'm kind of afraid to ask."

Micah runs a hand over his buzzed hair. "We might've

kicked his ass into the next country." His lips curve into a slow grin that transforms his face into a replica of his identical twin's.

"Might have? The whiner ran all the way to London with his girlfriend. My guess is he won't be back until the Gathering."

Austin is watching them carefully. "Are you not with the Sons then?"

Micah shakes his head. "We don't believe in killing hot babes, if that's what you mean."

The twins are pacifists. Or, as Jeremy puts it, they'd rather make out than make war with the bandia.

"Is there any way for you to avoid the Gathering?" I ask. Jeremy pops another cake into his mouth.

Micah's face grows serious. "I don't know. But it doesn't matter. They can't make us fight."

A wave of nausea rolls through me. "You might not have a choice. I won't fight you. But the other bandia will."

"Nah. Not when she gets a load of this face." Jeremy waggles his eyebrows. "She'll be too busy swooning."

Micah laughs along with us, but his eyes are dark. When he thinks everyone is looking at Jeremy, he bites his lip.

I want to hug them both. They may be Sons of Killian, but they're not fighters. They don't want to be part of this war any more than I do. I turn to Micah, keeping my voice low. "Maybe Blake can get you away from here."

"Have you seen him lately?"

I nod.

Micah leans in close, lowering his voice to a whisper. "He's not the same without you."

"He'll be okay." I hope it's true.

I catch Austin watching me. Nothing's the same—not Blake, not me. But maybe, just maybe, things are going to turn out okay. I reach for Austin's hand. His answering smile is crooked, and sad, and somehow perfect. A war is coming. We might not be able to stop it. But at least for now, we've made our own peace.

And for the rest of the afternoon, a fuath, a former god, a bandia, and two Sons of Killian share tea and cakes and laughter.

It has to mean something.

FORTY

The next day, I make arrangements to meet Joe at the ruin. I sit on the low wall and watch as he emerges out of the mist that covers the trail, wearing a long raincoat as black as his hair. He pushes a branch away from his perfectly smooth pompadour as he ducks under a tree and enters the clearing.

The sky is gray again, the clouds covering the sky in a blanket of dampness. The mist curls through the grass and covers the wall.

Joe takes a seat beside me. "It's been a long time since I've seen this place."

"You know it?"

"Magic places are hard to avoid." He puts his hands in his pockets and stares at the ground. "Portia came down to breakfast yesterday wearing your necklace."

My stomach twists into a tight knot. "It's not mine. I gave it back to Blake."

"It doesn't belong to Blake any more than it belongs to Portia." He turns to me, his eyes serious. "You're the one who needs it."

"I don't." It's nothing more than a reminder of Blake. "We've both moved on."

"You shared a soul once. That means something."

I wish I had my power now. I want to set something on fire. "Blake and I were never meant to be anything but enemies. You should know that better than anyone." I dare him to argue with me. "And now Portia has the necklace. You do the math."

Joe's expression doesn't change. He still looks calm as ever. "So you know about their bond."

"It doesn't sound so special anymore, does it? The whole bonding thing is just what happens when a Son and a bandia hook up." The truth hurts more than it should. Jonah once told me that I would've bonded with any Son who got me on my back. I hadn't wanted to believe it at the time, but now it's hard to doubt it.

Joe stretches out his legs. "I've seen it before." Of course he has. He's been watching the Sons for how long, centuries? "You and Blake were different," he adds.

"How?"

"The bond always ends in death. You're both still alive."

"It did end in death. I killed him."

Joe smiles. "You're only half right."

"I was there. He was dead."

"Last time I checked, he looked pretty spry." Joe takes

a cigarette from the pocket of his long coat. "But it might change if you don't get that necklace back."

"What does my having the necklace have to do with Blake living or dying?"

Joe stands up and puts the unlit cigarette between his teeth. The sky darkens above us. "Portia will kill him."

"Not if Blake kills her first."

"Same difference. Rush won't stand by quietly after his daughter's been killed."

While I knew that Blake and Portia had bonded, all I saw was how it degraded what Blake and I had shared. It hadn't occurred to me that Blake could be in trouble, that it could kill him. Joe's right—there's no way for this to end well for Blake.

But Blake got himself into this mess. He can get himself out. That thought is smothered by the part of me that can't bear for Blake to die. Even now. "What am I supposed to do?" I ask, my voice angrier than I intend. "I can barely lift a broadsword."

"As I said, get the necklace."

"I'm still not following."

Joe puts the unlit cigarette between his lips and takes a step toward the trail leading into the forest, his back to me. "You will always be a bandia. Nothing can take it away completely."

"I can't access any of my power. I've tried."

Joe looks back over his shoulder. "The necklace."

I wait until Joe disappears down the trail before I move

off the low wall. He thinks the necklace will help me access my power? How?

I test this theory against what I already know. After I'd used the reversal spell to save Blake, my power was supposed to disappear by halves until I couldn't access it anymore. But instead, it seemed like I was stronger than I'd ever been. Right up until I gave the necklace back to Blake, that day in his room over the Ornery Knight. And then my power was gone.

Had my power been declining all along, but I didn't notice because the necklace helped to magnify it? Was that even possible? If so, the wolfsbane pendant was infused with some serious magic. Just like the wolfsbane charm on my bracelet that had once kept guys from noticing me.

And the little horse charm, that lets me travel a thousand years back in time.

I stare at the matching carving in the stone wall. I can't believe it's too late to change everything. I place the horse against the carving and let it carry me into the mist.

I close my eyes until I feel warm sunshine on my face and solid ground beneath my feet. The field is empty so I venture forward, into the trees and down the hill that will take me back toward Lorcan Hall. At a break in the trail I see the house, an imposing wall of stone even then.

A tall figure approaches through the trees. I duck behind a thick bush. Mick strides past, dressed in form-fitting wool pants and a simple green tunic. His red hair is long, all one length that brushes his shoulders, and his face is clean-shaven. He looks younger without the thick sideburns.

"Mick?" I step onto the path behind him.

"Mikel," he says, in the same stern tone he always uses, before he turns around. When he sees me, his eyes go wide. "Are you the mystery girl?"

"The mystery girl?"

"The girl from the future that everyone speaks of?"

"Who's everyone?"

"The master and Gwyn and Bronwyn, and their mother."

"Danu? She knows about me?"

Mick's lips quirk. "Aye. And you had best stay far away from her. She is not at all happy that her matchmaking has been thwarted."

"Is that all?" At least Danu hasn't heard about my so-called murder plot. Then it occurs to me, maybe Danu is exactly the person who needs to know about the future.

"It is enough." He walks forward. "Are you here to see the master then?"

I shake my head. "I don't think so. Do you know where I can find Danu?"

"You wish to test your fortune?"

"Looks that way."

"I do not suppose there will be any talking you out of it?"

I shake my head. If I can warn Danu, she could protect herself. She could stop Austin.

I freeze.

What would stopping Austin mean? Could she hurt him?

Mick walks along the trail a few feet. "You coming?"

What if preventing the war means hurting Austin? Could I do it?

"Mick!" Austin calls from the trail below us. Or Aaron.

It's hard to think of him as anything but Austin. He runs up through the trees, but stops when he sees me. "Oh."

I smile at his uncertainty, so at odds with the arrogant confidence he throws around so easily. "Hello to you too."

He walks the rest of the way to me, lifting a hand to touch my cheek, but he drops it before his fingers make contact. "You came back."

I don't know how long we stand there, just staring at each other, before Mick clears his throat. We both turn to look at him at once.

"I was just going to check on the flock in the eastern field," Mick says. He turns and walks up the hill quickly.

As soon as Mick is out of view, Austin takes my hand in his, lacing our fingers together. "I was not sure I would see you again."

"You will. Maybe not so soon. Eventually."

"Ah yes. My future."

"What if I really could change everything? I could stop a war."

"Is that a rhetorical question? Because right now all that matters to me is that you are here."

"I thought all you cared about was finding a way to let the gods out of the underworld."

Austin laughs. "If my future is so bleak, please find a way to make me mortal and put me out of my misery."

My smile slips. I can't stop it. Austin has no idea how close his joke hits to the truth.

He squeezes my hand gently. "I'm not serious. If you

know me in the future, surely you know how crazy you sound."

"You don't want to bring the gods back to earth?"

"I did not say that." Now he sounds like the Austin I know. "I would like nothing more. Believe me. It is why I spend so much of my time here, leaving Pwil to rule below."

Pwil. Liam. "Is he still your friend?" I bite back the question that I really want to ask: *Do you have a lover in the under-world?*

Austin tilts his head to the side. "Still? You mean Pwil and I are mates in the future? I find that unlikely."

"No, you're not. I just wondered if you two are friends now."

Austin guides me to a clearing between the trees and sits down in the grass. I sit beside him, folding my knees to my chest. "Pwil and myself . . . it is a long story."

"You never told me about it."

"Would you like me to?"

"Yes." At least I think so.

"My friendship with Pwil ended like many do. A girl came between us. Although it seems wrong to call Morrigan a girl."

Morrigan. His lover was a goddess. I wrap my arms around my knees and stare out at the hillside. Austin lived for how long? Thousands of years? Of course there were other girls. It's not like I can complain. I've only been alive for seventeen years and I managed to bond myself to another boy.

Austin reaches for one of my curls and twists it lightly

around his finger before he lets it go with a springing bounce. "Are you jealous?"

"Maybe."

His grin is sweet and not the least bit smug. "So there is hope for us, in the future?"

I can't help smiling back. It would be so easy to lean forward and kiss him now. But I need to know what happened between him and Liam. And this Austin will tell me. "Tell me about Morrigan."

Austin looks out at the trees. "She is a goddess of great power and wrath. She had a special talent for manipulating things, especially me. Morrigan is a goddess of war, so it's no surprise that she left blood in her wake."

"Yours?"

"In a manner of speaking. After the Milesians defeated the gods, she could no longer wage war on the humans. Her dark side, with no outlet, grew restless. She resented my ability to walk with the humans. And so she waged a new war, inciting the gods against me. Convincing them I was not doing enough to free them."

"An uprising?"

"Led by Pwil."

"But he was your friend?"

"Morrigan can be very persuasive. Still, the revolt was ill-conceived and short-lived. I control the underworld and the gods can do little against me there. The only casualties were my ties to Morrigan and Pwil."

"You don't seem upset."

He shrugs. "It was a long time ago."

Hearing him tell the story, I'm not jealous at all. I'm furious. Austin's best friend and girlfriend betrayed him in every possible way. "I hate them both."

"You need not." Austin lifts his hand and lets his fingers graze my cheek. I turn toward him and his lips hover just inches from mine. His breath is hot against my mouth. "Tell me if I presume too much."

I lean closer, meeting him halfway as his lips brush mine softly. His hand slides behind my neck and his thumb rubs gently against my throat. He growls against my mouth. Then he kisses me so deeply that I can do nothing but yield to his tongue and claw at his shirt as I pull him closer.

I'm dizzy with his kiss, spinning until I'm back in the gray mists and the moment is lost to the past. To the future.

FORTY-ONE

I find Austin in his favorite sitting room, reading a weathered book. He takes his glasses off as I storm in and sit on the couch next to him.

"Tell me what happened to Danu."

He sets the book on the table next to him, taking his time. "Knowing the future won't change it."

"The future? It happened in the past."

Austin looks away. "Of course."

"What? Something is going to happen in the *future* that will lead to Danu's death?"

"As you said, it's already happened." His gaze falls to my chest and his solemn expression is transformed by a wicked smile. "I know that sweater."

I glance down at my powder-blue V-neck. I bought it in Cath, and it's the first time I've worn it. He could only "know" it from this morning. From a thousand years ago. "You remember this?"

"God, yes." He leans forward and inhales. "You smell the same. Like the forest."

"You told me about Morrigan."

He brings his hand to my shoulder, his thumb tracing a circle near my collar. "I know."

"Why won't you tell me about Danu?"

"The past is done, Brianna."

"If it's done, then there can't be any harm in telling me what happened. You didn't want to kill Danu. I know it. You *weren't* hellbent on starting a war between the Sons of Killian and the bandia. And you didn't want Danu dead."

"All true." Austin's hand slides to my wrist. He turns it over and brings it to his lips, pressing a soft kiss against the smooth skin as he pushes the sleeve of my sweater up to my elbow.

"Are you trying to distract me?"

He licks a path from my wrist to the edge of my sleeve, glancing up. "Is it working?"

"Yes." I pull my hand away from him. My skin still tingles. "Just tell me."

He sighs. "I'm not going to win this, am I?"

"You trust me, right?"

"With my life." Austin says it with a certainty that leaves no room for doubt. I believe him.

"Then tell me the truth."

"Okay." The worry lines between his brows are back.

I reach up and smooth them away. "I can handle it.

I'm not going to hate you." I know Austin. And now I understand his willingness to kill to protect what he loves. "I forgive you," I whisper.

"I didn't kill Danu."

Shit. Not what I was expecting. "Well, it wasn't Killian," I finally manage to say. "And no one else had a reason to—unless—oh my God. Was it Gwyn?" Is this my fault? Did I cause Danu's death by trying to stop it? Did Gwyn really kill her mother to spark a war?

"No."

"Who, then?" I'm shaking. I can't stop the tremors that roll through me.

He takes my trembling hands in his. "It was you, Brianna." He closes his eyes. "It was you."

FORTY-TWO

I can't imagine killing Danu. But now that I know it was me, I know I can stop it. I can control what I do. And no matter what happens, I won't kill her. I can stop the war from ever happening.

I could not go back to the ruin at all. If I'm not there to kill Danu, then it can't happen. For once, avoidance feels like a real option.

It's easy to stay away from the ruin. It's harder to keep myself from going into town and snatching my necklace back from Portia. But we have time before the Gathering. God knows that I don't want to waste it on the Sons or the bandia. I just want to live.

The next few weeks go by in a blur of sword fights and horseback rides and kisses. I work on accessing my power without the necklace, but it becomes increasingly clear that it's never going to happen. The idea of confronting a bandia while powerless is daunting enough. It's harder when I know how much said bandia hates me, so I put it out of my mind as long as I can.

I'm actually surprised when the week of the Gathering comes. As if Austin and I could block out the world forever.

We can't.

We have two days.

I've gotten better with the broadsword, especially after Austin made me a smaller one, more proportionate to my size. I might even be able to defend myself if it's one-on-one. But we will be outnumbered. Unless I can get my necklace back, Austin and I are lambs headed to slaughter.

Unless we make a different decision.

"Maybe we should leave." I barely touch the eggs on my breakfast plate. "We're no good to anyone dead."

"Is that what you want?" Austin has never asked me not to fight, but his voice is laced with hope.

"Can Liam force us in, now that our powers are gone?"

"I don't think so. I can't feel the gateway anymore."

"Okay." Is it really so simple? Can we just walk away and leave the Sons to their battle? Leave Portia to the necklace that is the key to my power?

Austin lifts his cup but doesn't take a drink. "Okay?"

"These last few weeks, without Liam or the Sons. I want more of them." I want more of him.

"I'll have Mikel make the arrangements."

And just like that, we have tickets to Rome.

Austin stops me in the hall a few hours later. "Have you been back to the ruin?"

"No. I've been packing."

"You came back again. The day Danu—" He stops himself from saying it.

"What if I don't?"

"You do. It's already happened. I was there, remember?"

"There's no point in forcing it."

"It will happen whether you force it or not. And I only ever saw you here. At Lorcan."

"So?"

"If we leave, you won't be able to travel to the past to visit me. But you do. Which means we don't leave until that happens."

"But we have to go now. There's not much time left."

"I'm not saying I don't want to. We can try. I'm just saying I don't think it will be possible. The past has already happened. It has to happen."

"The theory of compossibility."

"In English?"

"If you're right, if there are no paradoxes, then some things are impossible to change because they've already happened. For instance, I couldn't go back in time and kill my mother before I was born, because then I would never have been born to go back and kill her. I could try, but it wouldn't work, because it would be impossible for both my mother to have died back then and me to have been born to come back to kill her."

His crooked smile nearly melts me. "This is what I get for falling in love with a scientist."

"How many times did you see me? In the past?"

"Five." He doesn't hesitate.

"And I've been back four. So that means I go back one more time?" But I won't. Ever. It won't matter if we leave today or a month from now. Going back would mean putting Danu's life in danger, and am I willing to risk Danu's life for the chance to build a future with Austin?

I don't want to kill her, but what if I can't stop it?

Austin puts his hand on my shoulder and I lean into him, letting him pull me into a hug.

"You're not going to leave until I go back, are you?"

He kisses the top of my head. "It has to happen this way."

"Okay, fine. I'll go down to the ruin now. I'll get this over with and then we can leave tonight." I walk past him, not feeling nearly as confident as I sound. I don't have to hurt her. I can make the choice.

But if Danu doesn't die, and there is no war between the bandia and the Sons, will Austin still be here for me? Will any of this have happened? Does changing everything mean changing *everything*?

"Wait." Austin doesn't let me go. Is he thinking the same thing? That everything will be different? "This isn't right. You were wearing something else."

"What?"

"You wore a dress. A shimmery gold thing, with one sleeve and a skirt that touched the ground."

"That doesn't sound like anything I own."

Austin looks frustrated. "We didn't talk about where it came from. You just wore it."

"Maybe it was something I got in the past?"

"No. It wasn't of that time. It had a slit on one side that went above your knee. I could see your leg when you walked."

"Okay. I'll go see Shannon at the shop in town."

"It's too risky to go now. The Gathering is too close. Everyone will be restless. The Sons will kill you on sight."

"I obviously make it back to the past for you to see me in the dress, right? It's already happened. I must survive getting the dress."

"Your theory of impossibility?"

"Compossibility. And it's your theory. I still want to believe I can change things." I have to. How many lives could be saved if the war never starts?

Austin pulls me into a deep kiss. I don't want to be anywhere but in the present, soaking up every second and keeping it close. I'm caught off guard, but it only takes a second for my lips to part and let him in. He presses me against the wall so I can feel everywhere our bodies touch.

"What was that for?" I ask through ragged breaths.

He kisses my throat. "You have no idea how much I want you to be right."

"But you don't think I am."

He doesn't say anything. He doesn't have to. His message comes through the urgency of his kiss. We're running out of time.

FORTY-THREE

I look at every dress in the shop, but I don't see anything resembling the dress that Austin described. Maybe it's in Rome. Who's to say we can't come back here? I don't have to go to the ruin now, if I can go later.

Shannon comes out of the back room with an armful of dresses. She smiles as she lays them across the table. "Did it work then? The broomstraw?"

"Like a charm."

She smiles at my joke. "Keep it close. Something's brewing. I can feel it in my bones."

"I will." Even the humans can feel the coming battle as the magic hour approaches.

"Are you looking for something special? These just came in." Shannon holds up a red satin sheath. As she twirls around, I notice a scrap of gold in the pile behind her.

"Do you have a gold one?" My stomach buzzes with anticipation.

Shannon works through the stack and pulls out a yellow dress with gold trim. It has long sleeves and a short golden skirt, nothing like the dress Austin described.

Maybe Austin is wrong about the dress? Or maybe I just don't go back. If Austin is right, and the past can't be avoided, at least I can keep it at bay for a little while longer. The longer I put it off, the longer we'll have.

"You like this one?" Shannon asks.

"I was thinking of something more formal. With one sleeve and a slit up one leg?"

"You have very specific taste."

"Do you have anything like that?" I want her to say no. I want to do more than change the past. I want to change my future.

She shakes her head. "I'll keep an eye out."

As I walk out onto Main Street, I can't help smiling. Austin and I will go to Rome. Maybe Paris. I'll do my senior year of high school in England, apply to MIT. I'll stay far away from the ruin. Have a normal life.

Jonah steps out of an alcove, stopping me in my tracks. "Hi, bandia."

I back up a step.

"What's the matter? I thought you'd be glad to see me."

"There's no place in the known universe where I would be glad to see you." I try to keep the shakiness out of my voice. I'm unarmed and he knows it.

Jonah puts a hand on my shoulder and slides it down

to my elbow, his grip hard. "You won't say that after we've bonded."

Is he serious? Does he still think he can force me into a soul bond? I would never willingly have sex with him. But it's not like Jonah ever cared what I thought. My leg starts to tremble.

"Or can't you bond anymore?" Jonah's smile is terrifying. He leans forward so his breath is in my ear. "I guess there's only one way to find out."

I break from his hold just as Sierra and Mallory step out of the alcove behind him. I don't think I've ever been happy to see Sierra, but I want to kiss every last cherry-red stripe in her dark hair as she throws her arms around Jonah territorially.

"How are you even still here?" Mallory is as charming as ever.

I won't be for much longer. I force a smile. "Magic."

Mallory's heel wobbles in a cobblestone. She catches herself before she falls, but she looks shaken. Not as sure of herself as she wants me to think.

I cross the street before they can say anything more. I talked Austin into letting me come into town to buy this stupid dress, on the theory that I must survive it in order to visit him in the past, but now that I'm almost convinced I can change the present, coming here seems beyond stupid.

I'm nearly to the car when I see Blake. He's sitting alone at a small iron table outside the Ornery Knight, sipping from a tiny espresso mug. He doesn't see me. There's no reason he would—I'm half a block away, and he's looking down the street toward the ocean, his gaze distant.

I should tell him I'm leaving. It's what he wanted. I take a step forward, but stop when Portia emerges from the pub, a rare smile on her face. She turns her head and stares at me, almost as if she knew I'd be here.

Her smile grows wider as she moves toward Blake and wraps her arms around him from behind, leaning forward so her breasts rake the back of his neck and her hands drift down across his chest. He leans his head back and closes his eyes as she kisses him.

I want to turn around and walk the other way, but Jonah is behind me and the Porsche is on the other side of the block. I'll have to walk right past them.

It's my chance to get the necklace. Blake probably wouldn't let Portia kill me, and she might not even try in such a public place. But getting the necklace back, and presumably my power, would mean staying to fight at the Gathering. I'm not ready to concede that Austin and I can't escape all that.

I keep my eye on them as I walk by, knowing better than to turn my back. I can almost feel sorry for them both. From the outside, it's easy to see how miserable they are together. They're both shadows of themselves, their beauty a thin veneer over the dark emotions that eat at them from the inside. Still, there's an ache in my chest when I look at Blake. I don't know if I miss him or just mourn for the piece of my soul that died with him on that beach. The piece of me I lost when I killed him.

Portia looks up at me, her lips twisting into a bleak smile. Blake sees me too, and when our eyes meet, his poker face is nowhere to be seen. I see the murder in his eyes as clearly as if I could feel it in my soul.

I just wish I knew if it was meant for me or Portia.

FORTY-FOUR

Mick opens the front door before I can ring the bell. His normally perfect neckcloth is a twisted mass. "Oh thank the gods!" he says when he sees me. "We have to find Lord Lorcan."

"What do you mean? Isn't he here?"

Mick puts his head in his hands, rubbing his eyes with his palm. "I couldn't stop them."

"Slow down. Stop who?"

"Liam and his witch."

"What happened?"

"I tried to keep them out, but she came through like a tornado. I couldn't stop her."

"And Austin?" I run past Mick, past the cracked marble table that lies on its side, over bits and pieces of broken glass and porcelain.

Mick trails behind me. "They took him."

"Was he—?" I can't bring myself to say the word dead. I can't bear to think it.

"He was breathing." If breathing is the best thing Mick can say about Austin, he must be hurt bad. I should've grabbed that stupid necklace while I had the chance.

"Do you know where they took him?"

Mick collapses in a heap on the floor, amongst the shards and debris. "Liam has been staying at Dunfield Abbey."

"Is that where they went?"

"I don't know. She walloped my head with something heavy. I tried to compel her, but I couldn't think straight."

I grab the keys and run back to the car. Rain spatters the windshield as I pull out of the drive. The car fishtails as I turn onto the road back into town, but I keep my foot on the gas and hang on to the steering wheel as the car skids through the next curve.

I leave the car in front of the Ornery Knight even though the road is not nearly wide enough for parking. Blake and Portia aren't outside anymore. I glance at the bar, but Blake isn't among the smattering of tourists drinking warm Guinness. I go upstairs and pound on his door.

He opens it on the third knock. He looks worse up close. His face is gaunt, his eyes hollow. He pulls me inside and slams the door behind us. "What are you doing here?"

"I need the necklace." *I need my power.*

"What are you talking about?" Blake blinks.

"The necklace you gave me. I need it back. Now."

"Why? Do you need a memento? Because I was under the impression that you'd moved on."

"Please, Blake. I don't have time to argue. Just trust me when I say it's important. I'm asking for your help."

"I'm supposed to trust you now?"

"What's that supposed to mean?" But I know exactly what it means. Nothing has changed. Blake still doesn't trust me, and he's not going to help me. I don't know why I thought that he would.

"Forget it," he says. "And anyway, I can't give it to you. Portia has it."

"I know. I need it back. Please."

"I can't. She'll freak. She hates you."

"This is a matter of life and death. Your girlfriend will get over a stupid necklace."

Blake looks skeptical. "Who's life?"

I look down at the floor.

"It's him, isn't it?"

I meet his gaze head-on. "He has a name."

Blake picks up a cell phone from the nightstand and hurls it at the wall. "I knew it!" He grabs me by the shoulders. "Are you in love with him?"

"Do you really want to have this conversation?" If Blake won't help me get the necklace, I need to find Portia myself.

He drops his hands and sinks down on the bed. Defeated. "He doesn't deserve you."

And Blake has a say, because? He's the one who sent me away. He's the one who won't help me now. He's the one who thought that hooking up with Portia Bruton was a good idea.

"I know about the bond," I say.

He lies back and sighs. "It's unbearable. She's awful. All I feel when I'm around her is anger and bitterness. I'm not even sure she likes me. But she's obsessed with wanting me to love her. She's worse when I see you. I can't hide anything from her."

I know exactly what it felt like to have Blake's emotions tied to my own. How much he could influence what I felt and vice versa. Sharing a soul with Portia couldn't be easy. But I don't have time to talk. I move toward the door.

Blake sits up, pinning me in place with his eyes. "I have to end it. She'll kill me if I don't. One way or another."

"Rush will kill you if you do."

"I can handle Rush."

I nod, even though Blake doesn't look like he could handle a butter knife in his current condition.

He stares at me. "I messed up everything, didn't I?"

"It doesn't matter anymore."

"How can you say that? Of course it matters. I should never have sent you away. I should've come here with you."

At the time, I would've agreed with him. Now, everything is different. What I had with Blake wasn't love. What I have with Austin might be. "I need the necklace."

He looks away. "But not me."

"I have to go." I put my hand on the door. "Be careful, okay?"

When he finally looks at me, a hint of a dimple appears on his cheek. "It's what I get for letting my soul get tangled up with a bandia, right?"

I don't need to ask whether he's talking about Portia or me. It's me he watches walk out the door.

FORTY-FIVE

I search the pub for Portia. I don't find her anywhere and I don't have time for this. I need to come up with a new plan. I call Braden but get his voicemail. I leave a message before jumping into Austin's Porsche and navigating my way to the narrow road that will take me to the village of Dunfield. The sky turns dusky gray. The clouds block out any sunlight, casting everything in murky shadow even though the sun won't set until nearly midnight.

The rain comes down so hard, I barely see the road. I keep my eyes on the faded white line on the left side, hugging it with a tire. I don't have magic, but my fingers curve around the hilt of the broadsword in the passenger seat. It's something.

The white line fades to gray. The road and the forest merge in a curtain of rain and darkness until I can't tell where the road begins or ends. I hit the brakes just as the left front tire drops off the road. I grab the wheel and swerve back to the right. The car spins around hard, sending the back end into a tree with a crunch. Airbags go off around me with a bang that stings all over.

I take inventory as the airbags deflate. My left arm is bruised where one hit. My face feels like I was punched in the nose. Otherwise, I appear to be in one piece. The car is a different story. I try to open the door, but it doesn't move. I have to smash the driver's side window with the heel of my boot and climb out through the opening. The left headlight lights up the driving rain for about two feet before the shaft of light is swallowed by darkness.

I drag the sword out through the window and move away from the car. I'm soaking wet, but I've seen enough car explosions in movies to want to keep my distance. I wait on the side of the road. It doesn't look like anyone else was foolish enough to drive down this narrow, curvy road in this weather. I start walking toward Dunfield.

The farther I get from the car, the darker the road becomes. The trees on either side would block out the light if there was any, but the driving rain ensures there's none. It's not until the rain lets up to a slow drizzle that I even make out the gray line in the road. I'm still at least six kilometers from Dunfield. I'd make better time without the sword, but I clutch the hilt tighter. I won't have a chance of rescuing Austin without some sort of weapon.

A twig snaps in the forest to my left. I drop into a stance and bring the sword front and center as I turn toward the sound. A flash of light is visible through the branches.

"Who's there?" I call.

There's a movement, and a beautiful white horse comes through the trees. Braden. I want to throw my arms around his neck, but I'm still clutching the sword. I lean the blade on the ground. "You got my message."

He drops to his knees so I can climb onto his back. I set the sword across my lap and grab a handful of mane as he trots and then canters along the side of the road. Eventually he turns off the main road, up a long drive that leads to a huge church and an even larger building behind it. It looks like a castle, but I assume it's the abbey.

A giant stone cross stands between the two buildings. This is where Liam is staying? It would be odd, since it was the church and the crusades that brought the Milesians to Ireland. But then, Liam is the type who cares more about appearance than substance. The abbey is at least as grand as Lorcan Hall. Grander.

As I slide off Braden's back, I can't help glancing at his tail. He looks exactly like a regular horse except for his tail, which is covered in fur and ends in fins like a whale's. It's strange and beautiful.

The horse disappears, fading into white light, and Brandon appears in its place. "So what's the plan?" he asks.

"I guess I should start by finding out where they're holding him. My best chance is to sneak in and break him out without them knowing."

"The abbey is huge." Braden glances up at one of the tall towers that flank either side. "But I'm guessing Liam is a traditionalist. If Austin is their prisoner, he'll be in the dungeon."

"There's a dungeon? In an abbey? I thought monks were peaceful types who transcribed books."

Braden laughs. "You're such an American."

"Hey. So are you."

"Salvation came to Ireland on the blade of a sword. There's nothing peaceful about the history of religion here. You're on the front lines of a war that's never really ended."

"So the dungeon's where? In a basement?"

Braden points to a turret reaching high above the stone walls. "Actually, the Celts liked towers."

"How do I get up there?"

"Through the front door." Braden smiles. "Mikel called in reinforcements."

We huddle under an eave behind the church. The rain stops, but the wind batters my wet clothes. I'm cold from the outside in. I reach inside myself for fire, for warmth, but it's locked up tight. All I can do is stare at the tower and shiver.

A car turns from the road and rolls into the drive. It turns off its lights and pulls around the back. Mick, Joe, and Sam step out. It's funny to see the three giolla together. They're all tall, a good three inches over six feet. Joe's pompadour makes him look even taller, and Mick's ginger mutton chops make him look older. Sam looks close to normal, but his eyes are the weariest, as if keeping up with the times has taken its toll. They're dressed in identical black trench coats that hit them mid-calf.

I can't resist smiling. "So, you guys hang out?"

"Is there something odd about that?" Sam asks.

"Aren't you all on different sides?" Mick has been Austin's caretaker, on the side of the gods, while Joe is the Sons' historian. Sam hangs with the fuath.

Joe shakes his head. "It's not our fight. Never has been."

"Then why are you helping me now?" As far as I know, a giolla has never aligned with the bandia.

Sam pats Mick's back. "Technically, we're helping Mick."

"Oh."

"If it makes you feel any better, I'm here for you," Braden says.

Joe puts a hand on my shoulder and squeezes it lightly. I smile at him in the darkness. I don't miss how he scans my collarbone for the necklace.

"I tried." I hope he doesn't see the guilt behind my eyes as I say the words.

Joe lifts his chin and looks back up at the abbey. "Let's go."

Braden and I fall in behind the giolla. They march up to the front door and ring the bell. I feel silly, clutching the sword like I'm ready for battle, but I'm not leaving it behind.

A heavyset woman in a gray uniform pushes the door open a few inches and peeks at us through the crack. "We're closed. Tours are on Tuesdays." Her words are clipped, but her voice has a tinge of desperation to it.

Mick waves a hand in front of her face. "We're here for the boy. You want to help us."

She steps aside and opens the door the rest of the way. "Poor thing."

Mick stares at the woman like he's looking right through

her. "He's in the tower," he murmurs. "In pretty bad shape, if her memories are accurate."

I push past Sam, but Joe stops me before I can run ahead. "Easy. It's a long way between here and there. We'll get him."

As we turn down a hallway, a man runs up to us. "You can't be here now."

Sam holds out his hand, and the man immediately steps back without saying another word.

"Show off," Mick says.

Joe takes a cigarette out of his pocket and sticks it in his mouth. He gestures toward an alcove in the corner. We fall in step behind him, moving single file to the winding stairway.

We climb up and up and up. Every fifty steps or so there's an opening onto another level, but we climb higher. After we pass the sixth opening, I start to wonder how much higher we'll have to go. My wet jeans chafe against my skin and my quads are screaming at me with every step.

I stop on the eighth landing. Braden looks over his shoulder. "You coming?"

I wave him forward. The giolla are already half a flight ahead. "I just need to catch my breath. I'll be right there."

He shakes his head and calls up the stairs. "Sam, hold up."

I lean back against the wall, and suck in a breath. I really wish my training had focused less on trying to access my power and more on cardio.

I barely feel the shift in the stones behind me. I stand up straight, thinking I'm dizzy from being out of breath. Then a hand grabs my arm and yanks me back. Hard.

I expect to slam against the wall, but there's nothing but darkness. Then the wall closes back into place in front of me and everything is black.

FORTY-SIX

One arm is around my waist, another is clamped down on my neck, choking the air out of my lungs. I slash the air with my sword, but the threat is behind me.

"You bandia are so predictable." Liam's thick accent cuts through the darkness. "I knew you wouldn't be able to stay away."

He jerks my wrist and the sword falls to the ground with a clatter. I'm dragged down a winding pathway that seems to go on forever before it finally levels off. Liam keeps his arm tight around my throat. Just when I think I'll pass out, he leans back against a wall and a crack of light appears behind us as a doorway opens against his weight. He lets me go, and I stumble into a candlelit room.

I move away, gulping in the incense-infused air. We're inside a small church, with rows of empty pews and a huge stone crucifix carved into the back wall. Sherri stands at the altar, her dark hair piled on her head in an elaborate arrangement of loose curls. She wears a long red dress that flows to the floor, the same one she wore the night Sasha died. She holds a small dagger in her right hand, waving it in the air as she mumbles a series of Gaelic words I can't understand.

She sees me and stops, holding the knife suspended in the air. "I was getting worried you weren't going to make it in time." Her smile is terrifying.

"Be quick about it," Liam says, pushing me forward.

Sherri pins a loose strand of hair into the mass of curls. "It will take them hours to search the abbey. No one saw us move him here."

Him. Austin. "Where is he?" I move forward without any prompting from Liam.

Sherri points the knife at the altar. A white blanket covers a lumpy form.

I run forward, grabbing the blanket and throwing it off. Austin lies on his side, curled in a fetal position. He's stripped down to his boxer briefs, his face swollen and dotted with angry bruises. Blood runs from his lip to his chin. His eyes are closed, but his chest rises and falls with his breath.

Sherri runs her free hand through Austin's hair, pushing it away from his face. "Such a shame," she says. "He really is beautiful."

My gaze follows the knife in her other hand. "What are you doing to him?"

She lowers the knife to her side. "As it turns out, nothing."

I feel Liam's hand on my hair, gathering it behind my neck. "The spell will be stronger coming from you."

I jerk away, breaking his hold. Austin stirs on the altar. He moans and tries to lift his head without success, letting it fall back onto the marble with a thud. He opens his left eye, but his right eye is swollen shut. "About bloody time," he says.

I brush a finger across his puffy cheek, pulling my hand away when I see him flinch. "I'll get you out of here," I whisper.

Austin swallows. "Save yourself."

Liam grabs my wrist. "Don't worry. You'll put him out of his misery in just a minute. But you can't perform the ritual looking like that." He nods at Sherri.

Sherri looks me up and down, taking in my still-wet hair and clothes. "Jesus, Paxton. Did you swim here?" She bends over and pulls a white gauzy cloth from a bag at her feet, throwing it at my chest. I clutch it out of instinct. "Change into that. And do something with your hair."

Sherri is still holding the knife in her hand. There's no way I can get to her before she could hurt Austin. Not to mention that she's got all the powers of a Seventh Daughter, and I've got no weapons and no plan. My best hope is to stall them until the giollas and Braden find us.

I place a hand on Austin's shoulder and give him what I hope is a reassuring squeeze. Then I walk behind a screen on the left side of the altar and change into the dress Sherri gave me. It's too big, hanging low across my chest. The skirt brushes the stone floor. There are no pockets, so I take the little packet of broomstraw from my jeans and tuck it into my bra. I plait my hair into a thick braid that stretches to the middle of my back, taking as long as I can.

Liam steps around the screen. "Enough. This will have to do." He grabs my arm, his fingers pressing so hard I'm sure I'll have a bruise.

Sherri points to a huge book open on the pulpit. "She'll need to learn the words."

"There's no time. The ritual must be done at least forty-eight hours before the Gathering or it will be of no use." Liam pulls me until I stand directly in front of Austin. "She can repeat after you." He takes the knife from Sherri, forces it into my hands, and covers my hands with his own, applying so much pressure it's a wonder my fingers don't break. He holds the knife above Austin.

I kick and thrash against his hold. I can't get any leverage. Liam is too strong for me to do any real damage.

"Don't worry, bandia. Your affection for Arawn will not be wasted. A blood sacrifice is only as powerful as the bond that is severed. The higher the price, the greater the reward."

"For the love of all that is sacred," Sherri says.

I twist and try again to break free of Liam's hold, but he pulls me hard against his chest.

Austin rolls onto his back. "Did you go to the ruin yet?"

"No."

"Good," he whispers. "You will live." He closes his eyes again.

"You will too," I say, but Liam has moved my hand so the knife is directly above Austin's heart.

Austin grins up at me through his split lip. "Let him do it, Brianna."

What? Has Austin lost his mind? I am not going to let Liam force me to kill him.

Liam laughs. "Even Arawn recognizes that he is worth more to the cause dead."

Austin winks the eye that isn't swollen. "*A thousand years of otherworldly night,*" he says, quoting the spell I used to banish him to the underworld. Does he think that Liam's role in his death will lead to Liam's banishment? He might be right, but I'm not about to let him die to find out.

"No," I whisper. We'll find another way; I can get Liam to the gateway. If I can get the necklace back, I can use the banishment spell on Liam.

"For the love of all that is sacred," Sherri says again, more emphatic this time.

"Say it," Liam growls in my ear. "You'll be doing him a favor. If he dies as a tribute, he will be given a special place in Avalon. Will you leave his soul to fade with the masses?"

I can't fight Liam off. So I go with the truth. "I can't do it. I don't have magic."

Liam laughs. "That has been painfully obvious for some time. This is your chance to make yourself useful. The blood of the deity who once ruled the gods will be a powerful sacrifice in itself, but your loss will be personal. Blood magic doesn't require anything more than that. It thrives on suffering."

Sherri steps forward, wind whipping around her skirts,

and another curl of hair falls into her face. "We're running out of time."

Austin raises an eyebrow, then winches at the pain. "You did say this would end badly."

"I never said that. You did."

"Shut up!" Sherri sends a blast of wind so powerful that Austin flies off the altar, straight at Liam and me.

Liam lets go of me to get out of the way. I can't do anything but put my arms out and toss the knife away as Austin crashes into me. We fall to the floor in a heap.

My elbow hits first, slamming against the stone. My back hits next. Austin lands on top of me. He barely gets his arms out to break his fall, but he rolls to the side when we hit, doing his best to minimize the impact.

I struggle for breath. Pain shoots from the center of my shoulder blades. I scream out before I realize I'm breathing again.

Sherri stands over me, her hands lit with blue fire. "You are such a disappointment."

Austin rolls onto his stomach and stretches toward the dagger. I try to distract Sherri. "A disappointment? To you?"

Sherri sends a ball of flame at the dagger just as Austin reaches it. He pulls his hand back with a gasp. "To every Seventh Daughter that came before. You are a pathetic girl who lets stupid crushes take precedence over everything else. When the gods are back you can have any boy you want, but for now you must do what you were born for."

I clutch at my chest, fumbling for the little packet of broomstraw. It's not a weapon, but it is a shield. Once I have it, I clench my teeth against the pain in my shoulder and crawl until I'm directly in front of Austin, between him and Sherri. It takes all my concentration to plant my feet and pull myself up off the ground. I stand to face her. "I'm the only one who gets to decide what I was born for."

Sherri's smile is hideously beautiful. She raises a fiery hand in my direction. "Then I guess I get to decide what you die for."

The ball of fire comes at me so fast, I barely register the blue blur before it slams against my chest and explodes in a burst of purple and indigo. The force of the blast sends me backward. I hit the ground hard, but my chest feels okay. No burning and no pain. Not even a hint of smoke or flame on the white dress. I push myself up on my elbows. "Or not."

Her smile falters. "What the … how did you do that?"

"Stop!" Liam roars from behind Sherri. He moves past me and grabs Sherri by the neck. "Her fate is not yours to decide."

Nice of him to step in *after* Sherri landed her fireball.

Sherri's eyes are huge as Liam throws her against the altar. "I alone decide whose blood will spill." Apparently I'm worth something now that I've survived a shot to the heart.

Liam spins around, abruptly letting his hands fall from Sherri. I stand up, doing my best to deflect his attention away from where Austin still lies.

Liam's eyes are wild. "I've underestimated you."

I hear Austin moving behind me, but I keep my gaze on Liam. "Not my problem."

He narrows his eyes at me. "You have magic."

The doors to the church swing open. Braden, Joe, Sam, and Mick come through all at once.

I smile. "I have something better. I have friends."

FORTY-SEVEN

Liam takes in the trio of giolla walking calmly up the aisle. He grabs Sherri by the waist and drags her in front of him like a shield.

Joe lifts his chin slightly. "Liam."

Liam shrinks back, even though Joe hasn't done anything remotely aggressive. Then he catches himself, thrusting his chest out to try and cover. His eyes flit from Sam to Mick. "Only three of you left?"

Joe takes a new pack of cigarettes from the pocket of his coat and taps it against his palm. "It's no concern of yours."

"Isn't it? You've failed so badly that nearly all the demi-gods are extinct."

Failed? At what?

"Not all." Joe tears at the plastic wrapper around the pack.

Liam stands straighter. "Three bandia. And of those,

only one is worth anything. The others fell prey to that damn bonding curse. But it hardly matters. We will bring back the gods and restore balance to the earth."

Austin struggles to his feet behind me. Once he gets upright, his arms wrap around my waist. It's not clear if he's holding me or if I'm holding him up. Either way, it's a relief to feel his warmth.

Joe stuffs the plastic wrapper in his pocket. "It's not your place to question our methods. We have prevented chaos. And we will continue to do so." He walks around Liam, toward Austin and me. He places his hand on Austin's forehead and whispers something in Gaelic. "Now, there are more."

Austin stands up straighter behind me.

Joe looks from Austin to Liam. "You tread very close to the line."

Liam curls his upper lip into a sneer. "I am well aware of my limitations. I haven't killed anyone."

Joe takes out a cigarette and puts the pack into the front pocket of his long coat. "Killing is not the only sin that leads to banishment. I suggest you watch yourself." He nods to Austin.

Austin takes my hand and leads me through the church, past Liam and Sherri, past Sam and Mick. Austin's gait is surprisingly smooth considering the beating he's taken. Braden holds the door open for us, winking at us as we walk across the threshold.

I glance up at Austin as we get into the giollas' car. Dried blood still stains his chin, but there's no sign of the cut on his lip. Both his eyes are open and clear. The bruising on his face is already faded to a light shade of brown and getting lighter. I bring my finger to his cheek just as the last of his injuries disappear.

"How did you do that?"

"Magic." He laces his fingers with mine. "Either Joe is really pissed at Liam or he wants to make sure I'm at the Gathering. He gave me access to my power."

"I don't understand." Joe gave Austin access to his power? How? Joe is a freaking historian.

The car doors open and Mick slides into the back seat with us. Joe and Sam take the front.

"Where's Braden?" I ask Mick.

"You see room for a bloody waterhorse?"

"Watch it, Mick." Sam turns around to face us. "That bloke is my charge."

Mick waves him off. "Don't look at me. I'm not the one who returned magic to a sodding god so he could fight a bloody war."

Joe puts the key in the ignition. "Don't think you can call him a god anymore, regardless."

Mick snorts from the seat next to us. Austin squeezes my hand.

"What the hell just happened?" I look at the four boys in the car.

"Joe restored Austin's magic," Mick says. "It's our job to keep the balance, and Liam had too damn much power."

I try to process this. "Just what kind of magic do you guys have?"

"We have only what we need," Joe says from the front seat. "When we need it."

Austin laughs. "I don't know whether to love you or hate you."

Joe stares at the road. "It's not my concern."

Mick takes my other hand and squeezes it, and it dawns on me what Austin meant when he said that Joe wanted to ensure that he was at the Gathering. Austin has his power back—he won't be able to ignore the Gathering. He's back on the front lines of the war, whether he wants to be or not.

In this case, restoring the balance meant arming a soldier for battle.

I don't say anything as we drive the rest of the way to Lorcan Hall. The mess Liam made has already been cleaned up. The table in the front entry even has a new vase on it, complete with fresh flowers.

Austin doesn't let go of my hand as he leads me down the hall and up the stairs. He doesn't stop until we're inside his room with the door shut and locked behind us.

"What the hell were you thinking, coming after me like that?" he asks.

"That I couldn't let them hurt you?" *That I couldn't bear to lose you.*

"And you were going to stop them, how?" Austin raises his voice. "With logic and reason?"

"I had a sword. You taught me how to use it. I didn't realize I was supposed sit back and let them kill you." Not that I ever could.

The little creases between his eyebrows are back. "It helps no one if we're both dead."

"Stop acting like a whiny, domineering god. Just because you got your power back doesn't mean you can start bossing me around."

"Is that what you think I'm doing?"

"Aren't you?"

"Maybe." He flops down on the leather couch, still dressed in only his underwear. "Since when do you care what happens to me?"

I feel caged. Trapped. "What?"

"I'm the bastard that got you to kill your boyfriend, remember?"

"Why are you bringing this up?" He's really going to do this now? He has to know that things have changed between us. Of course he does—he told me he loves me, and we both know that I haven't exactly said it back. He wants to force my hand.

"And you tried to kill me yourself," Austin goes on. "Now you want to save me?" His eyes are pained, accusing. "You can't help me anymore. Your power is gone. You need to get out of here while you still can."

"I won't let you fight by yourself." The words come easily. Why can't I just admit that what I feel for him is something more than like. More than lust.

"That's the stupidest thing you've ever said." Austin's face turns haughty. He looks every bit the obnoxious god I used to loathe. "I've got powers now. I'll be fine. You won't survive five minutes."

"I won't leave you."

"Why not, Brianna?" Austin is on his feet again, stalking me like a predator. I back up until the wall stops me. He keeps coming closer, until his bare chest nearly touches me. "Why won't you leave me?"

I reach up to rub away the dried blood that still sticks to his chin.

"Why?" he asks again.

I know what he wants, but I can't give it to him. I want to be with him—these last few weeks have been perfect—and can't that be enough? At least for now? "Don't make me say it," I whisper.

I stretch up to kiss him and he kisses me back, pressing me into the wall. Into him. His tongue thrusts into my mouth with a force that steals my breath.

"God, Brianna," he says, his breath hot in my ear. He licks a line of kisses down my neck and along my collarbone, pushing a gauzy sleeve off my shoulder. "You were magnificent. I've never seen anyone, human or god, act so brave."

"I thought—"

"Shh." He lifts his head and meets my gaze. "I didn't get this chance at life so I could watch you die, Brianna. Don't take chances with your life for mine."

"I'm not letting you go to the Gathering by yourself."

"Tomorrow, and tomorrow, and tomorrow." He slides the sleeve of the dress from my other shoulder, baring me to him. "We have all of tonight before we need to worry about tomorrow. I've waited over a thousand years for these moments

with you, and I don't plan on wasting another second."
His lips blaze a trail to my breast.

I tangle my hands in his hair and pull him closer.

I can't give him the words, but I can give him tonight.
For now, it's enough for both of us.

FORTY-EIGHT

In the morning, Mick greets me in the kitchen with a steaming mug of coffee. I walk past him and pour a cup of tea.

He pushes the mug at me again. "I made it with the steamed milk you always say you miss. And some vanilla syrup."

"You've been pushing tea on me since I got here. I'm kind of used to it now."

Mick lifts the corners of his lips in that almost-smile. "So I guess bribery is out."

"Since when do you need to bribe me?"

He sits down at the counter across from me. "What if I told you there was a way to stop the war? To prevent the battle that Liam has planned from ever going forward?"

"I'm listening."

"Last night, Joe told me about a bandia and a Son of

Killian who bonded and lived to tell about it." Mick passes me a bowl of sugar cubes.

Me and Blake. "Old news."

"But it's never happened before. The bond always ends in death. Always."

"Didn't Joe tell you that part? It did. End in death, I mean."

"It *should've* ended there." Mick gazes at me thoughtfully. "In the normal course of things. At the end, the bandia and the Son always want the other one dead. They pray for it. But you brought him back. Even after sharing a soul, you cared enough about the son of a bitch to bring him back."

"It doesn't mean anything."

"It means everything."

"You're losing me."

Mick picks one of the sugar cubes out of the bowl and turns it over in his hand. "The result of the bandia's curse was that the Sons and bandia could never really love each other. They could feel only feel lust."

"Loost?"

He laughs at my bad translation of his accent. "Attraction. Not love."

"Got it." I watch the cube of sugar dissolve in my tea. "Been there. Done that."

"You and Blake, however ... you didn't grow to hate each other. You grew to care for each other. It's the only explanation for why you both lived."

"We weren't in love." The sugar disappears in my tea, the brown liquid absorbing it as easily as my words absorb the lie.

"Your souls didn't try to overpower each other, either. You had something more. You survived the bond. I think that together, you could change everything."

"What are you saying?"

"That you and Blake—if you gave it a chance—could break the curse once and for all and bring the bandia and Sons together again. End the war."

"I love Austin." The words come so easily in the light of day.

Mick closes his fist around the sugar cube, crushing it into powder. "I love him too." When he looks at me, his eyes are wet. "But this is bigger than him. You can stop the bloodshed. You cared for Blake once, enough to keep the soul bond from eating you alive. That is the most powerful magic I know."

"No." I meant it when I said I wouldn't leave Austin. I want to spend my life, whatever's left of it, with him. "If you care about Austin, you won't ask me do this."

"Just consider it. Joe is not wrong about things like this."

I walk out of the kitchen without looking back.

Austin is waiting on the other side of the door. His face is a mask of indifference, but the crease between his brows is there.

I bring my hand to his forehead and smooth the crease away. "How much of that did you hear?"

"Enough."

"Enough to know that it doesn't matter."

He grabs me by the shoulders. "It should. If Mick is

right, you could end the war. Unite the Sons and stop Liam. It's what you want."

"You're what I want."

He pulls me to him, holding me against him. "You could stop a bloody war."

"I couldn't."

"I don't understand. Mick said—"

"Maybe Blake and I could have loved each other once. Too much has happened. And I don't know if you've noticed, but Blake has bonded himself to another bandia. And before that, he sent me away, knowing the Sons would try to kill me." I run my fingers in the wild curls at the back of his neck. "And then I found you."

"He would take you back if he could."

"He wouldn't." *And I wouldn't have him.*

"I would."

"Yeah, but you're a flipping lunatic who doesn't know how to handle human emotions."

Austin laughs into my neck. And then I kiss the smile right off his face.

We have to find another way.

FORTY-NINE

Austin and I spend the day like the weeks before it. We take the horses for a gallop in the large field and race back to the barn. The last of the daylight clings to the sea as we spar with swords near the edge of the bluff.

"Keep your sword up." There's an edge to Austin's coaching tonight. We both know that I have little time left to get it right. The Gathering is tomorrow.

I block his swing with the blade, and then spin around so my sword comes flying at his chest before he can regain his balance. He barely has time to disappear in a flash of gold light before my sword would have sliced his chest.

He reappears behind me.

"Was that okay?" I ask, slightly breathless.

"Just okay? Shouldn't we be aiming a little higher?"

I laugh.

"It's a good thing I have my power back or you might've really hurt me. Perhaps we should take a break for now."

We lay down our swords. Austin takes my hand, leading me along one of the stone paths and down a trail to a plateau about twenty feet above the beach. A firepit has already been filled with a roaring fire. At least a hundred candles in glass cylinders line the pathway down to the ocean, growing brighter as the sun slips behind the sea.

"This is beautiful," I say.

Austin sits down on the low wall that faces the sea below, pulling me into his lap. His hands rub up and down my arms as he looks up at the sky. Stars peek through a break in the clouds. "I never get tired of gazing at the heavens."

"You like stars." I'm reminded of the glow-in-the-dark stars stuck to the ceiling of his room back in Rancho Domingo. Of the first time Austin kissed me there. My first kiss.

"A wise person once told me that the stars are distant suns, each one watching over its own worlds. The stars remind me that we are all small. Even the gods."

"Is this humility? Because it feels like a new thing for you."

"We can't forget that no matter how strong we think we are, there is always someone or something stronger." The firelight dances around Austin's face, worshipping.

"You can access your power now."

"But I remain mortal." He runs his thumb over my wrist. "My heart bleeds as well as any." His touch ignites a fire inside me, a flicker of heat that draws me closer. He looks past me, to the sea. "The ocean reminds me of you."

"Of me?"

A wave crests over a boulder, sending a spray of sea water in all directions. "Beautiful, fierce, deadly."

"I'm not sure how to take that."

"You've always been strong, Brianna. As powerful as the elements you command."

It's what I've felt since we got here. The wildness of this place speaks to something deep inside me. Yet now, without any power running through my veins, I feel tiny. Invisible. Like I could disappear into the landscape without anyone realizing I was gone. "I don't feel so strong these days."

"Don't doubt yourself. Not many people would risk their mortal life to save someone who has already lived for too long." He brings his finger to my lips, tracing the line of my mouth. "To save me."

"Strength or stupidity?"

"Courage. You stood against me when you believed I was wrong. You stand against Liam and an army of Sons now. It's not your power that gives you strength." He drops his finger to the center of my chest. "Your strength comes from here." His thumbnail grazes across my collarbone, scratching a promise into my skin. "We may only have tonight."

I feel tears sting at my eyes. "We can't stop the Gathering, but I'm still planning on getting us out alive."

"I like your plan."

"But?"

He brings his hand to my cheek, running his fingers

through my hair until they rest at the back of my neck. "For tonight, I am going to live one hundred and ten percent in the here and now." He lowers his face to mine until I can feel the warmth of his breath on my cheek, taste the salt of his skin on my lips. I kiss his cheek and his neck and his ear and his mouth, and then he kisses me and I am lost, lost, lost.

"Ahem." Someone clears their throat.

Austin and I pull apart. I leap off his lap and turn to face the intruder.

Blake stands in front of us, his blond hair wild and sticking out in every direction at once. He wears a pair of dark jeans and a U.R.D. sweatshirt that reminds me of home. He looks thinner than he did yesterday, his cheeks sunken in. It's impossible to tell if it's the night or if there are more shadows under his eyes, but he looks like he hasn't slept in days. His smile is a grimace, a painted-on artifice that's more grotesque than real.

"I'd ask to join you, but I think Portia might smite me down on the spot." His laugh is hard.

Austin stands and puts himself between Blake and me. "You shouldn't be here."

Blake takes another step toward us. "Says who? Didn't Brie tell you that she came to ask for my help? She needed me, and now I'm here."

Austin looks back at me, his eyes full of something that looks like panic. "You asked for his help?" His voice is quieter than it should be. I barely hear him over the sound of the waves as they crush boulders into tiny pebbles.

"Yesterday. You were in trouble. I didn't know what else to do."

Austin keeps his eyes on the ground as he reaches for my hand and squeezes. "You could still change things."

"No." He can't seriously think I could go back to Blake. Not now.

"Think about it, Brianna. An end to the war." Austin lets go of my hand and turns back up the trail.

I rush after him. "Austin!"

Blake grabs my arm. I pull away, but Blake's words stop me. "I've got the necklace."

FIFTY

"What?" I ask. Austin is getting farther away. I need to explain.

"The necklace," Blake says again. "You said it was a matter of life and death. Although the guy looks healthy to me."

I turn to face him. "Portia gave it back?"

"No." His eyes spark silver. "I took it."

I look back up the path. Austin has already disappeared onto the bluff.

"Damn it, Brie." I don't need to see the vein on the side of his neck to know what this costs him. "I got the necklace. It's what you wanted."

"Did you kill her?" I can't believe I have to ask.

"No." His eyes are hard. "Would it matter if I did?"

I don't know the answer to that question and it scares the hell out of me. "Can I see it?"

He reaches into the pocket of his jeans and thrusts his

hand at me. There's no way to avoid touching him as I take the broken chain. Our eyes meet as my fingers brush his palm. I wait for a shock of heat where our skin brushes, but there's nothing but a sad familiarity. A dimple appears on Blake's cheek, but his smile is eclipsed by the shadows in his eyes.

I listen to the sounds of the waves as I close my hand around the wolfsbane pendant. The elements assault my senses in a rush. The ocean pounds through me in beats I feel from the inside. The chill of the air and the damp of the sea converge in my blood, flowing through me in icy waves. Power rages against my chest like an inferno, stronger and more insistent than I remember it. I reach out to a passing breeze, curling it around me until my hair blows wildly.

Blake looks stricken.

I stop the wind.

"Do you remember the first night we went to the beach?" he asks.

"Of course." Our first date. The night we bonded.

"You did that same thing with your hair when I kissed you." He reaches for my hair, taking a curl between his fingers. For a second, I see the boy I knew, looking at me like I was the most beautiful girl he'd ever seen. Making me believe it. Is it possible to go back? Could we have found a way to love each other? But we tried. Blake didn't trust me.

I step back. "Don't."

He drops his hand. "When did I become the invisible one?"

I rub the silver pendant between my fingers. A thousand words hang in the air between us, none of them right.

It's impossible to see Blake the way I used to. Too much has happened.

"Thank you," I finally say, holding the necklace to my chest.

I notice a shift in the air. Before I can find its source, a blast of wind hits me square in the chest, pushing me off my feet. The momentum sends me off the plateau and into the empty air. The rocks below wait to catch me in their jagged jaws.

I grasp for my own connection to the wind. I call it until it flows beneath me in spirals, spinning faster and faster, creating a cushion of air that slows and then stops my fall a few feet from the beach below. I lower myself to the ground and make my way to the switchback trail that will bring me back up.

There's a silver flash above my head. I start to run. If Blake is as weak as he looks, he's going to need help.

I crest the bluff at the trailhead, north of where I went over, trying to stay in the shadows. Blake is in his demigod form, illuminated by silver light, draped in his family plaid. He looks more like himself in this form, his hollow cheeks no longer visible. He stands with his broadsword raised, his eyes shining. He looks like an angel of death as he circles his prey:

Portia.

She sends an arc of blue flame sailing at him. Blake disappears before it hits him. He reappears at the plateau where I fell, looking down over the rocks.

"Oh, poor baby." Portia struts across the grass, even more gorgeous than usual. She's dressed in a long black dress with soft sleeves that stretch to her wrists. Her chestnut hair glows auburn in the silver light. She looks every bit as strong and powerful as Blake had looked weak and depleted, almost as if she's been draining him. "Pining for your ex-girlfriend until the very last." She sends another fireball in Blake's direction, aiming squarely for the middle of his chest.

Blake vanishes in a flash. The fire hits the ground, sending bits of rock up in a blue blast. He reappears twenty feet away. "You're going to have to try harder than that, bandia." He says the word like a curse.

Portia moves down the trail. "Why wasn't I ever good enough?"

"Maybe it would help if you didn't hate me so much." Blake's voice is almost musical in this form, making the words sound soothing. He looks over the edge again. He doesn't see Portia raise her hand. The earth shakes beneath his feet, knocking him to the ground before he can dematerialize. Portia aims a ball of blue flame at Blake's prone form.

"Stop!" I yell, drawing her eye away from Blake before she can make a lethal strike. The split second is all Blake needs to recover and disappear again.

Portia sends the fire at me instead. I throw up a wall of water. The fire disappears in a hiss of steam. The wind shifts. I meet it with a healthy blast of my own before it can hit me. The two forces create a mini tornado, sending glass and candles smashing to the ground.

A flash of gold light from the house thrusts the bluff into near daylight before it goes dark again. Then it's bright again as Austin appears behind Portia, his knife at her throat. "Stand down." He gaze flits around wildly until he spots me.

Portia drops her hands to her sides. I take a tentative step toward her, picking my way through the shattered glass. Blake reappears next to her, so she is flanked by silver and gold.

I can't stop staring at Austin. I've gotten so used to seeing him as a mere human, it's a shock to see him in all his power. The golden rays that surround him cast him in soft, warm light. He's like a piece of art come to life, a monument to beauty, strength, and love. I can't help the smile that crosses my lips. He raises an eyebrow in question. I'm not sure what he's asking, but I'm pretty sure the answer is yes. A million times yes.

Blake's melodic voice falters. "I don't believe it."

Portia looks from me to Austin. "Serves you right, lover." Her laugh is giddy.

"And you said I could never make you happy." Blake glares at Portia. "Glad my torment is working for you."

Portia is enjoying Blake's pain?

Austin disappears and appears again at my side in human form. "Perhaps you two can take your little spat elsewhere?"

Portia shakes her head. "We have some baggage we need to dispose of." She smiles at me. "Time to exorcise the ghost of bondings past."

Austin stands in front of me. "I should be more clear. Get off my property."

Portia rolls her eyes. "You don't get it, do you? It ends tonight." I feel the rumbling in the ocean floor before she even raises her hands over her head. Blake and Austin disappear at once, just as Portia charges me.

The ground shakes so hard I'm knocked on my back. A wave of water crests the bluff and hits me with such force I'm carried on its tide until my shoulder hits a boulder with a crack. I'm held against the stone by the surge of water. It relents for less than a second before I'm pulled over, spinning in the waves as the water retreats to the sea, carrying me with it.

I'm so dizzy that I lose sight of which way is up and which is down. I feel a tugging at my wrist and reach toward it, but no one's there. Something jerks on the chain in my hand. I pull back, desperate to hang on to my necklace, my power. I feel the ocean and do my best to calm the seas, but I'm fighting against Portia's control and the most I can manage is to create a counter-current that results in a whirlpool.

I tighten my grip around the chain, but it's slipping through my fingers. It's no use. Whatever grabbed the chain is strong, and it's not letting go. I'm running out of breath. I absolutely can't let go of the necklace. Not now that I finally have my power back.

My skin burns as the chain is ripped from my hand. I stare into the waters, but I can't see anything in the darkness.

A hand grabs my hair, pulling my head up and through the surface. I breathe in gulps of air as the water calms around me.

"You didn't think it would be that easy, did you?" Portia pulls me to shore, keeping hold of my knotted hair as she drags me up the path. "I want him to see you die." She stops near the soggy firepit. Broken candles litter the wet ground.

The firepit erupts in blue flames.

Portia grins as Blake appears in front of us. "Just in time to watch your witch burn."

Blake steps forward, then stops, watching the blue flame arc from Portia's hand as it hovers near my shoulder.

"Uh uh, lover."

Austin runs up behind me. "Brianna, thank—"

I need to give him an opening. The heat from Portia's fingers licks at my shoulder. "Do you think killing me will make Blake love you?"

"You think he's capable of love?" She waves the flame against my shirt. The wet material smolders and smokes, but doesn't catch fire. She doesn't take her eyes off the two boys. "Don't come any closer."

I raise a knee to her thigh and push her shoulders, knocking her away just as Austin and Blake disappear. They materialize on either side of her but she throws up a wall of flame, forcing them back. The blue flames in the firepit go out. Portia backs up a step before her gaze settles on Blake. "Did you just try to kill me?"

Blake flashes that dimpled, haven't-got-a-care-in-the-world smile. "Next time I won't miss."

Portia's face changes from fury to shock to tears in the span of a few seconds. She sits down on the wet, littered ground and buries her face in her hands. When she finally looks up, her eyes are red and swollen. "Well, what are you waiting for?"

Blake kneels down in front of her, leaning on his sword. "We could just go our separate ways. Like Killian and Danu. I could leave and—"

Portia shrieks and jumps to her feet. "You don't get it. You are ruined. You don't even have the decency to kill me and put me out of my misery. There was a time when you would've killed a bandia without thinking twice. Does my father know what a pathetic excuse for a Son you've become?"

Blake's face turns dark despite the glowing silver light, his anger rising along with Portia's. "Do you really think we should kill just because we can? Brianna is no threat to the human race. She never was. And I've seen every dark corner of your soul, but I still want to believe you'll make the right decision when the time comes. We're not our ancestors. We can make our own choices."

Black clouds gather above us, blocking out the stars. A bolt of blue lightning shoots down to the ocean with a jagged crack, illuminating the sea in an eerie shade of indigo. Rain starts coming in fat drops that scatter across the yard.

"You were supposed to choose me," Portia says, tears mingling with the rain on her cheeks. She turns and runs up the path, disappearing into the darkness.

I hope Blake is right about Portia. She may be a bandia, but she's also a person. Like me. She can still decide to fight with her family instead of against them.

It starts to pour.

I hurry up the path, stopping at the top. Austin and Blake still stand down by the firepit in the rain, illuminated in their own godly light, silver and gold. Blake turns to Austin, letting the tip of his sword fall to the ground. Austin drops his sword and lifts his chin in a short nod.

A truce of sorts, between the boy I love and the boy I might've loved if things had been different. I don't mourn what could have been with Blake. I haven't for a long time. Maybe Joe is right, and together we could've changed things. It's too late now, because when I look at Austin, even in this form, I don't see a god hellbent on reclaiming the earth. I see a boy who did what he thought he must to keep me alive, who gave up immortality to save my horse. The boy who waited a thousand years to see me again. Who trusted me after I gave him every reason not to.

People will die in the battle tomorrow. I might be one of them. But I will fight for what I love. I will kill for it. Maybe that makes me a bad person. I hope not. Because I couldn't change it if I wanted to.

My heart is full.

FIFTY-ONE

I'm up at dawn. I should probably be resting, but it's not like I can sleep. I make my way to the barn and set to work grooming Molly.

"Couldn't sleep?" Mick stands outside the stall, wearing the same black duster as yesterday. He's more pale than usual.

"You neither?"

"Guess not."

I run the brush along Molly's neck in soft strokes. Mick watches me, like he's trying to get inside my head. Hell, he probably could get inside my head if he wanted to.

"For what it's worth, I'm glad you're still here," he says.

"I thought you wanted me to stop the war." I step under the stall guard and come into the barn aisle.

"Joe is worried about you and Austin, yet I can't help but wish his lordship happiness. No matter how problematic." He leans a shoulder against the stone wall.

"Austin's happiness is problematic?"

"It prevents you and Blake from ending things peacefully." Mick reaches for Molly's bridle, pulling it down from the hook near her stall. "Let's go for a ride."

Neither one of us says anything until we're both mounted and halfway down the road that cuts through the pasture. Mick turns Tally toward the ocean, away from the trail to the ruin. I don't argue. I want to leave the past behind me. Today I want to find a way to ensure a future.

"The Gathering will be near the gateway," Mick says. "Low tide coincides with the sunset, near midnight. Liam will want to take advantage of the magic hour between day and night."

"Tonight, then." At least I'll have all day to look for the necklace. To arm myself for battle. We reach the edge of the switchback trail and head down to the rocky beach below.

"The bond was Danu's way of forcing Killian to love her, but it backfired. Quite spectacularly." Mick pulls Tally to a halt. He stares out at the ocean while Tally snorts and stomps his hoof. "The ironic thing is, she didn't need to bind Killian's soul to her. He loved her already. He just needed time."

I'd met Killian in the spirit realm, and I'd come to the same conclusion. Killian loved Danu. "If he loved her, why couldn't they make it work?"

"Killian was not happy about becoming the very thing he was sworn to kill."

"He forgave her," I say. I know he did.

"Eventually. But Danu didn't return to Ireland after she bound Killian to her. She took his rejection hard, and stayed in the spirit realm for nearly a quarter century. Killian had no choice but to move on. Even so, Killian and Danu survived the bond better than anyone after them did." He gathers the reins, increasing the contact on Tally's mouth. "Until you. You know about the prophecy?"

"The seventh generation of the Seventh Daughters will bring an end to the war. That's supposed to be me." Danu told me as much. "But no one seems to know *how* I end it. Or even who wins."

Tally stamps the ground again, ready to move on. Mick reaches down and pats him on the neck, but holds him steady. "We try to anticipate, but we don't know the future. Not really."

"You've been with Austin all this time. Even when he couldn't travel to this world, you've protected his place here. Why is Joe with the Sons?"

Mick pulls on the reins, turning Tally back toward the barn. He brings one gloved hand to his eyes, dabbing the corners. "Joe is strong. He can withstand watching so many die. It's harder for me. With Austin, I figured I was safe."

"Safe?"

"The losses add up. It's the way of things when time passes for everyone but you. We have to guard ourselves or we'll lose sight of the greater good. Joe has closed himself off from emotion, but I haven't always been able to do so. Serving a god made it easier to stay detached. And if I did let myself get too close, at least Arawn would not die." He looks down at the ground.

"Except now—"

Mick kicks Tally into a gallop and takes off across the field.

Molly surges forward, but I hold her back. I let him go.

FIFTY-TWO

I have at least eight hours before sunset. I walk out to the bluff and gaze at the ocean. I couldn't see well in the dark water, but something, someone, took my necklace from me. Who? Portia would have taken it if she could. No, she was the one who pulled me out of the water. Whoever took the pendant was below me, I'm sure of it.

The fuath are the most likely culprits. They like shiny magical things, the older the better. But whoever took it didn't seem to care if I drowned in the process. Braden wouldn't let me drown, would he?

Everything seems so far away. A millennium separates me and my power.

I don't hear Austin walk up behind me, so it's a surprise when he sits down on the wall beside me. I turn my head so that I can see the hint of his crooked smile forming at the corners of his lips.

"Mick thinks the Gathering will coincide with the sunset," I say.

"It is a magic hour. The tide will begin to rise as the sun touches the horizon." Austin's gaze flits to the bare spot at the base of my neck. "Did you not find your necklace, then?"

It's a rhetorical question, so I don't answer. I look out at the sea. "If Portia comes to her senses and fights with the Sons, they can defeat Sherri and Liam. I can try to forge a peace again, once the Sons see we're on their side in all of this." Or not. It's the best I can do under the circumstances.

Austin reaches for my hand. I let him take it. "I won't be able to stay away from the fight. With my power restored, the gateway's pull is strong."

I haven't thought of going to Rome ever since Austin went missing. We have to fight if we have any real hope of being together.

"No matter what happens, know this." Austin watches me, but he doesn't say anything more.

"Know what?" I press.

He takes a breath. "I have wanted you since the year 1009, when you were a mystery girl from the future who kissed me like I'd never been kissed. I waited for you for over a thousand years. I've loved you even longer. I will do everything in my power to keep you safe."

"I thought you fell in love with me when I flipped a quarter into your lap."

Austin laughs. "That too. I've already said too much. My past is still your future." The way he talks is almost wistful. Sad.

I lean my shoulder into his. "My future is our future."

His smile is warm. His hand comes under my chin, raising it just enough for his lips to cover mine.

When he pulls away, I'm breathless. "If you're going to kiss me like that," I say, "I think it might be a good idea for us to move off the edge of this wall."

Austin stands and holds out his hand. As I take it, he pulls me the rest of the way to him. "Better?"

I nod into his chest. "It might be even better if we were somewhere more private."

"Are you asking to come to my bedroom?"

"Actually, I was thinking of asking you to come to mine."

He raises his eyebrows. "Were you?"

I kiss his neck, letting my lips trail up to his ear. "It's closer."

He tugs my hand and leads me up the path and across the yard, pulling me through a back door into a foyer shaped like an octagon. As soon as the door closes behind me, he presses me against the wall and kisses me. His chest rubs against my breasts, his hips rub against my hips, his tongue invades my mouth and pushes closer, closer, closer.

I reach for his hair, his neck, his waist. He groans into my mouth as his hands slip beneath my shirt. His fingers dance along my skin, each touch a brand that marks me as his.

He moves his mouth to my ear, his hot breaths stoking the fire higher. "If we don't find your room soon, I'm going to embarrass us both by getting naked right here in this hallway."

"I know for a fact that you have nothing to be embarrassed about."

"A fact?" He kisses a trail from my ear to the V of my shirt. He undoes one button. Then another. "Don't say I didn't warn you."

I have never heeded Austin's warnings, and this time is no exception. Not even when we're breathless, with my bare back pressed against the cold marble floor. Not later, when we're safely shielded by the soft duvet in my bed. Not when he kisses me softly and tells me that he loves me.

He has warned me that this will end badly, but I give Austin exactly what he asks for. I give him everything.

FIFTY-THREE

With only two hours to go before the sun sets, I have one last chance to convince Portia to fight with us. Given what happened last night, Austin doesn't think there's much point in trying. He may be right, but something Blake said sticks with me. He's seen inside her soul, and he still wants to believe she'll do the right thing.

Some part of Portia still loves her family.

Mick waits on the drive with the big black sedan he used to drive me home from the airport. He nods at me in the rearview mirror as Austin and I slide into the back seat.

The Ornery Knight is busy. Nearly every table is full of locals and tourists, eating and drinking and laughing without a clue that a battle for control of the world is about to rage in their backyard.

Joe leans against the staircase to the rooms, blocking anyone from going up or down. He shakes his head at Mick. "We've done all we can."

"Don't look at me," Mick says. "I'm just driving my charge." He jerks his chin toward Austin. "You're the one who made sure he would fight. I'm not the one who restored his power."

"What if I was wrong?" Joe lets out a breath.

"Are you just now thinking that?" Austin asks. "Because the last thousand years have done little to allay my concerns about the giollas' ability to keep the peace."

Mick grins.

Joe's lips curve into an almost-smile. "I could do without the negativity." He puts his hands in the pockets of his black duster. "Sam says the fuath are still undecided."

"They won't take a stand until there's a clear winner."

Joe nods and steps to the side, letting Austin and me pass. "Try room 217."

I glance toward Blake's room. Is he preparing to fight?

We stop in front of Portia's door. Austin knocks lightly.

Portia's voice carries from inside. "I told you to leave me alone."

Austin knocks again. Finally, we hear footsteps and Portia thrusts the door open wide. Her face registers surprise for the barest of seconds before she glares at me. "Do you want me to strike you dead?"

"I want you to think about what you're doing."

"Do you? Because the more I think about it, the less reason I can think of to let you keep swooping in and destroying my life." Her voice quivers. Tears pool at the corners of her eyes. She nearly shuts the door, but I step inside her room before she can.

Her room is a disaster, with clothes strewn among the tangled sheets on her bed and scattered across the floor. The only surface that isn't cluttered with hair products and makeup is a small table next to her bed with one small framed photo. In the picture, Blake has his arm around her as they pose in front of Wolfgang Hunter's in Rancho Domingo. Blake wears his signature smile, dimples out in full force. He looks happy. Portia looks happy too. They're beautiful together, and my heart aches a little when I look at Portia now, her eyes clouded, driven by hate.

Maybe they could have been good together once. If I hadn't taken off my bracelet at Austin's party last spring— if I hadn't claimed Blake as my own, hadn't joined my soul with his. There's nothing I can do to change what happened. The past is behind us. All I can do is try to have an impact on what happens next.

"I'm sorry," I say.

"Sorry for what? That Blake loves you and not me? You really think I want your pity?"

"No. I just wish things were different. Maybe they still can be."

Portia barks out a laugh. "How? My father will never forgive me for this. Blake hates me. At least Liam appreciates me for who I am."

I take Portia's hand. "And who is that?"

Porta stares at my hand clutching hers. She doesn't squeeze back, but she doesn't pull away either. "I'm a bandia."

"No. The question is, who? Who are you really, Portia? Can you kill your own father?"

Portia's fingers tremble beneath mine. She jerks her hand away. "Get out."

I stand my ground. "It's your family. Blake wants to believe in you. I heard him say it. He could've killed you, but he didn't."

A tear moistens the corner of her eye before she can wipe it away. "He's an idiot. I'll kill him. I won't last another day feeling how much he hates me. How much he loves you. Every fiber of my being wants me to end this."

The words sting. Blake doesn't love me. How can there be love when there's no trust? But I understand what Portia is feeling. "You get to decide how it ends, Portia. You can fight with Blake or against him, but it's your call."

Portia pushes me hard in the chest, sending me backward. Austin catches me by the shoulders before I fall. She advances on me. "Exactly. You don't get to tell me what I should do. You don't get to tell me anything."

Wind swirls around her, sending her hair flying around her face. The picture on the table sails into the wall hard enough to crack the glass. Austin drags me toward the door, away from the maelstrom.

"Portia, please." My words are lost in the howling wind.

Austin pulls me out the door and slams it behind us. We both lean against the wall in the hallway, catching our breath.

"I think that went well." Austin looks at me sideways, his lips quirked in a smile.

He leads me down to the pub, keeping me behind him

while he makes sure the room is clear. He motions for Mick to bring the car around back. Just as we're about to duck through the kitchen, I see a familiar woman with short blond hair walking through the front entrance of the pub. The woman from the train. Corporate Tink. She's dressed in a sharp red suit that's cut to show off her thin frame, but my attention isn't on her outfit—it's on the silver pendant hanging from her neck.

My necklace.

I let go of Austin's hand and charge across the pub.

The woman sees me coming and clutches at her throat, covering the pendant with her hand. She turns and runs outside.

I chase after her. She has my necklace. My power.

She's easy to spot in her bright red ensemble, and she can't run very fast in her pointy black heels. She trips as soon as she hits the cobblestone. I dive after her, landing on her back. She disappears underneath me in a flash of white light.

Crap. I push up onto my knees just as Austin reaches for my arm, helping me to my feet. "Who is she?" he asks.

"Fuath," I say. "That bitch has my necklace."

Another flash of white lights up the street, half a block ahead. I take off after it.

A white horse with a thick tail that ends in a fin has appeared right in the middle of the street. It breaks into a run, galloping toward the water. I sprint as fast as I can even though there's no hope of catching her now.

The horse leaps over the three-foot fence that lines the

harbor and dives into the water a few seconds before I reach the fence myself. I stare out at the ocean.

"Do you know her?" Austin asks, breathing hard beside me.

"Not exactly. I met her on the train once."

"The fuath don't part with their treasures easily."

"It's mine. She stole it from me."

Austin puts his arms around me. "Maybe it's for the best. You don't have to fight anymore. I have power now, and I can fight better if I'm not worried about you." He squeezes me tighter. "I'll make sure nothing happens to Blake."

"Blake?"

"Don't tell me you wouldn't try to save him if you could."

I don't know the answer to that. "I wouldn't let him die if I could stop it. I wouldn't let any of them die. But who will have your back if I don't go? You're the one I'm worried about."

He brings his hand to my cheek. "You make me want to do something to deserve you."

"Like what?"

"I don't know. I wish I could take back all the things I did that hurt you."

"Are you apologizing?"

"I'm more selfish than that," he says. "I'm afraid I'm not sorry. I would do everything all over again if I thought it would keep you alive. If I thought it would bring us here, now."

"That doesn't sound selfish."

"Trust me, it is." His crooked smile is suddenly so close

that I could touch his lower lip with my tongue. "Whatever happens tonight, promise me you'll only remember the good parts."

"Don't talk like that. We're going to get through this."

His lips brush mine, so lightly I might be imagining them. "God, I hope you're right." And then he crushes his mouth to mine.

I wrap my arms around his neck and hold him to me. I may not have power, but I have Austin. It feels like enough.

I know it can't be.

But right now, it feels like everything.

FIFTY-FOUR

Austin watches the sun drop from the window in my room. He's dressed in a pair of gray slacks and a soft wool sweater, the kind with thick cables that I'll always associate with Ireland. "You can stay here," he says. "I'll come back for you when it's over."

I place my hands on his shoulders from behind, trailing my thumbs across the bare skin on his neck. We've already had this discussion three times. "I'll keep my distance," I tell him again. "And I have a sword if I need to defend myself. I'm not going to throw myself into the middle of the battle unless I have to."

He flashes that crooked smile. "It's the last part that concerns me."

"I know I'm outgunned. I won't do anything stupid. But it's not like I can end this war if I'm not there."

He nods and takes my hand. "Let's go."

We walk through the house in silence, our hands forged, drawing strength from each other. We're still alone when we get to the trail that leads across the field, but Austin says he can feel the others moving toward the beach from the sea.

By the time we get to the edge of the bluff, I see Liam standing on the rocky shore below. The tide is out, revealing the beach carpeted in small pebbles. Liam climbs atop a boulder. Sherri stands just below him, her hair pulled up in a tight bun. Her dress looks like a costume, with capped sleeves, a fitted waist, and a skirt that flares out just below the rib cage. It's blue, with silver ribbons dotting the hem.

I'm dressed for a physical fight, in thick black leggings and a black long-sleeved tee that will allow me to move. I carry nothing but the clutch of broomstraw tucked safely in my bra and the broadsword Austin gave me just before we left the house.

Austin stops at the firepit. "You'll be able to see everything from here."

I step past him onto the trail. "I won't be able to get down there fast enough."

"Fast enough to what? You're staying out of it, remember?"

I nod and keep walking. By the time we reach the beach, the sun is so low that it nearly touches the horizon. When I glance back up, I see the giolla on the bluff above. Sam stands in the middle, flanked by Joe and Mick. They look like avenging angels, dark coats flapping in the wind, but they're not here to fight. They're here to clean up after our mess.

A boat comes in from the south, the low tide keeping the water far enough from the cliffs that the boat can make it to shore without smashing into the rocks. The Sons climb onto the beach, led by Rush and Dr. McKay. Levi and Jonah fall into step beside them. Blake and the twins stay a few feet back. Micah flashes me a shy smile. Jeremy doesn't look at anything but his feet. I know they don't want to be here, but they're drawn along with everyone else, slaves to their DNA.

There's no sign of the fuath. I'm not surprised. Braden knows the outcome is far from certain, and if the fuath intend to wait for a clear winner to emerge, they'll stay away at first. Braden risked enough in helping me rescue Austin from the abbey.

The only person missing is Portia.

Liam raises his hand, and a loud cracking sound comes from the rocks behind him. Like the others, Austin moves toward the boulders. He turns to look over his shoulder at me, but it's clear that he's compelled to keep walking to the opening that's forming in the wall of rock. White light spills out of the fissure, illuminating the beach in an eerie glow.

A pebble rolls against my foot from the trail behind me. I glance up. Portia is picking her way down, her steps unsteady. Her hair is wild, blown into knots. Her jeans and sweater are caked with dirt, as if she's fallen somewhere on the way. Once she gets to the bottom, she runs to stand beside the others, who have formed a semicircle in front of the gateway.

Liam raises both of his hands and shouts into the wind, "*Fearadh na fáilte.*" The air lights up with a hundred strikes of lightning at once, crackling as they reach to the ocean in jagged arcs.

Obviously proud of his display, Liam smiles. "Tonight," he declares, "you are called to the source of all power, so that you may use the gifts that have been bestowed by your forefathers as it has always been intended. Tonight, the gods place their fate in the hands of their children."

I move closer, watching as the Sons move single file toward the opening, their eyes locked on Liam. Levi steps through the crack, disappearing into the light. Rush follows, then Jonah, Blake, and Dr. McKay. Micah and Jeremy trudge behind them.

They're going into Avernus?

Once the Sons are inside, Sherri takes Portia's hand and leads her in after them. Austin gives me one last glance before he follows.

I push my way through the boulders until I get to the opening. I hope I can still travel inside. I may not be able to access my power, but I still carry Danu's DNA. And I've been to the spirit realm before. To Avernus. To the past.

I take a tentative step into the blinding light. Then another. Blake's eyes meet mine from a flat boulder I recognize. The river, which winds through a ravine that separates the barren rock floor on this side from the equally barren landscape across the way, reflects the unearthly white light back at us.

Austin puts his hand on my shoulder. "Go outside."

"I can't do anything from the beach."

"You don't have any power, remember?"

Liam steps in behind us and the rock wall seals shut with a shudder. I couldn't leave now if I wanted to.

No one says a word. We're all trapped together. Seven Sons of Killian. Three bandia. A former god and his successor. Austin wraps his arms around me from behind. "You remember how to get out?" he whispers in my ear. "Through the river?"

I nod. Last spring, when I'd lured Austin into Avernus and banished him, he'd pushed me into the ravine, into the river that runs to the underworld, and I was washed back onto the beach outside. It seemed that as a mortal I couldn't pass through the river, which carries the souls of the dead to their final resting places.

Of course. Mortals can't stay in the underworld. And Austin's immortality was fading, which explains why he was able to come back just a few months after being banished.

"Do you remember the spell?" I murmur. Liam brought us through the gateway. The banishment spell should work here.

Austin shakes his head. "Only the end."

Liam turns on us. "Enough!"

Austin drops his hand and steps forward, drawing Liam's attention away from me.

"You should have forced this battle with the humans centuries ago," Liam says, stalking toward him. "Tonight you will rectify the error of your ways. You will make the opening strike."

Austin disappears in a flash of golden light, and Liam smiles. Can Liam command Austin here? Can he force him to kill?

Austin materializes in the same spot, his sword drawn and pointed right at Liam's throat. Blood spills from Liam's neck as he falls to the ground.

Not exactly the opening strike Liam expected.

No one moves.

Then Sherri screams, and a blast of blue fire sails at Austin's head. He disappears and the fire lands harmlessly on the rock wall behind him.

Liam grunts from the ground, his hand on his neck. He moves to his knees and then stands. Blood stains his shirt, but there's no longer any sign of a cut on his neck.

Austin appears again next to me. "Get to the edge of the river. Be prepared to jump."

I work my way closer to the edge of the cliff, clutching my sword.

Portia stares at Liam's blood-stained neck, frozen.

"What are you waiting for, bandia?" Liam turns toward her.

Rush steps forward, grabbing Portia's wrist. "You shouldn't be here. This is no place for a breeder." Portia's hand fills with fire, and Rush jerks his hand away. He stares down at his reddening fingers in disbelief. "Impossible."

Portia chokes on a sob. She points her fiery hand at her father, eyes wide as she watches the blisters rise on his palm.

Sherri lobs a fireball right at Rush's chest, sending him to the ground with a blast. Portia backs up, her hands still filled with fire, staring at her father's body. Silver flashes light up the bluff as the Sons all dematerialize at once.

There's no choice but to fight now.

Blake reappears first, next to Portia. He drags her away just as the rest of the Sons descend on the area where Sherri stood. But she's ready for them, moving off to the side and sending fire at the first flash she sees, making another hit on Levi.

Austin moves in front of me, his sword drawn.

Portia lobs her fire into the air wildly, aiming at nothing. It crashes into a rock before disappearing. She collapses against Blake, crying.

A silver flash to my right is the only warning I get before Jonah appears at my side. I thrust my sword forward, barely blocking Jonah's knife as it comes at my throat.

Austin steps behind Jonah and holds his sword at Jonah's neck. "We're on your side," he growls. Jonah disappears as soon as he realizes that Austin hasn't cut him.

Sherri runs toward us, yelling "I could use a little help here." Dr. McKay flashes to her right. She hits him with a blast of wind, knocking him backward.

But when Jeremy flanks her on the left, charging with his sword, Sherri loses her footing. She falls to the ground, away from Jeremy's blade, and there's an explosion of blue fire. Jeremy flies through the air. His head makes a sick cracking sound as he hits a wall of rock. He lands on the ground in a heap. Micah screams and runs to his brother's lifeless body. A pool of blood is forming beneath Jeremy's head. Micah pulls at Jeremy's hair, trying desperately to keep it from getting bloody. Jeremy would hate that.

I stand frozen next to Austin, too stunned to move. Rush is dead. Jeremy isn't moving. Levi lies whimpering on the ground. Blake is still trying to keep Portia together, holding her shaking form, but at least she's staying out of the fight.

Jonah and Dr. McKay materialize near Sherri, but even with Portia out of the battle, their momentum is lost. Sherri is already on her feet, fire licking at her fingers. The Sons are losing. Liam grins at the carnage from atop a large boulder.

I reach for Austin's shoulder. "We have to fight. They need our help."

Austin holds his sword in front of us like a shield. "You are not fighting anyone without your power."

"We can't let Liam win."

At that moment, Sherri sprints toward Blake. I raise my sword and charge after her. She turns on me, hitting me with a blast of wind that knocks me back. I fall hard and roll to the side, taking the brunt of the blow with my shoulder. Pushing onto my knees, I'm just in time to see Sherri send a blast of wind at Blake and Portia, blowing them both into the air at once.

Blake lands on his back, temporarily stunned.

"No!" I scream just as Sherri raises her hand to send a ball of flame at him. Before she can get the shot off, there's a flash of gold to her left and a sword at her chest. Her blue dress turns a dark shade of purple as blood soaks through.

The air goes still.

Austin lays Sherri on the ground.

No one says a word. Austin stands with his sword still dripping blood, staring down at Sherri's lifeless body like he half expects to be dragged back to the underworld for another thousand years.

He didn't let her kill Blake.

Liam slides down from the boulder and moves toward Austin with grace befitting a god. "What have you done?" His voice is so quiet, I have to strain to hear it. "You are a failure in every sense of the word. It shouldn't come as a surprise after all this time, but still, I find myself at a loss."

Austin steps forward. "I've chosen a side, friend. Or didn't you understand that when I slit your throat?"

Liam laughs. The sound echoes across the stark bluffs until it's finally swallowed by the river below. "You were a pathetic excuse for a god, and you're even worse as a human. A traitor to your own cause. For what? For a mortal who will die anyway?"

Austin raises his sword as Liam gets closer.

"Your sword can't hurt me for long." Liam circles Austin. White light arcs from his fingers. "You are a disgrace, Arawn. It's only fitting that you will die like one. A true death."

Jonah and Dr. McKay move toward Micah and stand together. Blake crawls over to Portia. She's sitting up, trembling as she stares at Sherri's bloodied body.

I step forward, trying to deflect Liam's attention away from Austin.

Liam smiles at me, and my stomach twists into a tight knot. "Is this your moment, then? Will you end the war with the Sons?" He pushes Sherri's body to the side with his foot, clearing a path for me. "As a sacrificial lamb?" He sends a bolt of white light at my chest.

A burst of gold light flashes in front of me, sending me flying backward. I land on my back, breathless. I reach for my chest, but I'm fine. It's not until I sit up on my elbows that I see Austin on the ground.

No.

No, no, no.

Austin materialized in front of me.

I scramble to him. His body is still quivering from the shock of Liam's blast. His skin is red where he was hit, but his chest still rises and falls as he sucks in air. I look for Dr. McKay, pleading with my eyes. *Help him.*

Liam laughs again. "Utterly predictable. Arawn's fall at the hands of a girl. Did you give up immortality, Lord Lorcan, so you could die for her?"

"At the hands of a tyrant." I glare at Liam as he moves closer. "You know you can't kill him. You'll be banished."

"He's not dead, is he?" Liam kicks Austin hard in the ribs. Austin curls away and lets out a grunt. "Didn't think so. He'll just wish that he were." He kicks Austin in the small of his back, right over a kidney, and then turns to me. "You will do the deed for me."

I leap to my feet, my sword at Liam's throat. I slash. Blood splatters everywhere. In my hair, my eyes, my mouth. The iron taste is thick and sour. I spit at the ground, but I keep slashing, hacking and chopping at his neck. I don't stop until he lies on the ground, unmoving. I stand over him, my sword still pressed against his neck. His skin grows back over the gash, repairing itself before my eyes.

Liam coughs and sputters. "Stupid girl. You can't kill me."

"Maybe not. You'll just wish you were dead." I cut his neck again, then hack away until he's unconscious, ignoring the second wave of blood that sprays on me.

I wait for the skin to regroup. Then I do it again.

And again. I keep going, chopping until I feel spine. The muscles in my shoulders ache from the effort, but I push past the pain, past everything.

A hand rests on my shoulder.

"Stop." Austin stands beside me. "You have to stop sometime."

I drop the sword and throw my arms around Austin, hugging him to me, feeling his warmth. He hugs me back, undeterred by the blood that covers my clothes and hair.

"I love you," I say.

He laughs in my ear. "It's okay. I already knew. I've been waiting for you to figure it out."

"I should have told you."

"You did." He lifts his hand to my face, wiping a drop of blood from my lips. "A long time ago."

The movement behind me barely registers, but I catch it out of the corner of my eye. I spin around to face Liam. I raise my sword, but he's too far away.

All I'm aware of is white light as it comes at Austin and me.

A crack of pain as we fall to the ground.

Then nothing.

FIFTY-FIVE

Everything hurts. My head throbs in time to the sharp stabs in my chest. My hands and feet are numb, but prickles of pain poke along my skin, threatening to prod my nerves into an all-out assault. My mouth feels hot, tinged with the taste of rusty metal.

"She has a pulse." I recognize Dr. McKay's voice, although it sounds tinny and far away. I can't be sure if he's talking about me.

"Kill her, then," says another male voice. Maybe Levi. I can't be sure. "It's what we came for."

Everything goes numb at once. Then I'm floating, drifting. I open my eyes, but there's nothing to see but foggy blankness. It's cold and disorienting.

Then I see him, just a silhouette in the clouds, reaching for me. I know him now. Once, he was just a shadow in the fog, but now he's my heart. My Austin.

I stretch to reach him. Our fingers brush and his hand closes around mine, pulling me the rest of the way to him. His touch ignites something primal and strong inside me, filling me with a strength that has a magic all its own.

"You can't stay." I feel the soft lilt of his voice inside my head. It's as if we're trapped in a dream where nothing is truly physical. Everything happens on the inside.

I don't argue with him. I'm completely out of my element here, surrounded by an icy mist that threatens to swallow me whole. "Come back with me," I say.

His sigh is a vacuum, stealing my own breath, smothering me. "You already know I can't do that."

My heart doesn't make a sound as it shatters. I don't cry or scream or even beg for things I know I can't have. I just hold on.

A silver thread of light moves through the fog, breaking up the gray, inching toward us.

"I have to go." His words are resigned.

The light moves closer. It brushes my arm, wrapping itself around my wrist, pulling me. I fight against it, not wanting to let go. Not yet.

He lifts my hands from his shoulders. "Remember your promise to me." He once asked me to stay alive, no matter what.

"I never said I would do it." I can barely get the words out.

"You have your whole life ahead of you."

"So do you."

"You know that's not true," he says softly.

The silver thread tightens. I grab Austin's hand and cling tightly to it.

He brings my hand to his lips. His voice in my head is warm and melodic. "I would die a thousand deaths for the life I had with you."

I cry out as he lets go of my hand. His shadowy form retreats, floating backward until he disappears into the haze.

I'm pulled in the other direction, along a trail of silver light. But when I close my eyes, all I see is gold.

FIFTY-SIX

Blake kneels over me, his hands pressed against my rib cage. Even with all the silver light that surrounds him, I can see the shadows that line his face. His lips are fixed in a hard line. "She's awake," he says.

Awake? As if I'd been sleeping. Dreaming. As if none of this is real.

Austin lies next to me. No one needs to tell me he won't be waking up. He's on his stomach, his arm still draped across my waist. Liam's blood puddles around us.

I sit up too fast, sending a rush of oxygen to my head. Blake's hand stops me from reaching for my sword. "It's over," he says. As if to demonstrate the point, he vanishes and then reappears in street clothes. The remaining Sons follow suit. All but Micah, who sits hunched over Jeremy's body, still wearing the same plaid his brother wears.

"Where's Liam?" I look around the rocks frantically, but I don't see him anywhere.

"They took him. After he killed—" Blake looks at the ground.

"They?"

"The dogs. The ones we saw that night, at the gateway back home."

"Arawn's hounds," I murmur. The three giant wolfhounds that guard the river. "Liam was banished, right?" Killing a mortal is an offense with a hefty price, and Liam had killed. I try not to think about what that actually means, even though I already know the answer.

"I think it was more than banishment." Blake's cheek twitches.

"I don't understand."

Blake lifts his head, and his face is pale. "The dogs didn't just herd him to the river. They took him. In pieces."

"What?" Liam is a god. An immortal. But the hounds are creatures of the underworld too. And Arawn was their master.

Blake looks from me to where Austin's body lies. "I'm sorry."

I look around the bluff, anywhere but at Austin. Portia sits huddled on a rock, her face in her hands, shaking. Sherri's neck is bent at an unnatural angle where she lies slumped over a boulder, in a pool of her own blood.

Levi is limping, but he manages to help Jonah lift Rush's body and take him to the side of the ravine. They say a few words I can't hear and then throw him into the water below. Portia screams.

Micah stays on the ground, Jeremy's head cradled in his lap. As Levi and Jonah approach, he leans forward, shielding Jeremy's face with his chest. "You're not taking him."

"It's already done," Levi says. "He's on the path to Avalon whether the river takes him or not."

"No!" Micah's cheeks are wet with tears. "Jeremy doesn't even believe in the war. He can't die this way."

I push myself off the ground, forcing myself to my feet. My shoulders hurt. My heart hurts. Everything hurts. I try not to look at Austin as I step over him. I focus on Micah, placing a hand on his arm, ignoring the stickiness where my bloody fingers touch his skin. I'm careful not to touch the swath of plaid across his shoulder that matches Jeremy's. I know words are meaningless now, so I say nothing. I just take him in my arms and hold on.

He cries, and I wish I could cry with him. Not just for Jeremy, not just for Austin. For Rush. For Sherri. For the Sons of Killian and Seventh Daughters who have fought and died and killed for the last thousand years. But I can't afford tears. We're far from out of this.

Finally, when he's too exhausted to cry anymore, I let go. "He didn't die for nothing," I tell him, not sure if I mean Jeremy or Austin. "He ended a war."

I feel the eyes of the Sons on me. All of them. Blake tilts his head. It dawns on me that I have no idea what he's thinking, but I'm not trying to feel him anymore. It takes all my effort to keep from feeling my own emotions. They hover near the edge of my composure, waiting to pull me under and drag me into darkness.

I turn my attention to Portia. She lifts her head to watch me, her eyes wary.

I weigh my words carefully, thinking about what Blake said. "Liam is dead." I put my hand on her shoulder. "The last remaining Seventh Daughter is right here, and she's more than just a descendant of Danu—she's the daughter of a Son. She chose not to fight against her family. Not to kill the Son she bonded to her."

"The last?" Jonah moves toward me, a sick smile on his lips. "Aren't you forgetting someone?" He lunges forward, but Micah is on his feet with his sword raised, preventing Jonah from getting closer.

"I haven't forgotten," I say. "But I'm no threat. I lost my power after I broke the bond with Blake."

"Is this true?" Levi looks to Blake for confirmation.

"More or less," Blake says.

"Which is it?" Equivocation won't work with Levi.

"She can't access her power," Blake says. He leaves out the part about my necklace, even though I don't think he knows the fuath took it.

Dr. McKay nods. "We saw as much at the pub, and again tonight." He looks at Portia. "But she came here to fight."

Portia glances over her shoulder, at the gorge where her father's body was dropped into the river. She buries her head in her knees and starts crying again.

The sun drops the rest of the way behind the rocks, casting us in shadows. Only the glow from Micah keeps us from descending completely into darkness.

"Tell them," I whisper, but Portia doesn't acknowledge

me. I square my shoulders. "She was called here like the rest of you. She couldn't stay away. She tried to. That's why she was late."

Portia lifts her head and stares.

"She didn't attack anyone," I continue. "She's one of you."

"God help us then." Jonah smirks.

Portia picks up a rock and throws it at Jonah's feet. He steps out of the way easily, but Levi laughs. Dr. McKay smiles. Just like that, the tension is broken.

Levi and Dr. McKay take Sherri's body to the ravine, and then walk toward Jeremy.

Micah holds up a hand. "I'll do it." He sets down his sword and brushes a long strand of hair away from Jeremy's face, then lifts his brother's shoulders off the ground. Dr. McKay comes around to takes Jeremy's feet, but one look from Micah is all it takes to wave him off. Hugging Jeremy's back to his chest, Micah drags him to the ravine on his own.

Once there, he hesitates. He leans forward and kisses his brother's cheek. And then he lets go, with a shrill scream that echoes throughout Avernus.

A howl responds in the distance.

The dogs. "The hounds will be back," I say. "We need to get out of here."

Blake takes a step in my direction.

"Don't." Portia turns toward Blake, her voice so quiet I'm not sure I heard it.

I look away from them, too fast, catching a glimpse of Austin out of the corner of my eye. I know he's already moved on, that this body is not him, not anymore. Still, I'm not as strong as Micah. I don't go to him.

I stare at the ground as Micah motions for Blake to help him move Austin's body to the ledge. I close my eyes tight when they push him over. I don't even hear the splash of his body hitting the river, indistinguishable as it is from the sound of the water rushing below.

I walk in the opposite direction, to the crack in the cliff wall that should lead back out to the beach. There's nothing but solid rock. It won't be as simple as walking out of here, without Liam to open the gateway.

The howls get louder. Closer.

Micah walks up behind me. "So that's it? We're all going to die in here anyway?"

I run my hand along the wall, looking for any opening even though I know I won't find one. "There's another way out."

Dr. McKay looks around the vast wasteland. There's nothing but rocks and cliffs, and water and waterfalls. Nothing alive but us.

A growl echoes in the wind. Us and a trio of very angry hellhounds.

"We don't have much time." I make my way to the edge of the ravine. I take a breath, afraid to look down, although I know there won't be anything down there but water. The current should have dragged Austin halfway to the underworld by now. I force myself to look. Just water—water and giant boulders I don't remember seeing before. The water is at least fifty feet below where I stand. Jagged rocks line the walls of the ravine, like teeth ready to rip and tear me up on the way down.

The last time I did this, it was easy. It wasn't by choice. Austin pushed me. Plus the water was rising then, so the fall was only half as far. Still, I remember the way the water grabbed and spun me, nearly choking me as it spat me out on the beach. And that was in the comparatively calm surf back home. The coastline near Cath is far less forgiving to a human body.

Austin isn't here to push me now. And he isn't here to get me out of the currents, either. Why is it so important for me to stay alive now? So someone will be here to mourn him?

I look over my shoulder at the five remaining Sons and Portia. "This river will dump you into the ocean on the other side," I shout. "As soon as you hit the waves, look for the beach. You'll have a better chance if you can dematerialize to get to the shore."

I'm just going to have to take my chances.

The howls turn to barking as the three dogs lumber around a boulder. We're out of time. I back up a few steps, then run as fast as I can to the edge of the ravine and jump.

FIFTY-SEVEN

I close my eyes as I fall, concentrating on leading with my feet. The air rushes by so quickly that the sky feels like a part of me again. My stomach floats into my throat, but I force myself to breathe, sucking in the oxygen I'll need once I'm underwater.

My left foot hits the water first, slapping against it with so much force that I'm thrown to my side. The impact on my hip is hard, but the shock of the cold water as I plunge downward is worse. I have to fight to keep from opening my mouth to scream. It's several seconds before I feel the current move around me. It pushes me and drags me deeper, spinning me around until I'm no longer certain which way is up. I resist the urge to kick. I could just as easily be kicking myself deeper instead of moving to the surface.

My lungs start to protest, searching for their next hit of oxygen. A rock appears out of nowhere. My knee slams against it. My mouth opens before I can stop it. Water rushes in. I close my mouth, but it's too late—the water pushes down my throat. I can't stop the cough, which only causes more water to come in.

My body fights to breathe. To live. But all I can do is panic.

I reach out and my hand finds something soft. Not rock. I can't make out anything more than the color white in the blue darkness, but I grab hold of a handful of coarse white hair and cling to it with all the strength I have left.

One.

Two.

Another cough bubbles up. I fight it even as water starts to fill my lungs.

Then I break the surface. I open my mouth and cough. Water comes out even faster than it went in, in one massive retch. I gulp the air, taking it in with giant watery breaths as a weight below me keeps my head above water.

I collapse on the beach, lying on my stomach in the rocks. When I'm convinced I'm going to keep breathing, I push myself up on my elbows.

Braden kneels beside me, his hand tapping the spot between my shoulder blades. "That was a dangerous stunt, even for you."

"You're such a smartass." Another coughing fit keeps me from thanking him. I don't need to tell him what I'm feeling. He already knows.

"Who's winning?" He gets right to the point.

I roll onto my back. "I should've known you didn't save me out of the goodness of your heart."

"What can I say?" Braden grins. "I'm a multitasker."

There's a silver light beside us as Blake lands in a heap on the shore. He kneels there, retching.

"I guess that answers my question." Braden raises his eyebrows as he looks from me to Blake. "No clear winner." He holds out his hand to help me sit up. I place my palm in his. Something hard and cold presses into my hand. "If anyone asks, you didn't get this from me." Then he turns and leaps into the water, disappearing into the waves.

"Who was that?" Blake's hands are buried in the rocky beach, his arms bracing himself as he recovers from the near-drowning.

"A friend," I say. Braden has risked enough by coming here. I don't feel guilty for keeping his secrets. And I have my own. I keep my fist closed tight, but I know exactly what he gave me. I can already feel the ocean water flowing in my veins. My body is no longer fighting it but embracing it, calling to it. "Where are the others?"

"They thought you were crazy." Blake pushes himself into a sitting position.

"Didn't you?" I ask.

"No." Blake shakes water out of his hair. When he glances at me, I see a hint of the old Blake, a dimple, appear on his cheek. "I always knew you were."

A scream breaks through the darkness. Then it's gone, swallowed by the waves.

Blake is on his feet, running back into the water. Before

I realize what I'm doing, I'm calling the water, feeling it, pulling it. The silence is the first thing that tells me it's working. The waves no longer crash against the rocks. They no longer crash against the beach. The water is smooth. Calm. Like a lake with giant rock islands.

Jonah breaks the surface.

My enemy. My enemies are out there. The people who ostracized me, who wanted me dead. I could turn around, walk back up the hill, and leave them to fight the ocean and the rocks as the tide comes in. Some may survive. Some may not. But none of it, none, would be my fault.

Or I could end it all. Make the current stronger, the waves more powerful as they bash against the rocks. Prevent the Sons from ever catching sight of the shore.

That thought scares me so much, I drop my necklace onto the beach. The waves start to churn again just as Blake reaches Micah, who's struggling against the current. I fall to my knees and run my hands along the rocky shore, becoming increasingly frantic as I hear more yells from the water.

My fingers close around a rock, then another. *No. I have to find it. I won't let them die.* At last, I grasp cold silver. Holding the wolfsbane pendant tight, I stop the waves once more.

Three, four, five heads pop out of the water. All the Sons. No Portia. Blake pulls Micah the rest of the way to the beach. Jonah and Levi follow. Dr. McKay comes in next.

Still no Portia.

"Where is she?" I ask Blake as he helps Micah lie down.

He shakes his head. "I guess she didn't want to jump."

"She had to jump. The dogs—"

Blake looks back out at the ocean. It's eerie in its calmness. "I still feel her."

Then, as if he's called her to him, Portia's head bursts though the water. Blake dives back in while I keep the waves at bay.

And I wonder, not for the first time, if I'm doing the right thing.

FIFTY-EIGHT

The three giolla still stand at the top of the trail. Joe nods at me, a hint of a smile on his lips. I want to hit him. People are dead. Rush. Sherri. Jeremy.

Austin.

If Joe cared so much about ending the war, he should've ended it himself. I march up to tell him as much, but Mick steps forward, searching my face. I shake my head, answering the unspoken question that passes between us. Mick's face crumbles. He falls to his knees. I kneel beside him and he hugs me, ignoring the pebbles and the water and blood that still cling to my hair. By the time he lets go, everyone else has moved up the trail, leaving us to mourn in peace.

We sit and stare at the ocean for hours, holding hands as we watch the moon fall across the sky.

Mick finally breaks the silence as the sky turns from

black to a dusty gray that beckons the sun. "I don't know how much more of this I can take."

I just nod. There's nothing left to say.

"He wasn't supposed to die," Mick says.

It's my fault. Austin lost his immortality because of what he did for me.

"What will you do?" I ask.

"I don't know. You?"

The wolfsbane pendant is heavy in my hand. "I don't know either."

In the gray minutes between night and day, the waves build and crash against the rocks, destroying them one tiny pebble at a time. The rocks stand strong, oblivious to the tiny cuts that will be their undoing.

I stand and walk to the edge of the bluff. Wind blows through my damp clothes. I push it away without thought, letting fire fill my veins, warming me from the inside. Blue flame arcs between my fingers, dances along my skin. I let it grow, let the fire burn until I don't think I can stand to hold it in another second.

But I do. I hold on to it until I can't see anything but blue spots, until I can't feel anything but searing pain. I let the heat consume me until I pass out, until I'm floating in the gray mists of the spirit realm ... and beyond, to Avalon.

The field is empty, but I am undeterred. I walk toward a long stone wall in the distance.

"Austin." I say his name, as if I can conjure him from thin air. "Arawn."

Nothing.

The wind picks up. Flowers beat against my legs. There's howling in the distance, and it grows closer. A tendril of mist curls along the ground ahead, swallowing the field as it goes.

I've never come here intentionally before, and it might not be the best idea now, but I still hold out hope that he's here. If Danu and Killian reside in Avalon, why not Austin? I call his name again.

Shapes move in the distance. At first, I think they're people and I move toward them. As I get closer, I see they stand on four legs, huge beasts moving in a pack of three. I don't need to hear the snarls to recognize Arawn's hounds as they move through the mist.

I back up a step, then another, fighting the instinct to run. The three dogs get closer, close enough that I can see their lips curling back, revealing sharp canines.

"Sit."

They keep coming. Apparently Austin didn't bother with obedience training.

I startle when I feel a tug on my wrist. Killian—all six feet gorgeous of him, with his long blond hair and golden smile— leads me toward a large rock on the side of the field. I follow without question, as the dogs snap their teeth behind us.

Killian gives me a leg up onto the massive rock, encouraging me to keep climbing. I climb at least twenty feet before reaching a ledge large enough to sit on. Killian climbs up beside me. The three wolfhounds circle the rock at the bottom, teeth bared.

"Thanks," I say.

Killian nods and looks down at the dogs. "They're harmless unless you try to go somewhere you don't belong."

"That would be me they're after."

"So I surmised."

I kick the rock with my heel. "Have you seen Austin here?" When he wrinkles his forehead, I add, "Arawn."

He sighs and looks out across the field, which is now entirely coated with a layer of fine mist. "You waste your talents."

"What?"

"Arawn is no help to you now. You would be better served to focus on what's going on topside."

"I'll tell you what's going on: a truce. The Sons and Daughters have broken the curse."

"Why would you think that?"

"Because Portia is aligned with the Sons. She didn't kill anyone when she had the chance."

Killian laughs. "There is time enough for her to kill."

One of the dogs howls from beneath us.

"Portia was devastated when her father was killed. Blake protected her. That has to mean something."

"They are still bound?"

"I guess so."

"Then they are still cursed." He looks at me. "And you are still alive."

"But the gods can't return. The gateway is sealed. Not even the god of the underworld can cross over for the next thousand years."

Killian's smile makes him look more god than human. "Don't confuse a victory in battle with a victory in war."

The fog closes around us. I can't see the three wolfhounds circling below us anymore. I can barely see Killian. And then I'm lost in the mist, floating, spinning. "Wait," I call to no one in particular. But I can't stop it.

When I feel solid ground again, it's dawn. Mick stands over me, holding out his hand to lift me off the wet grass. "You want to tell me what that was about?"

"Later." I reach for my cell, but it's been soaked in the ocean and is completely useless. I run toward the house.

Mick follows. "What?"

"Blake," is all I can say. I don't stop running until I get to the car. I grab the keys to the sedan from a hook by the door and jump inside. I'm probably doing permanent damage to the leather interior.

I drive as fast as I can, considering I've had no sleep. When I burst into the Ornery Knight, a few local fishermen eye me over their morning mugs, but they don't say anything about my wild look. I take the stairs two at a time until I get to Blake's room.

I knock on the door. Once. Twice. Three times, before I hear footsteps from the other side.

Okay, okay. Footsteps are good.

Blake opens the door partway, his eyes wide. My hair is knotted and still damp. My clothes are stained with Liam's blood. Blake rubs the back of his neck with his hand. "Is everything okay?"

Nothing is okay. I step into his room and sink down

on the floor, exhausted. "I thought—" I shake my head. "I don't know what I thought." *I thought Portia might try to kill you?* It sounds silly now that Blake is here and whole.

Blake sits down on the floor across from me. "I'm sorry about Austin. I guess he turned out to be kind of okay."

A tear sneaks out of the corner of my eye but I wipe it away. I'm not ready to cry. I'm afraid if I start, I won't ever be able to stop.

Blake stares at the dark stains on my shirt. "You need to get out of those clothes."

I laugh. I hate myself for laughing, but there's something absurd about that statement. Maybe it's the innocence behind it, the complete lack of tension between us. I wipe my nose on a bloody sleeve and wince at the metallic smell. "Can I use your shower?"

I stand under the hot water until the bathroom is filled with steam, watching the water turn from red to brown to clear again as the blood washes out of my hair. By the time I comb the last tangle out of my hair, change into a pair of Blake's sweats, and fasten my necklace, I can barely keep my eyes open.

I'm too tired to drive back to Lorcan Hall. I'm not ready to face Austin's big empty house. His room. "Is it okay if I stay here for a little while?" I ask.

Blake sits on a wood stool, watching me as I sit down on his bed. "What are you doing Brianna?"

"I just need a friend right now."

"Then go find one."

I'm frozen. My mouth opens but no words come out. Everything is a jumble of pain and grief and confusion.

"You can't just show up in my room, change into my clothes, and ask to stay with me," he says. "We're not friends. I get that you're upset. We all lost people we loved last night. But I'm the one person in the world who can't help you through this. Don't you get that?"

Blake and I aren't friends. I don't even know what we were, let alone what we are now.

"I'm sorry," I finally say. "I didn't mean to—I just came here to make sure you were okay."

Blake laughs. "So now you care about how I'm doing?"

"I saw Killian. He said that Portia—"

I don't get to finish my sentence. The door to Blake's room opens, and he's blown against the wall along with the stool. Portia sends a flaming ball of fire at my head.

FIFTY-NINE

I drop to the floor. Portia's fire lands on the bed, igniting the duvet. I douse it with a wall of water.

Blake slides to the floor with a crash now that the wind has stopped, but Portia ignores him. Her anger is firmly directed at me. "You didn't waste any time making your way back to Blake's bed. Your boyfriend is not even cold—"

I slap her. It feels far more satisfying than using magic.

She comes at me with a tornado, wind that picks up everything in the room and hurls it in my direction.

I catch a vase as it whirs past my head.

Blake climbs to his feet. "Stop!"

Portia laughs. "Or what?"

Silver light fills the room, making it hard to see at first. Then Blake appears with his sword drawn, its tip angled at Portia's chest.

"Well?" She curls her lip, but the wind stops. "Man up and do this already."

Blake swallows, withdrawing his sword. "I don't want to kill you."

"You don't want to love me, so you might as well kill me." Portia sits down on the soggy, charred bed. "My dad is dead and I did nothing to stop it. Nothing. I just froze and huddled in the corner like a baby. I hate this. I hate all of it." She grabs a pillow. "This has to end. Now. I'm not going to sit here and have to feel your shallow heart break for this useless excuse of a bandia a second longer."

I sense more than see the wall of fire that comes at me. I reach for water, but it's wind that flows inside me, unbidden. The wind chases the fire away, but sends it straight back to Portia.

She falls back on the bed, her chest lit with blue flame.

Blake curses and doubles over, dropping his sword. He screams along with Portia, clutching his chest. He disappears in a flash of light, then reappears in his pajama pants, unconscious on the floor.

I find water too late, stopping the fire only after it's done its damage. Portia's chest is black and red and blistered. She lies still. Staring at her brings me a twisted sense of déjà vu.

She's dead. I'm a killer.

Again.

I turn away, focusing on Blake, who still doesn't move. His heart is beating, but I hold his wrist, counting every pulse as if it will be his last.

He opens his eyes and smiles at me. "Am I dreaming? I'm dreaming, right?"

I shake my head. "She's dead."

He scrambles to his knees. "Did I . . . ?"

"I did."

He stares at Portia's body. "Shit."

"That pretty much sums it up." I can't believe I let it happen again so easily. One second the wind was there, and the next Portia was dead.

"What are we going to do?"

"Not we. *Me.* I killed her."

It should be easier this time. I don't love Portia. I don't even like her. But the nausea and horror don't discriminate. I feel sick.

Blake takes my hand, and I let him.

"She's really gone." Blake sounds like he can't quite believe it. "It's like a giant vise clamped around my heart has been released. I can breathe. God, I can feel."

I let go of his hand. "I'm glad you're feeling better, but you're missing something kind of important here. I just killed your girlfriend. She's lying right here. Dead." Again, I quell the urge to vomit.

"She was never my girlfriend."

Like me? I keep the words locked up tight. "Can you look a little less relaxed? I'm a little freaked out here."

"Hang on. If you're the one who killed her, you can save her, like you did me." Blake says the words I've been avoiding thinking since the ball of flame hit Portia in the chest. I can reverse the magic that killed her and bring her back. It will cost me nothing, now that I have the necklace to sustain my power.

I don't move.

"We can't trust her," I say. "She tried to kill me. She hates you."

Blake finally looks shaken. "So that's it? She's dead?"

"Mick will help us get her body out of here and cover her death."

"Listen to yourself." Blake puts his hand on my shoulder. "You're not a killer."

"It's not fair," I snap. Austin is dead—no one is bringing him back. Why should Portia be any different? Just because I can doesn't mean I should. "What if I bring her back and she kills you? Or me?"

"If she wanted to kill me, she would've done it weeks ago."

"Well, that's great for you, but she's already tried to kill me." Multiple times, but who's counting? "So forgive me if I'm a little skeptical. I'm calling Mick."

I walk out of Blake's room, letting the door click shut behind me. I'm not even sure if I *could* save her. The fire that killed Portia was hers, not mine. I probably couldn't bring her back if I tried. At least that's what I tell myself.

I make it down the stairs and halfway to the car before I stop. And even though I'm fairly sure I'll live to regret it, I turn around and walk back into the pub. This may be the stupidest thing I've ever done in my life, but I'm not sure if I can live with myself if I don't at least try to bring Portia Bruton back to life.

Blake opens the door on the first knock. "Change of heart?"

"You will not mention this to anyone. Ever. Got it?" I walk over to Portia's body and place my hand over her heart. I feel the warmth just beneath the surface, the magic that still lingers even after her life has left. I say the words that will reverse the magic that killed her. "*Draiocht leasaigh.*"

Nothing happens. There. I tried. Can't be done. Guilt trip over.

"Are you sure that's it?" Blake sounds nervous.

From the bed, Portia coughs.

Blake jumps back.

"What the hell?" Portia says, sitting up. She stares at Blake. "I can't feel you."

"It's over," he whispers.

"This is your fault." Portia lunges for me, unleashing a torrent of wind that pushes me against the wall.

I can't move. I can't breathe. I can barely keep my eyes open as the wind beats at my face. But I do. Long enough to see the ball of flame arc in her hands. Long enough to see the flash of silver light behind her. Long enough to see her slump to the floor as Blake pulls his bloody sword from her chest.

The wind stops abruptly and I fall to the carpet.

Blake stares at the blood pooling around Portia's body. "Call Mikel."

SIXTY

Joe meets us at the top of the trail, his face a mask of placidity. I've seen so much blood in the last twelve hours that I'm numb to it as I watch Mick and Blake unwrap Portia from the hotel sheets and carry her down the bluff.

"It's still not over, is it?" I say to Joe.

Joe doesn't look at me as he pulls a cigarette from the pack he keeps in the pocket of his long black coat. "I don't know."

"But I'm the last one. Officially."

"Looks that way."

On the beach below, Mick and Blake maneuver Portia up on one of the boulders. The tide is in now, but receding enough that they manage to climb up without too much difficulty.

"Who will lead the Sons with Rush gone?" I ask.

"Dr. McKay will have the votes. Levi will make a push for it anyway."

I silently hope that Levi's "push" won't get very far. Blake and I might not be friends, but I'm pretty sure we're still on the same side of this. There's no chance of Levi working with me, but Dr. McKay might. "I'll propose a new treaty."

Joe just nods in silence. Neither one of us says anything for a while.

"Did you do it?" He gestures to where Portia's body is now draped across the boulder.

"It was self-defense." I don't know why I don't tell him the whole truth, but something keeps me from mentioning the fact that Portia died twice.

Joe puts the cigarette between his lips and stares down at the ground. "So it wasn't Blake who broke the bond?"

At least that much is true. "Does it matter?"

"I wish I knew." Joe finally looks at me.

"Mick said the curse ensured that the Sons and the bandia could never love each other, but that if they did—"

"Mick talks too much."

"What is he going to do now?" Who will Mick take care of without Austin? I try not to think of what I'm going to do without Austin, but the thought is there anyway, ripping at me until all I feel is shredded.

"Find a new alliance."

"And if he doesn't?"

"He'll opt out." Joe says the words with finality.

"What does that mean?"

"It doesn't get any easier. Not for any of us, but it's harder on some than others. The giolla are only here as long as they want to be."

"Liam said there were only three of you left." Did that mean there were more? Did centuries of loss wear them down until they couldn't handle it anymore? Mick basically told me as much. He chose Austin because Austin couldn't die on him. Until he could. And did.

Joe puts his hands in the pockets of his coat. "There were twelve, originally. That was a long time ago."

So nine have opted out? "How long ago?"

"Long enough."

"The Sons think you serve them."

Joe squats down to the grass and brushes it with his fingers. "We serve no one." He plucks a blade and then stands, holding it out to me. "And everyone."

On closer inspection, it's not grass at all but clover. "A four-leafed clover?"

"They're not so rare." Joe blows on it, sending it into the wind. It catches a draft over the bluff and floats over the beach, drifting down until it comes to rest on the rock where Blake and Mick are holding Portia. They wait for a wave to crest and then swing her body out, letting go just as the wave comes into the rock. Portia floats on the surface until a second wave crashes over her, dragging her under.

Joe bows his head.

The ocean no longer looks beautiful. I see only its dark, destructive side. It's like me. I close my eyes and say a prayer for Portia. For Sherri. For Rush and Jeremy.

For Austin.

When I open my eyes again, the waves still crash against the rocks, the same way they did a thousand years ago, the way they will for a thousand more. It occurs to me that if I'm like the sea, the giolla are the rocks, solid and unflinching. Destroyed one pebble at a time.

Eventually, so much living, so much dying takes its toll. I don't judge the giolla who opted out before Mick, and I'll understand if Mick decides not to continue. I would do it myself if I could.

Austin thought I was strong, brave, but I don't think I can ever be the fighter he thought I was. It doesn't feel like there's anything left to fight for.

Blake and Mick make their way up the trail slowly. When they get to the trailhead, Mick pulls out his cell and makes a call to report a boat wreck in the cove that claimed five lives. The authorities will find the wreckage of the boat the Sons took to the Gathering. They'll find Portia's body, but not the four others, who will be deemed lost at sea.

We stop at the top of the drive. I just want to go inside and collapse on the nearest soft surface, to sleep for the next week. The next year. There's just one thing I need to do first.

I reach behind my neck and unclasp my necklace.

"Joe," I say. Blake, Joe, and Mick all watch as I unfold my palm. "I think you should have this back."

To his credit, Joe doesn't argue. He takes the pendant and nods silently. "You're opting out?"

"In a manner of speaking."

Blake steps toward me. "You'll be defenseless."

"I'll be offense-less too." I won't kill again.

"You need your power." Blake's eyes dare me to disagree.

"Having power didn't save any of them. I'm done fighting."

Joe curls his fingers around the charm. "Rush was right about one thing."

"What?"

"You're the least like a bandia of anyone I've ever met."

Mick sets his hand on my shoulder. "Come inside. You need to rest."

Joe places the necklace in the pocket of his duster and heads down the drive toward a silver SUV. Blake doesn't follow. Our eyes meet and hold. I see only grief in there, and I'm sure my expression is no different. We've both lost so much.

Mick gives my shoulder one last pat and walks inside without me.

Blake's eyes search mine as if he's looking for answers to the questions neither one of us is ready to ask. "So this is it?"

"Good luck saving the world." My smile is forced.

"What will you do?"

"Sleep."

"And then?" A dimple appears on his cheek. Now that the bond with Portia is broken, he's already starting to look more like his old self. Part of me is glad. I want him to be okay.

"I don't know. Senior year? Maybe MIT. I won't be tied to any one place." To any one person.

"For what it's worth, I'm sorry." Blake looks at the ground. "About everything."

I close my eyes against the reminder of what happened to Austin in Avernus. It's not that I wish Austin hadn't saved Blake from Sherri. I would've done the same if I could. Austin would've probably died anyway. Liam wouldn't let him live. All I know is that now, when I look at Blake, I only see what he's not. He's not the boy who trusted me when I gave him reason to doubt. He's not the boy who loved me even when I made mistakes. He's not the boy who was willing to sacrifice everything he had for the chance to love, even if he failed.

He's not Austin.

I don't know how long I close my eyes, but when I open them again, Blake has his back to me. He climbs into the SUV and never looks back.

When I turn around to walk inside the house, neither do I.

SIXTY-ONE

I spend another week at Lorcan Hall, just going through the motions. I sleep and eat and ride, but I don't dream or taste or feel. I've taken to sleeping in Austin's room, where his smell still lingers in the closet, the pillows, the sheets. Even that's disappearing, as time erases him.

Tomorrow, I'll fly back to Rancho Domingo. In two weeks, I'll start senior year, right on schedule. I'll bury myself in books and theories and logic, but my heart will remain here. As permanently as the wall that was once a castle. As ruined.

We haven't had any visitors, so it's a surprise when Mick comes into the sitting room and announces Shannon. Mick is the master of the house now, since Austin left everything to him, but I guess some habits die hard.

Shannon carries a large box, big enough to fit a pair of riding boots inside. "How're you holding up?"

"Do you want some tea?" I deliberately ignore her question. She's just being polite. No one really wants to know that I'm breaking into pieces and losing little bits of myself that I'll never get back.

"I can't stay." She holds up the box. "I hope you don't mind that I did a bit of personal shopping for you."

"What?"

"It came in yesterday, and I knew you'd want first crack at it." She opens the box and a slip of shiny gold fabric peeks out.

I catch my breath.

She unfolds the dress slowly. It's even more beautiful than what Austin described, with a swath of metallic fabric across one shoulder, a fitted waist, and a flowing skirt with a slit in the front that should hit just above the knee.

"It's perfect." I run my fingers along the delicate material.

"It's exactly like you described. Did you see it in a magazine?"

"Something like that."

I don't blink as Shannon tells me the price, even though I'm fairly certain my parents won't approve of my spending so much money on one dress. But from the second that hint of gold peeked out of the box, I knew I would buy it.

It's a memory I didn't know I had until I saw it: a piece of Austin wrapped up in gold.

It's even more beautiful when I put it on. Staring at myself in the mirror, I see myself as Austin must have seen me a thousand years ago, a ray of sunlight in the thick fog.

My feet carry me out the door and onto the trail to the

ruin before I realize where I'm going. There are risks to going back, I know. But nothing could keep me from seeing him one last time—before I leave this place, and him, forever.

I pause at the ruined wall, fingering the little horse charm on my bracelet. Part of me wants to rush in. To find Austin and never let him go. But I'm terrified of what it might do to me. I don't know if I'll ever be ready to lose him again.

Yet I'm more afraid of letting this moment pass, so I slide the charm into the faded slot.

The fog surrounds me, covering me in a damp blanket. I tremble as I float. The field gradually comes into focus. I feel the wall of the ruin at my back, hard and scratchy against the thin material of my dress.

The field is empty, except for the purple wildflowers that dot the meadow. I wait for a few minutes, but no one comes. I'm alone.

I walk toward the hill. The path is wider and easier than it was on the way up, paved by thousands of hoofbeats that make a daily trek form Lorcan Hall to the field beyond.

I see a flash of brown hair in the distance. I pick up my skirt and start running.

I run headlong into Austin, throwing my arms around his shoulders and hanging on tight. His arms come around me as he struggles to stay upright against my assault. He steps backward and loses his footing, falling sideways into the grass, carrying me with him. He rolls onto his back and I lie on top of him.

He opens his mouth to say something, but I don't give him the chance.

I kiss him.

He tastes exactly like I remember, like smoke and heaven. He kisses me back, his hands in my hair. We roll in the grass until his weight is over me. I close my eyes and try to memorize the feel of him, running my hands along his cheek, his shoulder, his waist.

When he finally ends the kiss, his crooked smile nearly breaks me. "That was a welcome for all time."

It will have to be. I bring my hand to the flop of hair that hangs in his forehead. "I missed you so much."

"Did you now? I cannot imagine that I would ever leave you for long enough to miss me. If you kiss me like that in the future, I am quite sure I follow you around like a puppy."

I laugh and kiss him again, softer this time. Sweeter. "I love you." A tear falls down my cheek before I can stop it.

"And this makes you sad?" Austin rubs my cheek with his thumb. "What have I done?"

You died. You made me love you and then you died. I shake my head. "Nothing."

"Lying to me is not a good way to start this relationship."

It's the beginning for him. I'm jealous of all that's ahead of him, even if he does have to wait over a thousand years for it. I kiss him again, as much to touch him as to keep from having to tell him my secret.

Austin props himself on his elbows, lifting some of his weight from my chest, but letting his hips sink deeper. "If you do not tell me what I've done in the future, how can I try to make sure it doesn't happen when I get there?"

"You don't believe the future can be changed. You always say that fate will out."

Austin laughs. "I sound like a sodding fool."

"A bloody fool."

"That too. So you are unhappy with me in the future?"

I keep my words wrapped up tight. No one wants to know that they're going to die. Not the when. Not the how. What did Austin say? *Knowing the future steals hope.*

"But you love me?" he asks.

"Very much."

"Then I imagine we will get through it."

I can't stop the tears.

Austin kisses them away. "I cannot wait to meet you for real." His hand brushes my hair away from my face. His brown eyes light with gold. "To know you."

"It ends badly," I finally admit.

His smile is warm. "Then we'll have to make the most of the time we have."

We won't. I'll bind my soul to another boy and Austin will hurt my horse and my friends and me. We'll only have each other for a few precious weeks before he's gone, gone, gone.

Before he leaves me forever.

I force a smile. "It won't go so smoothly at first. Don't give up on me, okay?"

"I am fairly certain that you will not be able to stop my pursuit."

I laugh, burying my hands in his hair and pulling him closer.

"What in the gods' names is going on?" Gwyn is standing over us, her hands on her hips.

Austin straightens my skirt before he moves off of me, standing to block Gwyn from my line of site. I scramble to my feet, finger-combing my hair.

"What brings you to Lorcan, Gwyn?" Austin's voice is laced with a superior air, as though Gwyn is the one who has committed the indiscretion.

She lifts her chin sharply. "I've been thinking." Something glints in the sunlight where her hand is resting behind her skirt. I move forward, but I can't see what she's holding.

"A dangerous pastime for a girl of your stature."

Gwyn ignores Austin's insult and smiles as her mother and a younger girl walk up behind her.

Danu's dark hair is crowned with yellow and purple flowers, just as it was the first time I saw her in Avalon. She's as beautiful as I remember, but less serene-looking. She glances at my dress and my matted tangle of curls. I pull a dried leaf out of my hair self-consciously.

"This is the girl you would take over Gwyn?" Danu's question is directed to Austin, but her anger is leveled at me.

Austin moves in front of me, shielding me from Danu's withering stare. "You set your sights too high, even for a halfling."

The younger girl steps forward. She looks like Danu, ethereal and dark. She must be Bronwyn. Gwyn takes Bronwyn's arm, but keeps her other hand firmly behind her skirt.

Danu turns her back on her daughters to make eye contact with me. "Gwyn's lineage is uncompromised. There is no better match for a god to start a new line."

Gwyn straightens her shoulders and grins. I see the glint of light from behind her again, the ivory handle as she moves her hand, but by the time I see the silver blade, she's already lifting the knife to strike, poised to literally stab her mother in the back.

I charge her.

I run as fast as I can, using my head as a battering ram. I knock her forward, sending us both careening to the ground. The knife falls out of Gwyn's hand.

"Have you lost your mind?" I grab for her wrists, but Gwyn strikes me hard in the face, knocking me backward.

Bronwyn drops to her knees and grabs the knife, slashing at my face. I roll away from the blade and push myself back to my feet. I'm hit by a strong blast of wind. It knocks me straight back. My head hits something hard, and my vision blurs to nothing but gold light.

I push up on my elbows, struggling to see. Bronwyn kneels over me, the knife raised. I kick out, making contact with her wrist. She drops the knife and I scramble for it. Gwyn jumps on top of me, her arm around my throat. I strike her in the ribs with my elbow.

Gold light shines behind us. Gwyn turns to look over her shoulder, giving me the opening I need to break her hold and grab the knife. I spin onto my back, holding the knife in front of me. Gwyn backs away as I get to my feet.

Austin appears in his god form, his sword aimed at Danu's chest.

"No!" I yell.

He turns toward my voice, letting the tip of his sword drop.

"How dare you!" Danu's face is filled with fury. Her hands fill with fire. She raises her palm toward Austin. I don't have to do the math to know how this equation ends.

I throw the knife as hard as I can, watching helplessly as it lands perfectly in the center of Danu's chest. The fire in her hand dies as she falls to the ground.

From somewhere behind me, Gwyn laughs.

Bronwyn crawls to her mother and pulls the knife from her chest, but it's too late. Danu is dead.

I killed her.

Bronwyn lifts the bloody knife, her face twisting into a grotesque mask. She runs toward me with the knife drawn.

The movement barely registers. I know I need to defend myself. To run. Something. But I'm too shocked to do anything but note the familiar hue of grief in Bronwyn's eyes.

I close my eyes, waiting for the knife to hit. Before it does, there's a flash of gold light behind my eyelids. When I open them, Austin stands over Bronwyn's lifeless body, his sword dripping with blood.

The sky above us turns so gray it's almost black. Fat drops of rain start to fall all around us.

"I'm sorry," he mouths.

The rain becomes a deluge, a wall of water so thick it's impossible to see anything but shadows moving behind the sheets of rain. I see the outline of Austin, his sword at his side. Perfect. Strong.

Then he's swallowed by the darkness.

I sit down in the mud, letting the rain pelt my skin. With Gwyn's laughter fading behind me, I finally cry.

SIXTY-TWO

Rancho Domingo High School feels different to me now. It's not just because I'm a senior, not just that people don't look past me like they did for most of the last three years, when magic hid me from the world. It's that everything is dull and washed out, coated in a gauzy film of indifference.

Austin thought life was precious because it ended. Such an easy thing to say when you have your whole life ahead of you. All I can think is how pointless life is without him in it.

Haley and Christy find their new lockers and coordinate a spot for our lunch meet-up, but I barely listen. This is what Austin and I fought for. Humanity. Normalcy. And I can't help wondering if this flat gray existence was worth the price.

"Whoa. Hot guy alert." Christy stands up straighter and flips her dark hair over her shoulder.

Haley turns her head. "Dibs. You already have a boy-friend."

I can't bring myself to care enough to look up.

"He's coming over here." Christy bounces on her heels.

I keep my eyes down, studying a patch of dirt on the floor.

"Brianna?"

The soft Irish lilt jolts me to life. I lift my head and almost forget that it can't be Austin. That it never can be.

Mick stands a few yards away, his red hair cut into a modern style, short on the sides and slightly ruffled on top. His hands are stuffed awkwardly into the pockets of black jeans. Even without the mutton chops, he stands too straight to pass for a high school boy. I feel the beginning of a smile.

"You know him?" Christy watches me with new respect. I haven't told them much about my summer in Ireland—they know there was a battle and people died. And that I don't want to talk about it.

I wave Mick over. "What are you doing here?"

He shrugs as he walks toward us. "It seems I inherited a house nearby."

Austin's house. Of course. "That doesn't explain what you're doing at R.D. High," I say.

Mick's eyes flit to Christy and Haley before they settle on me. "I thought I'd stay awhile."

I nod, letting the full weight of his words sink in. Mick is not going to opt out of his role as a giolla. He's going to try to stay on earth for at least a little while longer. I guess it makes sense that he'd want to be close to Joe now. And Sam will be with Braden at U.R.D.

I barely have time to introduce Mick to Haley and Christy before the first bell rings. My friends head off in the direction of their first-period dance class, but Mick doesn't move. "The horses will be here next week," he says.

"You're bringing the horses?"

"I was hoping you would help me train them to jump. I think Tally, especially, could benefit from the extra exercise."

"Okay." Molly will make a cute hunter. And Tally's athleticism will probably make him a fabulous jumper, if I can figure out how to rein him in. "What makes you think I can get Tally under control?"

"This from the girl who brought a god to his knees?"

My heart constricts in my chest. No one has mentioned Austin since I've been back.

"Sorry, I didn't mean..." Mick pulls a folded piece of paper out of his front pocket. "Maybe you could help me find my first class?"

"You're really going to high school?"

"I thought you understood."

"I'm not following."

"If I stay, I have to align myself with someone."

Me? "A giolla wants to align with a bandia?"

"It's not the first time."

I'm guessing there's a story there. "I don't think I qualify anymore," I say.

"You qualify, whether you want to believe it or not."

Although Mick looks different with his new haircut and clothes, it's still impossible to look at him, impossible to hear his accent, without thinking of Austin. Before I can stop myself, I blurt out, "I miss him so much."

He swallows. "Me too."

Students move around us, racing to stake out seats in their new classes. Mick and I stand frozen. I see the answering sadness in his eyes.

"There's no one to talk to," he says. "No one who knew him."

He's right. It's been so hard to keep it all inside. There's no one I can talk to about what happened with Austin. No one who will understand.

Mick pushes the crumpled schedule at me.

I take it from him and unfold it. "You have AP Calculus?"

"Don't sound so surprised. I was educated at Oxford."

"When, in the 1800s?"

"And the 1960s. Most recently in 1998."

I laugh. It's a foreign sound on my lips. "I had you pegged for a Cambridge man."

He opens his mouth in disbelief.

"You know you don't have to do this."

"I don't have to do anything. I'm a giolla." His posture changes, becoming impossibly straighter. As he says the words, there's no question of the power he wields. The power to compel human behavior. To maintain a delicate balance. To restore a god's power. What else can he do?

"Is there a way to bring him back?" Could Mick bring Austin back to me?

He takes the schedule from me. The second bell rings and he looks around the empty campus. "We're late."

"If we're going to hang out, you can't dodge my questions." I can't hide the desperation in my voice. I can't stop the tide of hope that rises in my chest. Mick is more powerful than a god.

"It is forbidden."

"But possible."

"The giolla cannot afford to indulge self-interest. It would upset the balance."

"I don't care about balance. I care about Austin." It feels good to say it out loud. I want to scream it at the top of my lungs. I'm tired of holding it in.

"You should care about balance." Mick rests a hand on my shoulder. "It's the only thing that keeps this world from falling into complete chaos."

My chest floods with warmth, a soothing heat that blooms from the inside and floats outward. I smile without knowing what I'm smiling about. I break free of Mick's hold and the warmth is gone. "Are you using compulsion?"

"I'm trying to help."

"Don't."

"Fair enough." He looks back down at the crumpled paper in his hand. "Shall we do this?" He's staring at the schedule, but I know he's not talking about high school. He's asking to become my ally.

"That depends. Will you let me call you Mick?"

He almost smiles. "You are going to do it anyway."

"Okay, Mick. Is that it? No blood oath or allegiance spell?"

"That's it."

"Then I guess we better get you to Calc before it's too late to pretend that you're just learning your way around campus."

"I am learning my way."

"You'd think that after a couple thousand years, you'd have things figured out."

Mick does smile now, a true one. "You would think."

He doesn't say anything as we make our way to class. We have to sit a few rows apart, since we're too late to pick our seats, but every once in a while I glance up and see him scribbling on his notepad as if this class is the most important thing in the world to him.

It's all review from last year, so I don't have to pay much attention, which is good because all at once the world is in Technicolor. The green of the chalkboard, the threads of pink running through the beige carpet, the deep blue of the ink spilling from my pen all compete for attention, forming a rainbow of promise.

Of possibility.

About the Author

Talia Vance has worked as a horse trainer, a freelance writer, and an attorney. She is analytical, practical, and a hopeless romantic. She lives in Northern California with her husband, children, and a needy Saint Bernard named Huckleberry. Talia always thought she'd grow up to write "the Great American Novel," but her tastes ran more along the lines of torrid romances and fast-paced thrillers. So did her life. But that's another story.

Visit Talia online at www.TaliaVance.com.